THE BERENGERS

Death and Sex at a Country House Weekend

Louise Van Hamm

CHAPTER 1

My Great Uncle George always slept on the floor, even as a very old man. On arriving at hospital during his last illness there was an unholy fuss when they put him in a bed. He died on the floor, at home, aged seventy-nine. At the funeral my great aunt explained that his strange sleeping habits resulted from a very, very – and she stressed both 'verys' – terrible experience on a bed, during his youth.

I felt I couldn't pursue the matter, it hardly seemed the time or place, but my usually reticent aunt had drunk quite a bit of sherry and was feeling loquacious.

"You know, of course," she leant closer towards me on the sofa, her voice warm and excited, "that I am one of the Berengers of Leatherboys Hall?"

"No, I didn't know that." I did sort of, though it was a family secret, but she seemed so desperate to tell me that I didn't want to spoil it for her - not today, at her husband's funeral.

"Yes. Leatherboys Hall... I haven't been there for years, your uncle never liked the place. He said he never felt at home..." she sipped delicately from her glass and gazed into the distance.

My great uncle's feelings came as no surprise; he had been a bus conductor- rising to inspector in his later years - and had lived all his life in Palmers Green. He had been born and had died in this very house, surrounded by his close family and with the rhubarb he had harvested for decades languishing unpicked outside the french windows. But I had always wondered how he came to marry a member of the aristocracy.

"The family are still there, you know," she glanced at me slyly, "they wrote to me last week offering me a home back with them, if I wanted."

"Will you go?" I was amazed, aunty rarely went anywhere anymore.

"Oh, no, I shall stay here with all of you. You've become my family over the years. I haven't seen any of them for ages and ages. Do you know, I never even went back for the funerals. I just read all the obituaries in The Times." She waved a hand airily, smiling, but then, she always smiled. At the graveside, crying as the coffin was lowered, she had been smiling through her tears. It was something to do with the cast of her mouth and the set of her blue, amazingly unwrinkled, eyes.

She had been a beauty in her youth, the painting over the fireplace and the pictures in the old photo albums proved it. There she stood, anchored against the brown felty pages by black photo-corners. In sunshine and in cloud, smiling for the camera; in the garden by the coal shed, or in front of the rhubarb, in the door of the Anderson shelter, crouched with one hand trailing in the tiny fish pond, in spring clipping the box hedging, or in high summer deadheading the rose bed. Photos of the garden from every angle over the years, with my great aunt sympathetically posed. There were very few entire photos of my great uncle as aunty never got the hang of the camera. He was frequently cut off at the knee or neck or represented by an arm flung along a fence top or a pair of crossed legs in a deckchair. Occasionally, a hawk-nosed profile or a quizzically raised eyebrow made it into the frame.

"Does Aunty want some fruitcake?" My mother leant heavily over my shoulder to ask me. The older generation have never come to terms with aunty's elevated beginnings and rarely address her directly. What they would do now there was no Great Uncle George to filter information and questions through, I did not know.

Aunty shook her head, "No thank you, Carol dear, I had to bake it with rather old dried fruit, I don't like to think what it will do to my insides."

"Oh, no, best not then. Don't tire your Aunty out." This last was hissed at me.

"I won't." The weight on my shoulder eased and I watched my mother go back to the dresser, where the huge fruit cake was waiting to be sliced and put it back in its tin. A few minutes later she was removing the tin surreptitiously to the kitchen.

"Will you write back to your family?" I wanted to get aunty back on track, becoming more interested in these Berenger relations.

"Yes I will, if you'll post it for me?"

"Of course. Did you meet Great Uncle George there?"

"Where?"

"Leatherboys Hall?"

"Not originally, no." She had finished her sherry and was curling her thin, surprisingly supple forefinger round the inside of the glass and then sucking it clean.

"Would you like some more sherry?"

"George will get me some." Something filmed over her eyes and she tapped her lower lip, "Oh, no he won't, will he?"

"I'm afraid not, but I will."

"Please," she held out her glass, "fill it up, there's a dear."

I found the sherry bottle in the kitchen, by the sink, and my mother sniffing loudly inside the cake tin.

"Does this smell off to you? I can't hand it out, can I?"

I sniffed, "It smells fine." It smelled of spirits, fruity and rich. "Who's that?" I had just noticed an old lady propped up in the corner by the boiler.

"I don't know, she won't say. I saw her standing all alone at the graveside and invited her along. I felt sorry for her."

I could see why. She was wallowing in grief, all rumpled in her funereal black, red-faced and sort

4

of saggy. "Would you like a sherry?" I offered. She clutched her drenched handkerchief and her lower lip wobbled, but nothing came out except sobs.

"Leave her be. I think it's best."

"She could be anyone, Mum." I hissed, "A burglar casing the joint."

"Don't be stupid," her eyes lighted on the full sherry glass, "Are you drinking all of that?"

"No, it's for Aunty, she said to fill it up."

"I've always known she tippled."

"Well we can forgive her today, can't we? It's so sad Mum, she keeps forgetting Great Uncle George is dead." I had to raise my voice above renewed wailings from the unknown woman. "She was going to ask him to top up her drink."

"Oh, I know, dear, when they get old they get very forgetful. Now, take her that drink before you spill it and I'll try to find those biscuits I brought just in case...."

Aunty had dozed off by the time I got back to her, one hand under her soft, powdered cheek, the other resting on her black draped knee, and the smile still curving her pink, very glossily painted lips.

"Doesn't she look peaceful?" My mother's brother Trevor asked everyone in general. "Like a baby."

There was a pause in the comfortable hum of family gossip and a dozen faces turned to look at her.

"How will she cope without him?" Someone

wondered aloud.

"He was her rock, her saviour, she once told me."

"He was a nice enough old bloke, but I wonder what she ever saw in him." There was a mutter of agreement.

"He was never an oil painting, that's for sure, and I'll say that even though he was my brother." My grandfather's quivering assertion caused a titter.

"She was lovely though, wasn't she," Trevor nodded at the heavily framed painting over the fireplace. It overshadowed the whole room, making the little grey electric fire below it, with the holiday souvenirs and the pipe rack on the mantelpiece, seem ridiculous. In the foreground, a young girl in a shimmering oyster satin frock stroked the gaunt neck of an Irish wolfhound. The smile was there, gently superior pitying us all.

"It's a very good painting." Grandpa assured me, grabbing my arm for support while he adjusted his Zimmer frame, "The only thing she brought with her from that place."

"Leatherboys Hall?"

"Yes. That's it at the back there," he pointed into the painting and I went over to have a closer look.

Beyond the seductive cream curve of my great aunt's youthful hip, a flat landscape, painted several shades of umber, receded under a smoky sky. Touches of blue showed between the thickly applied clouds and the turrets of a red brick house jutted up from behind equally claggy, oily-green trees. The faint line of a road wriggled between hedgerows towards the house, and as I peered closer, a little red open-topped car sped along it, sending up puffs of dust.

*****

"Am I driving too fast?"

"No!"

"Don't lie!"

"I'm not!" George had to shout, the engine was gunning and roaring by turns, but shouting meant opening his mouth wide and that meant swallowing gusts of grit. And she was driving much too fast. He had only been in one other car; a funeral car when his grandfather had died, and that had gone very slowly. "Whoa!"

Mags laughed, she had just missed a pheasant and turned round to see it shoot into the hedge, swerving again as she swivelled about in her seat. "Nearly there!" She told him, her yellow silk scarf rippling out behind her. "If you're nervy you can swot up."

"What?" In his terror he forgot to say 'pardon'.

"See that scroll on the back seat?"

"Yes!" He nearly lost his cap as he turned right round and clapped his hand to his head.

"Get it and open it up."

"What, now?!"

"Yes!"

He had to almost crawl into the back to reach the scroll, which slithered from one end of the red leather seat to the other as they sped round the bends of the lane. Mags squeezed his backside.

"Both hands on the wheel!" He yelled at her, finally catching the tightly curled scroll. He sat back again on his recently caressed buttock and chanced a kiss on her warm cheek. She laughed again. Mags was the most physical girl he had ever come across, and an Honourable too.

"Open it up."

"What is it?" His gloved hands fought with the thick parchment, rolled up for so many years it was reluctant to unwind.

"Family tree, it's best you know who you're going to meet!"

"God, there's hundreds of them!"

"Mostly all dead now!" She changed gear for a blind curve. "Just concentrate on the bottom few lines, see me?"

"Er... Yes, I've found you." He smiled across at her. She had an almost perfect profile. He had made a study of profiles, in his job you saw a lot of them. All the passengers in the front facing seats were only ever profiles to him, as they rarely looked up and round, full face, when paying for their tickets.

But she had been sitting on an inward facing seat and when he had taken her fare she had looked him in the eye and said, 'What lovely hands you have.'

It had been so unexpected that he had

blushed and checked around to see if anyone else had heard her (she didn't have a quiet, confiding kind of voice) but no-one had moved. So he'd wound on and punched her ticket with his usual aplomb and sung, as he always did, a lilting, 'Thank you,' as he gave it to her.

'The sort of hands one wouldn't mind being touched by.'

'I beg your pardon?'

'What are you doing at the end of your shift? Anything?'

'Um,' again he glanced around at his passengers and this time noticed the shocked rigidity of those close by, he grinned, 'No, nothing really.'

'So, what time do you finish?'

'Four.'

'Meet me at the Rendezvous Café, d'you know it?'

'   Yes.' It was a dusty little dive just opposite the station.

'I'll wait until half-past. I expect you have to change out of your uniform, or something...' Her smile was frankly suggestive.

Someone nearer the front rose to get off. George rang the bell and gave her his 'chirpy' smile, 'Right then, Miss 'The Rendezvous' soon after four.'

'I'm not a Miss, I'm an Honourable, actually. The Honourable Margaret Berenger, and you are number,' she flicked his oval, enamel lapel badge as he swung against her knees to allow the alighting passenger unnecessary room, 'six, nine, five.'

'George Pender,' he corrected her.

'George Pender,' she repeated.

'Are you going to take my fare, young man?' The man beside the Honourable Margaret enquired, then muttered, 'I don't think I'm the only one being taken for a ride.'

Now George squinted at the jiggling copper-plate script, his eyes for once off the road ahead and any possible – probable – disaster. The Honourable Margaret (his fiancée) had at least, he tried to count them up, seven siblings. Her mother was Lydia, her father Howard. There was an uncle; her father's brother, Lawrence, who had a wife and child. A second branch of the family had three sisters (all unmarried) and two brothers (both married) with issue of about the same age or older than Mags. Surely he wouldn't be meeting all these people? He knew it was supposed to be a big house but –

"There it is!"

He looked up, over the worn edge of the scroll and completely lost his hold on it, "Christ!" Then, "Christ!" again as the scroll sprung back into its accustomed tube and bounced out of the car.

"Don't worry, I'll send someone to pick it up."

"Blimey, Mags! It's bloody huge!"

"No need to shout, darling," she slowed the car to a purr and a popping in the open oval of the gravel drive and smiled at his astonishment. "It's not as old as it looks. Great-Great Grandpa built it in 1838. Gothic revival."

"It's me needs reviving. I never dreamed it would be anything like this. Turrets, look turrets!"

"Calm down darling."

"D'you have coach parties?"

"What?" Mags never said pardon, and this confused him because his mother always insisted that was the polite thing to say.

"Coach parties?"

"Good heavens, no." She stood up and jumped out of the car without opening the door, showing her suspenders as her skirt flared. "Mother would rather die. Get our stuff out of the boot will you, Smears."

"Yesh, Mish."

George twisted round and found his door being opened by a large man in morning dress. George got out and followed his fiancée up the flight of stone steps to a massive double oak door which stood wide open and swallowed them up into the darkness inside.

"Oh, by the way," Mags called back out into the daylight, "the scroll is on the drive again."

Smears nodded, his hands and arms full of their, well, her, luggage.

"It's very dark in here," George complained, feeling blindly for something to anchor him. He found her warm hand and squeezed it for comfort.

"It's because of the arras."

"The arrows?"

"The tapestries, they mustn't be allowed to fade. Just follow me." She led him confidently onwards, deeper and deeper into the murk.

"Good afternoon, Aunt Suzy."

"Ah, Mags, are you back again?"

George peered frantically into the shifting shadows, trying to locate a body to go with the high, whispery voice.

"Just till Monday."

"And who's this with you?"

"George Pender," she told her.

"George, how lovely to meet you..."

"Likewise," he screwed up his eyes, were they even open? Had he actually gone blind? Panic flooded him, then a door opened briefly across an expanse of polished floor. A figure flashed in the light. He made out a willowy shape in front of him and then Mags, more solid beside him. He smiled, able at last to shake the hand Aunt Suzy held out to him. "Likewise," he repeated, gently shaking the thin, cool hand which soon slid from his.

"I'll see you at drinks, I expect..."

"I'll look forward to it."

"Remember, Mags, the west wing is being decorated..."

"Ah, yes. Oh well, I'll take you up to the third-floor bedrooms, we'll find you something there. Come on." Her hand hauled him upwards and he stumbled at the foot of the stairs.

"Can you honestly see anything, Mags? I can't." He climbed unsteadily beside her, there was a larger than usual gap between each riser and as he got into the rhythm of it the gap changed.

"Well, not really, but I know where every-thing is."

"How will I ever find my way about?"

"Don't worry, Smears will have the lamps lit soon and all the bedrooms have got daylight in. Bugger!" her hand was wrenched from his. "Who put that there?"

"What is it?"

"Riding boots by the feel of them. Bloody Freddy. Ouff." The sound of heavy objects landing at a distance below echoed around them.

"Are you all right?" he asked.

"Yes. Onward and upward."

"Give me your hand."

"Baby." She teased.

They climbed for some while and breathing became difficult. George gave up all hope of ever reaching anything like a lighted room and wished he was at home in Palmers Green. Then a cold gush of air rippled round his frayed collar and made him shiver. Ahead, vaguely, a human shape material-ised, quivering and pale in the surrounding black-ness.

"Here we are, third flo-"

"Oh, my God. Mags?"

"What?"

"Is that- is that a ghost?"

"No. Leatherboys Hall isn't haunted. That's Ethel, the upstairs maid. She's been getting your room ready. Haven't you, Ethel?" She called down the corridor.

"Haven't I what?" She called back.

"Been getting Mr Pender's room ready."

"Not up here, Miss, no." She came closer, shielding her candle with a reddened hand. "You've missed the third floor, this is the attics."

"Is it? I thought it was colder," Mags found this very funny. "Oh, wait 'til I tell mother."

"You've got to go down two floors. D'you want my candle, Miss?"

"Perhaps I'd better take it. Come on George, down we go again. Now really, don't tell the others about this, I'll never hear the end of it," she set off with the candle, leaving Ethel in the dark and after a pause, George ran down after her.

"Will Ethel be all right, in the dark?" He worried. She'd seemed a nice, helpful girl and he had warmed to her. She had also whispered, in the seconds they were alone in the increasing gloom together, "I'm just along here, second door on the left, if you need me." George doubted that he would need her. He had Mags, often and noisily, ever since that first meeting in the café.

'Do you like sex?' She had asked over their pot of stewed tea.

'Eh?' George had blown out his cheeks, a habit his mother was always telling him to lose.

'Sex. Do you like it?' She repeated patiently.

'What do you mean by 'sex'? Generally, or in particular?'

'Very particularly with me. Would you like

14

that?'

He did it again, the cheek thing and hurriedly deflated to answer, 'Yes.'

'Well then let's, shall we?'

'Er, yes. When exactly were you thinking…?'

'Now. I booked a room at a little hotel near here while I was waiting for you.'

'Did you?' He was rather put out. 'You knew I'd say yes, then?'

'I guessed you would.' She smiled a little pouty smile which he found irresistible. 'I guessed right away that we were going to get on.'

Ten minutes later they had been pulling and tugging at each other's clothing in a room with regency stripe wallpaper and a red satin bed cover. They had still been there two hours later, during which time the Honourable Margaret 'commonly known as Mags' had initiated him into the various little treats and teasings that she particularly enjoyed, and which, to be fair, he found he enjoyed too.

'Just forget everything your mother ever told you about it making you go blind, there is nothing like synchronised masturbation,' Mags told him. 'Now, you go over that side of the room and I'll stay here on the bed. Ready?'

The mention of his mother and masturbation in the same sentence had almost stalled his ardour, but not quite. All in all, the Honourable Mags seemed to be pleased with him and he was certainly pleased with her, so they had begun a series of hasty, hot and sweaty meetings in various hotels around

Victoria bus station.

"Here we are, third floor corridor." She raised the by now stumpy candle and George could see an endless panelled hallway tapering away into nothingness as, down below him, over the landing banister, a gradually growing glow rose towards them. "Ah, Smears is lighting up, now you'll be able to see the arras."

George nodded, exhausted and tramped along the corridor behind her. She tried several doors, opening and closing them before he got to see inside, dismissing each with, "Urgh, green bed hangings. I don't see you with green bed hangings, darling..... No, too small..... Ahh, so that's where the bear got to..... How about in here, oh, no, someone already in residence. Sorry! We'll find you something soon," she smiled at him encouragingly over the willowing flame. "Now this is nice and look, isn't that your little case? Clever Smears, he's settled you in here already." She opened the door fully and stood back to let him in.

An unholy draught blew the candle out, curtains and bed hangings swung in the breeze from two open french windows. A vase of dead brown flowers rustled on the mantelpiece, a snarling tiger skin rug gaped up at him from the floor and his cardboard case lay open upon the overstuffed sofa at the foot of the iron bedstead.

"This is nice," he lied.

"Now you get unpacked and changed and I'll-"

"Changed?"

"You did bring a tux?"

"Yes, but-"

"Well, put it on and I'll see you downstairs in the long gallery for pre-dinner drinks at six," she kissed him hard and turned to go.

"Where will you be?"

"In my room, seeing Mummy, all sorts of things."

"But it's only four."

"Darling, don't whine. I can't be with you all the time, I told you that. I have family commitments."

"Well, at least tell me where the long gallery is."

"Down one flight, turn left, third door on the right." She caressed his cheek, "You look so lost." The thought seemed to cheer her and she skipped out with a sigh.

George slumped down onto the bed. Something lurched and pinged underneath him and, though at first he thought it was his own distress that had caused this sensation of sinking and pain in his backside, he soon realised that it was the bed and jumped up again. He pulled back the eiderdown to reveal a moth-eaten blanket and tested the mattress with the flat of one hand to feel the coiled fierceness of springs just underneath. Looking round – as if there would be anyone spying on him – he eased the blanket and sheets out from under the

17

mattress and peered beneath. Most of the mattress cover had rotted away, tufts of disgruntled stuffing adhered to the rusting springs here and there, and more had fallen straight through to the floor, some of it into the po.

He didn't know what to do, say or think.

He hadn't had much luck with thinking for some weeks now, ever since he had met Mags, in fact. Life had changed so drastically that he occasionally had to stop whatever he was doing; brushing his teeth, going to work, punching a ticket, and remind himself, 'I'm George Edward Pender, aged twenty-four, of 26 Linden Avenue, Palmers Green.'

He moved his case and sat down gingerly on the sofa, it was hard but safe. What on earth was he doing here? No-one at home knew where he was. Anything could happen to him and probably would - it often did with Mags. Lying had become a way of life. He who had been taught, 'Always tell the truth, Georgie, you'll only get found out and it'll be the worse for you,' now lied continually to everyone.

His parents and brother didn't know Mags existed and thought he had gone with Bill and Stan for the usual few days fishing. Bill and Stan thought he was in Eastbourne with his gran. No-one but he and Mags knew of their engagement, though he assumed they would be telling her family this evening, and even he wasn't entirely confident of it. He had certainly never asked her to marry him, the thought never having entered his head. Bus conductors might, occasionally, have sexual relationships with an Honourable, but they never married them.

He dropped his face into his hands and rubbed his eyes and cheeks. If he remembered correctly, he'd had her up against a violently patterned wall, her legs wrapped round his hips, his hands pinioning hers to yellow flowers on the wallpaper and she'd said,

'Oh, God,' in that particularly throaty way she had when aroused, 'I think I might marry you for this.' Then she had opened her eyes and stared at him so intently that he had blushed, 'What do you think?' Biting her lower lip in anticipation she had waited pointedly for his reply and he, as he always did with her, had agreed.

'Alright.'

He shivered, the air was autumn-cool despite the late afternoon sunlight, opaque and blinding on the dusty panes of the open French windows. Gusts of wind swung the open doors backwards and forwards, the hinges squeaking and adding to his unease. He got up to shut them and was surprised to see that he had access to a high balcony edged with battlements. Beyond, tree-tops and sky faded into a distant haze above Norfolk. He walked to the battlements and peered over. It was quite a drop, punctuated by yet another set of balconies one flight below, with muscular ivy branches twisting round gargoyles and drainpipes and, eventually, a paved terrace on which paced a man with a pipe and a dog. Mags' father he presumed and ducked back quickly.

Leaning against the battlements and looking up, grey rooves and turrets patterned the skyline and a flock of birds swooped from one cluster of chimneys to another. What a place to land up in, and if – when – he married into this family he would be expected to call it 'home'. He tried to imagine his parents visiting here, but couldn't.

He glanced at his watch, an expensive Swiss make which Mags had given him after their engagement. Ten past four. He had two hours to kill and nothing to fill them with.

He went back inside and started to unpack his case, which didn't take long as he didn't have much. One dinner suit (hired), one pair of trousers, three shirts, one tie, change of underpants and socks and his pyjamas. Hung up in the vast wardrobe it all looked very paltry, even with his pyjamas on separate hangers. On the other side of the room there was a wash-stand, on which he arranged his shaving kit and flannel, and then there really was nothing left to do and it was only - he checked slowly - twenty-five past four.

He began to clean out his jacket and trouser pockets, chucking bits of paper, fluff, sweet wrappers and old bus tickets into the empty open case, then not knowing what to do with it all. He could not tip it into the wastepaper bin; whoever cleaned up would think him pathetic, the contents of his little life laid bare in this mansion. It was a well-known fact that aristocratic servants were snobs.

They would laugh about him in the servant's hall and snigger as he passed them. So he picked up the open case and wandered out on to the balcony, whistling. He squinted up at the sky and pretended not to notice that the stiff breeze had picked up the balls of fluff, the crumpled sweet papers, the ticket stubs and spirited them away. Then in mock surprise, he watched a toffee wrapper twist and turn on its descent, only thinking to check if there was anyone below as the fluff and paper scraps floated and spiralled away on the breeze. It was alright, the man with the pipe and dog had gone.

He went back inside, shut the French doors, cut his hand on the latch, sat down on the hard sofa and wished he was back home. The passing half hours were announced by the chiming of a bell in a clock tower just out of sight from his balcony. He sat on and began to count the minutes between, sucking the cut on his hand as the blood gathered.

By five fifty he was washed, dressed and pacing the room bubbling with nerves and feeling positively sick from having sucked the blood on his hand. That awful metallic, dirty penny taste. A scab was forming, he practised in the mottled wardrobe mirror standing with his hand at an angle to hide the wound, without getting blood on the hired trousers. It looked odd with his right hand pointing outwards all the time but perhaps no-one would notice. Otherwise he looked smart, he was quite pleased with himself. Mags said he was handsome and this evening he almost believed her, if only the tuft of hair at the back of his parting would stay down.

As the last chime of six o'clock sounded he left the room, his haven of the last two hours and headed for the stairs. Down one flight, his thighs quivering inside the prickly worsted, the much-protected tapestries hanging drably to his side all the way. Turn left, and there was Smears, waiting - it seemed - for him.

"Ah, Shir," it was not so much a lisp, more a definite 'shushing' of every sibilance, "She hash been waiting."

"Am I late?"

"No, she wash early," he put a massive finger imperiously against George's sleeve. "Are you familiar with long galleriesh?"

"No, thish- I mean this- this is my first."

"Then let me exshplain," he leaned closer, smelling strongly of peppermints. "The gallery at Leatherboysh Hall ish unushual in being only twenty-three feet long. It ish, however, over a hundred and twenty feet wide."

George laughed nervously, two 'ha's' and dried. Smears nodded at him sagely, pulling down his fleshy lips, then opened the double doors with a flourish.

*****

I suppose our family has no more secrets

than the next; the uncle who was a mobster with the Krays, the second cousin once removed who changed sex and went into a convent, another cousin who disappeared for eight years with supposed amnesia, and Great Uncle George's aristocratic wife. I like secrets. I like having them but have an overwhelming urge to find them out - to shout them out. They therefore cease to be secrets and I lose interest in them, now there's a quandary of human nature for you. I am aided and abetted in this hidden vice by a mother who denies all rumours so vehemently that you know there's something in them and a father who has, at some time, known everything, but forgotten it all.

I am an only child. Perhaps that explains some of it. Although I am more complicated than that would suggest. James says I'm complicated. It's one of his.... excuses....

This child, in my womb now, will not be an 'only'. James doesn't know this yet. Oh, he knows about the baby, has been with me to see the scans, to ooh and ahh at the contents of my abdomen, but he doesn't know my plans. I should tell him, I suppose, he will have to play his part, if he's still around.
Is it wise to bring a child into such an unsure world? I know we can never be sure of anything, completely, but it would be nice for my little boy (it is a boy!) to know his father. My mother is in no doubt.

"It was all very well you living together before," she means before I wilfully got pregnant (one of those secrets I have trouble keeping the lid on), "but now why don't you do the decent thing? What's stopping you?"

I could say, 'It's too embarrassing to talk about.' She'd laugh, but it would be the truth. Instead, I say, "There isn't time."

"Isn't time?!" She stops vacuuming to look at me. "There's time for all your jaunts abroad." We've been to Paris twice and Mexico once this last year. "There's time for all your socialising." Yes, we do go out a lot; it's easier, somehow. "How long does it take to organise a wedding?"

"Ages, Mum," I know the offer is coming so I add, quickly, "And it's so expensive these days."

"Well, how much does it cost to pop down the registry office?" She stamps on the button again and the vacuum roars off with her after it.

That was a bit of a shock, actually. I never thought she'd suggest that or I'd have had an excuse ready. I always thought - church, flowers, dress, a hundred guests, marquee - that nothing else would satisfy her.

Once again, she has stumped me.

James isn't home, which isn't unusual - he often isn't home. He's a computer analyst, he works from his own flat eight stops down the line and comes to my flat in the evenings, mostly. I throw a cushion across the room. OK, so he can analyse computers, but he doesn't know a thing about me. This is pathetic, self pitying rubbish. I know it and enjoy wallowing in it for a while and end up on the sofa, humming and waving my legs about in the air (stomach and back exercises) wishing it was as simple as it was back when Great Uncle George proposed to his lovely debutant. Did it happen in the woodland surrounding the Hall, or inside somewhere? I close my eyes, take a couple of deep breaths and try to visualise.... A warm summer evening, sumptuous, Jean Harlow dresses, my great aunt blushing, Great Uncle George nervous, but passionate... in the long gallery.

*****

"George!"

He located Mags, with a young, bespectacled man, over by the nearest of the several fireplaces that lined the width of the gallery. He smiled and walked over. She was wearing a slip of pink satin so closely cut to her supple body that she could not possibly be wearing anything underneath it. As he got nearer George could detect the areola of her nipples, the fuzz of her bush beneath the thin material. He swallowed desire and kissed the cheek she angled towards him.

"Darling, you must meet George Pender."

George flicked a glance at this new 'darling', jealousy stirring, among other things.

"George, my brother, Harry."

"Ahh," George was immediately relieved and happy to shake hands.

"Nice to meet you George, I've been hearing all about you."

"Not much to tell."

"Oh, no? Pretty good in the bed department, I hear."

"Ahh," he blushed and shrugged, "thank you."

"Harry has just finished his latest painting," Mags beamed.

"Oh, yes, Mags- Margaret, mentioned that-"

"Everyone calls me Mags, darling. It's not just a bed thing."

"Right, er, what do you paint, Harry?"

"Still lifes, mostly."

"Things Freddy shoots," Mags explained. "Is he home, by the way? We found his boots on the stairs."

"Yes, he's about. Young Freddy is the first of the Berengers to go away to school," Harry smirked. "He's hating it, we knew he would, didn't we Mags? Where did you go to school, George?"

"Bowes Road Elementary."

"Don't know it. Freddy is at Harrow- same year as Lord Atterbury's eldest"

"George wouldn't know about that, would you, darling? He just knows about 'punching things'," she wrinkled her nose and pursed her lips at him. She looked stunning, desirable, but he had gradually become aware of someone crying in the distance and welcomed the distraction.

"Is someone...?"

"Oh, that's Mummy," Mags anticipated him. "There she is down there." She took his arm and swung him in the direction of the muffled sobs. All he could see, twenty or so yards away in the gas lamp glow, was the back of an armchair, beside yet another fireplace and a pale handkerchief occasionally wafting from the side of it. "I'll go and see her in a minute. What do you think of the gallery? Isn't it fine?"

"It's certainly very... wide."

"Mmm, isn't it? All this panelling was brought in from Burma."

"India." Harry corrected her.

"I'm sure it was Burma. Didn't the ship from India sink with all hands?"

"That was the porcelain from China. Honestly Mags, you do get confused."

"Well, I know I do. But you forgive me, don't you honey lamb?"

"Sometimes." Harry turned to George, excluding his sister. "Do you want to come up to my studio and see my painting?"

"Oh, not now Harry, George doesn't know anything about paintings anyway."

"Well, I do like Art, actually."

Mags looked at him tartly, "I'm sure you don't."

"I should think the chap knows what he likes and doesn't like without you telling him." Harry rushed to his defence.

"Well, I've never thought very much of what you think."

"Now, now, children...." A smooth voice, a heavily ringed hand on Mags' bare arm. "Introduce me, introduce me..." A man in clerical dress with a gold chain round his neck and a Bible under his arm smiled ingratiatingly at George.

"George, this is The Bishop, our eldest brother; Bish, this is George Pender."

"Mr Pender, I am delighted," he held out his hand, palm down, ringed finger wriggling. "Kiss the ring," he instructed.

George bent to do so and the ruby shot up, just missing his nose, and a fine jet of water hit him in the face. This was a considerable source of amusement to the others and while George fished in his pocket for a hankie, they flopped about laughing.

"They always fall for it!" The Bishop looked inordinately pleased with himself. "Poor George, I'm sorry. Well, I'm not really but we churchmen have a pretty miserable time of it, you know; funerals, weddings, synods, we have to get our laughs where we can. You should feel sorry for me."

"Should I?"

"Oh, look, you've made George cross. I've never really seen you cross. I quite like it. Let me do that." Mags took his hankie and dabbed at his by now dry face. "Don't be polite with us darling, or you'll get smothered," she whispered, pressing her body close then whizzing away. "But guess what, Bish?"

"What?" More sober but still smirking, the Bishop waggled his head at her.

"George, is a bus conductor!"

"What?" The smirk was wiped from his face immediately, to be replaced by a kind of awed reverence. "My dear Mr Pender," he advanced upon George and George backed off. "Give me your hand, you wonderful man," he grabbed George's wounded hand and made him wince. "Of all the wonderful jobs in the world, that is what I wish I could be doing. Had I not received the call at the age of ten, I would be a bus conductor now."

"Are you taking the mickey out of me?"

"Not at all!"

"No George, he's always wanted to be a bus conductor," Harry sighed and took a drink from the tray being offered round by Ethel.

"Here- have a drink," The Bishop gave George a glass. "Have two," he pressed another upon him. "I would never have played the trick with the ring had I known. Naughty, naughty Mags for not telling me, twelve Hail Marys."

Mags tutted but looked chastened. "When?"

"Now."

She sighed, "Hail Mary, Hail Mary, Hail Mary...."

"While she gets on with that, tell me," he grabbed George by both wrists, spilling sherry from both glasses, "what route are you on?"

"The twenty-fo-"

"The twenty-four," he grinned and took a deep breath.

"Hail Mary, Hail Mary." Mags shouted.

"That was only eleven," he told her.

"Hail Mary."

"Number twenty-four, starting at Victoria,

calling at St James' Park, Westminster, Charing Cross, Tottenham Court Road, Warren Street Station, Mornington Crescent-"

"All right Bish," Harry yawned exaggeratedly.

"That's very good," George told him, genuinely impressed.

"I know all the routes, all the London buses and the Suffolk, Norfolk and Essex routes. It's my passion." His eyes blazed, "And now, in our own home, a genuine London bus conductor." He put his hand to his mouth and closed his eyes in ecstasy.

"Mother's coming to a pitch," Mags told him. Certainly, the crying had got a lot louder. "Let's go and calm her down."

"One moment, Mr Pender, tell me honestly would you happen to have about your person a number twenty-four ticket?"

"No."

"Ohh..."

"I'm sorry."

"Not your fault, not your fault." He drew himself up. "Let's go and deal with Mother." He offered Mags his arm and they set off towards the next fireplace but one.

George looked at Harry, not sure how to take all this. Harry was on his third glass of sherry; he finished it and George handed him one of his.

"Thanks, you're a real gentleman."

They stood in silence for a while then George plucked up the courage to ask,

"Why is your mother so upset?" It had occurred to him that it might be due to his engagement to her eldest daughter. Mags must have told her earlier.

"It's because of Father."

"Is he unwell?"

"He's dead."

"Oh, right, I didn't know. I'm so sorry. Mags didn't say anything."

"Well, she might not - it was some time ago now - but mother still mourns, you know."

"Yes, I understand." George took his first sip of the sherry and decided it would be his last. "Presumably he was....?"

"Ill?"

"No, I was going to say, quite old."

"Twenty-six."

"Twenty-six?"

"He was in India at the time."

"Ahh, right." He took another sip in spite of himself, to buy time, and looked around. He felt a little disorientated and leant an arm against the mantle for support. Two very pale, very thin young girls slipped past and with a strange half run, half walk, their long, full lilac skirts brushing the floor, hurried down to where Mags was leaning into the huge armchair and The Bishop was reading aloud from his Bible.

"The twins," Harry informed him, "Joye and Gaye. They come after me and before Mags. But you won't have much to do with them, they rarely speak to anyone. Not even me," he laughed then bit his lip. "Bit odd that really, isn't it? I mean, they get on awfully well with Mother, Mags and The Beautiful Child, but they don't speak to us men at all."

"The Beautiful Child?"

"Yes, the youngest. She's only nine, you won't see her tonight, she had nursery tea with Freddie and Nanny at five." He gave George a friendly smile.

George felt bold enough to ask, "And how long ago then, did your father die?"

"Oh, must be nearly thirty years ago- Ah!" he grinned, "I see what you're getting at. Yes, must be confusing if you don't know. We're all posthumous children, you see." He slapped him on the shoulder.

George coughed and finished his sherry in one go.

Mags chose this moment to come up behind him, put her arms round his waist and nip his earlobe with her teeth. He nearly choked and she slapped him on the back, "Mother will see you at dinner, she's asked to have you next to her. A great honour." She kissed him on the jaw.

"Have you told her about-?"

"About you being a bus conductor? Bish has, he's over the moon. I knew he would be. And Mother's so excited about it, she's never been on a bus. She thinks you're terribly brave and avant guard. There's Aunt Suzy! Come and meet him, come and meet my bus conductor!!" Even for Mags this was a bit loud and excessive, jumping up and down clutching his shoulder and waving. George almost felt embarrassed for her then saw who was coming towards him behind Aunt Suzy and gasped. "Don't say anything!" Mags hissed in his ear. "Don't even look."

Harry took over the introductions, "Aunt Suzy, have you met George Pender, Mags' friend?"

"I have," she smiled at him, "in the hall earlier, although now I can see you. What do you think of our silly old ways?"

"I'm sure all families..." He trailed off, eyes inexorably drawn to the girl behind her.

"This is my daughter," she drew her forward, "Jane."

"How do you do?" asked George, trembling as he held out his hand, at the thought of her touch, but she tilted her head down, avoided his eyes and his hand and murmured,

"D'you do..."

"That's enough, go and see your aunt," her mother told her kindly, then turned to George. "I'm afraid my husband won't be down to meet you this evening-"

"Not another turn?" asked Mags.
George was staring after Jane as she glided to join her aunt and cousins. Mags jabbed him in the ribs.

"Sorry?" He turned to face Aunt Suzy.

"My husband... has turns and has to lie down, occasionally," she told him, softly. "You can see why," she nodded after Jane, her lower lip trembled and Mags left his side to comfort her.

George could not see why. Surely any man would be proud to have such an amazingly beautiful daughter but he asked, "Has he got a dog, and smokes a pipe?"

"A dog?"

"A pipe?"

They looked from one to another.

"No," Suzy patted his arm, "why should you think that?"

"Only I saw someone, on the terrace, this afternoon."

Three pairs of eyes slid away from his gaze.

"There's no-one like that here," Mags told him.

Smears entered with a brass gong, which he hit five times, very hard and loud. Everyone stood stock still and winced, then as the after shocks died away, began to move towards the far end - or rather side - of the gallery. Doors opened before them and the smell of roast meat billowed out. George's stomach growled, he was suddenly so hungry. Mags, hanging on his arm, laughed and rubbed his belly. He looked at her, her eyes were on his and she mouthed, 'Fuck me' at him, very slowly. Unfortunately, George could not 'fuck her' at that moment because her mother called his name.

"Where is this Pendar person I am supposed to like so much?"

Mags pushed him forward and he came up against a large bosom, a tangle of pearl ropes and a big smile.

"Mister Pendar."

"Pender."

"Hawkish," she told her daughter. "Approve your choice." A hand suddenly squeezed his scrotum. "Good balls. Come and sit with me."

She guided him to the top of a long, glittering table; just as well, because he was, at that moment, incapable of independent movement. Was this the woman who had so recently been crying over the death of a dear, thirty-odd years departed husband? She sat him down and with one hand resting on the top of his head directed the rest of the family to their seats.

"Mags there, don't want any competition, Harry, Suzy, Jane, other end of the table dear. Where are the old crones?"

"Here Lydia, here," three old ladies bustling together appeared from the throng and tried to sit in the nearest seats.

"Not there, not there, give me strength. Grace down one, then Hilda and Mattie over there. Oh, God for some more men! Joye and Gaye will you please sit on opposite sides of the table today just for me, just for Mummy. Don't start, don't start crying or it will be no supper again! What will Mister Pendar think of you, you silly girls! Bish, you sit here darling. Are those girls doing as they were told? I can't look they'll set off again."

Eventually the table settled and Mags' mother sat down heavily beside him. She smiled warmly,

"You can call me Lady Lydia straight away. I won't stand on ceremony." She looked him up and down in a most unsettling way and George caught something of her daughter in that look. He knew what it meant.

He cleared his throat.

The Bishop leant towards him across the table, "Tell me what sort of ticket machine you use? Is it a 158889 or a 267540?"

"I'm afraid I've never noticed."

It was a strange sort of meal. Overt sexual interest on one side, obsessive bus timetable questioning opposite, Aunt Suzy, quietly disinterested on his right, Mags loud and giggly with Harry away on the other side and the gorgeous, glorious Jane out of sight beyond one of the weird, silent twins and the gaggle of old women. But the food was good - leek soup, grilled sole, lemon sorbets, roast beef and Yorkshire puddings, spotted dick with thick custard and cream, then cheese; huge wedges of Stilton and cheddar with celery in a glass jug.

"You eat well," Lady Lydia noted, "Is it a life that calls for much physical exertion?"

"Not really."

"Come on, you're up and down those stairs all day," The Bishop reminded him.

"Up and down stairs? There are stairs on your bus? What's up them?"

"More seats."

"Seats? Are they comfortable?"

"Quite, but a bit rough."

"Rough?"

"The fabric covering them, I mean."

"Green, blue and red moquette, pattern number 2567." The Bish supplied.

"Up and down stairs all day you must have good thigh and calf muscles," Lady Lydia checked this out immediately. Her hand on his thigh was blatantly caressing, then she tried to lift his leg on to her lap. "Come on up, up - show us your calf."

George looked frantically over towards Mags for help, but she only waved and smiled, so he allowed her mother to rest his leg on her generous lap and roll up his trouser leg to reveal his calf muscle.

"Excellent. Good buttock development too no doubt, plenty of thrust," she winked at him. "Excuse an old lady her little foibles, young man," she slapped his calf, pushed his leg from her lap and helped herself to another slice of cheese.

"We only had the one child," Aunt Suzy decided to tell him. "Her father couldn't face another."

"I don't understand," he flicked down his trouser leg and tried to concentrate. "What do you think is wrong with your daughter?"

"Isn't it obvious?"

"No."

"She's... plain." The word cost her and she pressed her napkin to her lips.

"You think she's plain?"

"Of course she is."

"But I think she's beautiful."

"Oh, Mr Pender, you are so kind. So, so kind, but there's no need to shield me from the truth. Of course, you have picked the beauty from this family…" She gestured down to Mags who was hooting with laughter over something that Harry had just said.

"Oh, yes, of course, Mags is lovely-"

"A true English beauty," Lady Lydia asserted. "Not a blemish on her, as you will be able to attest, Mister Pendar?"

"No, not a blemish."

"Good breasts, firm rear and I defy a man to find a better inner thigh."

"Are you particularly fond of thighs?" George asked her bluntly.

She paused, a twinkle in her eye, "I like you."

His heart pounded as he sat back.

CHAPTER 2

I have just received a summons, a long and garbled telephone massage from my great aunt, left for me while I was in the bath. I suppose it must be very confusing for old people, all this new technology. Cars were hi-tech when she was a girl. I had to smile, sitting in my bath robe, warm and plumptious, listening to her.

'This is you, is it? How am I supposed to know? I could be speaking to anyone. Well, on the understanding that this is your phone Clover, I will leave my message as suggested by the kind lady who answered. What a job! Sitting there all day saying the same few lines over and over. Now, where was I?' Pause, during which it sounded as if she was blowing her nose. 'Clover, please come at once, or today at least. If that's not Clover listening then I hope you will forget all you have heard. Thank you.'

I called her back immediately to put her mind at rest, "What do you want Aunty, has something happened? Are you all right?"

"I'm all right my dear, don't worry. I need you to do a little chore for me that's all. And it would be nice to see you. Your mother and aunts and uncles come round quite often and, of course, I have my Bridge. I'm never lonely, but it's not the same. D'you know you're the only one who actually looks me in the eye? I miss that. George was always very good at that. He had lovely eyes, did you ever notice?"

"Yes, I did. He had very nice eyes indeed, very kind."

"Oh, I wouldn't say that. I always felt that he was undressing me, mentally..."

"Er... perhaps that was just the way he looked at you, Aunty."

"Yes."

"I'll pop in at six-thirty, is that OK?"

"Yes." She put the phone down rather abruptly- probably thinking about Great Uncle George's come to bed eyes.

Odd to think about old people having sex; rather nasty actually, though I suppose they enjoy it. After all those years together, the exciting separateness of another body conjoining with yours can no longer play a part, but the intimate knowledge of how that arm looks now and how it once looked, must add a poignancy.

Can't sit and think about that. James' body is still very separate, very exciting, though mine is probably... I slip the bath robe off and look at myself in the mirror. No mistaking that lump for anything but a pregnant tum, with my son growing inside.

I wonder why they had no children.

Aunty is waiting at her front window and hurries to open the door for me. She angles her cheek for a kiss and whisks me inside. There is a fizz of anticipation in the air. I smile at her and allow myself to be herded into the sitting room and on to the sofa.

"What's all this about? You seem excited."

"I'll make the tea." She's off.

No point in trying to stop her or tell her that James and I will be eating at his sister's this evening. I take off my coat and throw it over the back of the sofa. Up on the wall, over the fireplace, above the pipe rack, the beautiful young girl is still smiling down, knowingly. Uncle George must have found her absolutely luscious. I wonder where they did their courting, snatched their coy kisses. Perhaps in secret, in the woods round about the great house.

*****

"Where the bloody hell are you?!" George was getting very cold. It was late September, it had rained last night – he had heard every drop against his windows, sleepless on the hard couch – and once again, he had allowed Mags to manoeuvre him into a situation. He cupped his mouth, "Just whistle, or something, so that I know the rough direction!"

A distant trill of notes made him turn to his right. "Stay where you are!" he bellowed and began to pick his way through the leaf litter, thankful at least that he still had his socks and shoes on. Using one hand to part the low branches and russet-leaved thickets he protected his naked privates with the other. There was a breeze; splatters of cold water from the boughs above and the grass below sent shivers up from his buttocks to the small of his back and down again.

"Bloody stupid idea," he muttered.

'Let's have sex in the forest,' she'd suggested. And he, groggy with lack of sleep and annoyed that she hadn't come to his room last night, had agreed. But he hadn't reckoned on having to strip off and then find her amongst all the undergrowth, 'Oh, it'll be fun, Georgie, don't be such a kill-joy. I thought you were game for anything. I am disappointed in you...' The pout had come into play at this point and he had sighed and begun to undo his tie. 'There's a good boy! Mags will make it all worth your while, promise,' she had skipped off, flinging her hat into the bushes. 'Come and find me, chase me!'
'Oi, Mags!'

He slogged on hoping he wouldn't catch pneumonia and have to explain how to his mother. 'Well, Mum, I was chasing this titled mad woman through the woods in the buff...'

"Cooee!" Mags flashed through the clearing up ahead of him - pale, slim limbs pounding, breasts jiggling, hair bouncing - and disappeared again.
He found her knickers, turquoise silk edged with coffee coloured lace, hanging from a bush and snatched them up. He could always put them on, he supposed, give himself some protection. He

stood still, in a fleeting ray of weak sunshine, and stretched the elastic between his hands, judging the size. They would fit him, no problem. He lifted one knee. In front of him a low swoop of chestnut rustled and he glanced up, wobbling slightly. His mouth opened to complain to her about the cold and the stupidity of her suggestion, then snapped shut. Clutching the flimsy silk to his scrotum he turned tail, thrashing into the densest undergrowth and ducked down.

He could see the old lady, through the network of twigs and leaves. She swayed and the sun glinted on her round, gold rimmed glasses. Then she dropped her basket and pressed both hands to her pink cardiganed chest. He waited to see no more, but backed out of his hiding place, and ran.

He was out of breath, completely lost, wet, scratched and bleeding when he literally fell over Mags, laid out on a pile of damp leaves, and crashed down on top of her.

"Darling, you've found me!" she squealed and wrapped her arms and legs round him.

He might have been cross, dry-mouthed and cold but she wriggled and squirmed, caressed and aroused him so expertly that he forgot his bad temper and joined in enthusiastically.

"See how rough you can be with me? I really don't mind."

He was rough. He felt powerful and he didn't disappoint her at all.

"I knew this would be a good idea," she told

him afterwards as they lay on the leaves, in a soft bath of sunlight. "I find the wild woods so intoxicating," she sat up. "I forget all about the cold, the wet, the," she flicked a millipede off his raised thigh, "creepy crawlies. This is where we end up, in the ground, in the wild wood, part of nature. Rained on, snowed on, rooted out by pigs, grown through by tree roots, eaten up by worms and maggots. We're just a part of it, aren't we? Don't you feel it? I think you do. You rogered me like a wild man. I feel split in two with passion." She grabbed handfuls of leaves and rubbed them between her legs.

"Careful, Mags, you don't know what's on them."

"That's my point," she tossed the leaves over him. "Oh, George, can't you share this with me? Don't you know what I'm talking about?"

"Yes," he hid a yawn, turning to grab some leaves to throw at her, "I do know what you're talking about, it's just taking me time to… delve into the depths of my subconscious primitiveness, my wild man." He was talking through his arse, she would find him out, surely. But no, she sat astride him and rubbed her mucky hands over her breasts, spreading the mud across her smooth skin, raising her hands to the sky far above, flickering between the late summer branches. A little shower of orange and gold leaves trickled down over them and she laughed,

"I'm in my heaven," then she looked down, "with my darling boy."

He smiled.

George ran downstairs fresh from a bath run for him by the pertly plump Ethel and swung round the heavy oak newel post into the main hall. The double front doors were flung wide, the sun was shining in. It had turned into a beautiful day, even the arras had a bit of colour to them. Then Lady Lydia called to him from the open drawing room doors,

"You missed lunch."

"Yes," he slicked back his newly washed fall of hair and tried to smile cheerfully, "Mags was showing me the woods. We got lost."

"Rubbish, Mags knows those woods like the floor plan of Fortnum's. I know exactly what you were doing. Come here."

She waited for him in the door way and took his arm as he came up to her, "You must be starving. Walk me out to tea on the lawn, you wild man, you," she winked at him.

George felt himself redden and cursed Mags for telling all and sundry about their love-life. He must speak to her about it. He must speak to her mother about their engagement. He cleared his throat, "You do know the situation, between Mags and me?"

"I know all about it," she paused and altered the angle of a china dish on one of the innumerable little tables scattered throughout the room. "Don't worry your sweet little head about it. I am more worried about Hilda."

"Hilda?"   Was this another 'posthumous' child?

"She didn't turn up for lunch either, most unlike her."

"Have I met Hilda?"

"Of course you have."   She stopped him in the sunlight on the terrace and they reviewed the dappled lawns and white damasked tables, the cane chairs and people scattered about the greensward, "But you haven't met The Beautiful Child yet, have you?" She beamed at him, suddenly beautiful herself.

She can't be much more than fifty, he thought, smiling in spite of the danger.

"Sybella!" She called, her voice softer than when she had called to him.

A small child detached herself from a group near a noble cedar and ran towards them, her stringy plaits wriggling behind her like gaily tied snakes.

"My youngest," Lady Lydia informed him, "Come and meet Mr Pender, my dearest bird of love divine." The child arrived, breathless, and her mother took her by one shoulder, slowly rotating her in front of him so that he could fully appreciate the green smocked polka dot dress, the neatly parted brown hair and the scabbed, bony elbows. "Isn't she beautiful?"

"Yes," he nodded, "very."

"Are you Mags' beau?" The child asked, her voice tight and sharp.

"I am, yes, George Pender. Very pleased to meet-"

"I've heard all about you."

"Ah," he sincerely hoped not.

"The Bish thinks you're wonderful because you punch people on buses."

"Not people, no, just their tickets."

"How boring." She smirked and flounced off.

"Out of the mouths of babes." Lady Lydia simpered at him.

"It might be boring to you, but it-"

"Come and sit down, the food is arriving," she clasped his hand warmly and urged him on. "You know, I never cease to be amazed at how we can get through a massive tea at four and yet still have the room to eat dinner only three hours later." She led him firmly across the terrace, down the steps to the springy lawn and deposited him at the nearest small table. Leaving him without a word, she demanded of the two old ladies at the neighbouring table, "Have you found her?"

"No- "

"No Lydia, dear," they warbled.

George looked around for Mags. She was not down yet but the glorious Jane was. She caught his eyes upon her and lowered the brim of her white sun hat, he got up and went over to her table. As he sat, she made to move away.

"Won't you stay and talk to me?"

She edged back into her chair but didn't look up at him or answer. He had to content himself with the tip of her chin and the smooth curve of her throat above her dark blue dress. "This is an amazing house you live in," he began lamely. "Have you always...?"

"Always," she assured him.

"Is your father coming down for...?"

"No," she shook her head.

"Tea looks excellent." He nodded towards the trestle tables being loaded with tray after tray of sandwiches and cakes by a succession of maids and two footmen. Ethel was wheeling out a trolley with jellies wobbling on it, red and yellow in glass dishes, spoons jangling. "I have to admit to being really hungry. Mags and I got lost in the woods..."

"Liar." Her voice was a soft reproof.

He sat back and folded his arms, "Does everyone know what Mags and I were doing in the woods?" He was sorry for the curt note in his voice, sorry that she should hear it, but he was seriously angry with Mags now.

"Yes."

"Did she tell you?"

"Yes."

"Well I wish she wouldn't. Doesn't it occur to her that... I'm sorry- it's not you I'm angry with. Please forgive me? Shall we go and get some tea-?"

He glanced up at the trestles in time to see the trolley of untouched jellies being wheeled towards the house and the full plates of cakes and sandwiches being loaded back on to the footmen's trays.

"Excuse me." He got up and ran over to the

nearest footman, "Here, I haven't had anything yet."

"Go on then," the footman angled the loaded sandwich plate towards him, looking round to see if anyone was watching, "quick. I expect you're starving."

He grabbed two sandwiches off the tray, snatched a plate and went on to help himself to a slice of fruit cake from a china stand which was actually being removed from the table as he took his piece. The footman gave him a rather salacious wink and the maid who was loading the tray giggled. Smears boomed at him from behind,

"Ish shomething amish, shir?"

George stuffed a crab sandwich into his mouth and turned to him, "I haven't eaten yet. As you no doubt know, I was pleasuring the Honourable Margaret in the woods at lunchtime!" Crumbs splattered the butler's lapels.

Smears raised one bushy eyebrow, pursed his lips and half turned to point out, "Tea ish being sherved on the lawn, shir..." He brushed down his lapels and hissed, "I hope she was worth missing lunch for."

George swallowed his mouthful and narrowed his eyes at him, "What's happened to your lisp?"

"It was a requirement of the job, sir. If you get hungry you can always come down to the kitchen later."

"Thank you. I'll go and have some tea then. Very nice sandwiches, by the way."

"I'll tell cook."

They parted, George wandered back to Jane's table where a full cup and saucer awaited him. He sat down, offered her a sandwich, which she declined and said, "This is a very odd place."

"Yes. I was up in London the other week, to see the dentist…"

He looked at the crown of her hat, which was still all he could see, and waited for the rest.

"Near Victoria." She finished

"Ah, my bus runs-"

"I know. I always think when I come back, how odd it is here."

"Why do you come back?"

"Because of Mother."

"I see." Of course, father always having 'turns', mother having to cope, beautiful, loyal daughter helping where she could.… Her fingernails were oval perfection.

"Haloo, haloo, haloo!"

George looked round to see who was shouting.

"It's The Bish," Jane told him, "up there on the balcony."

"Ah yes," George waved back at the robe draped figure on the lowest balcony. "Is he a real Bishop?"

"No."

"I didn't think he could be."

"You are a Christian! A Christian gent!" The Bish assured him at the top of his voice.

"Thank you!" George called back.

The Bish arranged his robes carefully and sat on the balustrade, "Been meaning to have a talk." He bellowed.

"Come down then," suggested George.

"I'm waiting for Mags, you know what women are like! She was just saying..." Something caught his eye as he rested his hand on the balustrade and he leant forward. "Good Lord!" He leaned further forward.

"What's he doing?" George put down his cup. "Is he all right?"

"I don't know."

He glanced at Jane, her head was up and he could absorb her particular beauty; anyone could have such clear skin, such dark lashed eyes of deepest blue, but could anyone combine the two, the kiss of lash against fine grained pores, so intimately? He had never seen a mouth like hers, untouched by make-up, her delicately fawn lips were permanently parted as if she was about to smile or speak, perhaps to him. And then she did,

"What is he doing?" Her slim hand suddenly hid her lips from his view. He looked back at the house. The Bishop was now lying full length along the balustrade, reaching down into the blanket of ivy which covered the lower floor of the house. His white robes were billowing in the breeze, one foot was jerking about in the air, his ruby ring flashed.

"Watch out!" George and Jane jumped up together as The Bish rolled, oh so slowly, off the rail, his black bands fluttering for a brief moment.

Jane screamed.

There was a soft, dense crump, like a side of beef being unhooked and dumped on the chopping board.

George was aware of Harry running past him, of someone fainting at the old ladies' table, of Lady Lydia catching hold of The Beautiful Child as she ran screaming,

"Blood, blood!" Towards her fallen brother.

"Stay there," he told Jane. She dropped back into her seat, her face as white as her hat, and he caught Harry up at the body. There was blood, seeping quickly out from under the back of The Bish's head, almost black.

"Oh, my God..." George felt his gorge rising.

Harry turned to him, "Thank you." He bent slowly and knelt by his brother, the eyes were open but glazed. Harry took up one limp hand and kissed it.

Above them someone started to scream, rhythmically.

George squinted up and saw Mags leaning over the balcony, her face contorted. He ran inside, stumbled up the darkened stairs and opened every door he came to on the first floor till he found her. She was still there, leaning over and screaming. He grabbed her back from the edge and held her tight to him, her body was tense with shock and he rocked her, moving her slowly into the room.

"Hush, hush," his own legs were shaking; he

wanted to sit down, he looked round and saw a huge four poster bed, the sheets rumpled, the pillows dented. "Hush, hush," he rubbed the soft silk of her robe over her naked back and glanced again at the disordered covers. He shuffled her towards the bed, they sank onto it and she pushed away from him, burying her face in the embroidered pillows, her shoulders shaking with sobs, but quieter now. He stroked her hip, noticing her bare legs as the dressing gown slid open, and got up quickly. "Is this your room, Mags?" But he knew as he asked that it was not. In the corner was a complete pulpit, carved wooden canopy, steps and all. On the walls were paintings and drawings of London buses, one of them the number twenty-four.

She had ignored or hadn't heard his question, so he went back out onto the balcony. There was a lot of noise from below. Lady Lydia was sprawled across the dead body of her eldest, wailing. Harry was comforting her. The weird twins were skipping up and down the terrace steps, chanting, playing some kind of game. The Beautiful Child was being hauled off bodily by Smears, still shouting,

"Blood, blood!"

Both old ladies were flat out on the lawn, being fussed over by Aunt Suzy and a couple of maids. Jane was exactly where he had left her, immobile at the tea table and, in the middle of the lawn, a young boy was running towards the terrace, a gun in his hand, several dead birds falling from his game bag as he gathered speed.

George looked back down onto the terrace, to the spreading pool of dark blood and Lady Lydia, prostrate and something pink attracted his eye. It was the colour, the particular shade of pink, which made him gasp and look round quickly, back to the bedroom where Mags was still sobbing on the tousled bed, down to the terrace, out onto the lawn. Then he crouched down, as The Bish should have done, reached through the lichened stone rails of the balustrade and, shoulder, arm, fingers, fully flexed, tweezered up the stub of a six-penny bus ticket, route number twenty-four.

He pocketed it, got up, head spinning, and tottered back into the bedroom to try and deal with Mags.

*****

"I see you're looking at the painting." Aunty has come into the room behind me with a tray and my stomach gives a little lurch. As if I've been caught out doing something wrong,

"It is so lovely, you were…"

"And that's why I wanted you to come round. Just move those magazines off the table for me, will you?"

I move the jumble of BBC Homes and Gardens, Woman's Weeklys and Cosmopolitan – Cosmo? – from the teak coffee table and she puts the tray down. In the back of my mind is the hope, the idea, that she's going to offer me the painting. I would love it.

"You have milk and sugar, don't you dear?"

"No sugar." I pat my rounded tum.

"Oh, what a shame, it's a lovely top too."

"What?"

She hands me my tea. "Well, it's shrunk in the wash. Can't you pull it down over your tummy dear? We don't all want to see your, rather large belly, do we?"

"It's meant to be like this and I'm pregnant. You did know that, didn't you?"

"Pregnant?" She puts down the tea pot, "Your mother never said. Do you know who the father is?"

"Yes." I laugh nervously, "It's James. You've met James."

"Have I? Oh, at the wedding, I suppose."

"What wedding?"

"Yours and James', silly." She stirs her tea gaily.

"We're not married, actually."

She tuts, "Oh, dear," and get's up to go back into the kitchen. I sit and wonder whether the continuation of this conversation is going to make me inheriting the painting more or less likely. I decide and say nothing when she comes back.

"Forgot the cake," she explains. "D'you know, this huge fruit cake I made never got touched at the funeral? How it got overlooked I'll never know. Have some, do. It's awfully hard trying to eat it up all by myself, it affects my bowels." She proffers me a giant chunk.

I remember my mother suspiciously sniffing

the tin and, the oil painting firmly in my mind, smile as I take the plate.

"Now the reason I brought you here..."

Great, she's forgotten about the non-event wedding, though, if she's reading Cosmo...

"I want to get rid of that dratted painting."

"Oh, no, surely, it's so, so..." I am starting to get excited; I have a spot for it on the sitting room wall.

"I only ever allowed it in here because of your uncle. George was very attached to it and so I gave in, but I've always hated it. Don't look so surprised. Would you like it there, reminding you, hanging over you, day after day, year after year? I made my decision this morning, that's why I wanted you here soon, so that I couldn't change my mind." She sips her tea.

It's mine, it's mine, it's...

"I'm sending it back."

"Back?"

"Back to Leatherboys Hall. It's where it belongs and I want you to take it for me."

"Take it back to Leatherboys Hall?"

"Yes. It's the right thing to do. I can't trust the post with it. You've got a little car, haven't you?"

*****

"No, I haven't got a car." George was marooned halfway along the 'Long Gallery', dressed for dinner, sitting in an armchair opposite the youngest boy, Freddy.

"Oh." Such very deep disappointment, then, "I like cars." Freddy, red eyed and pale assured him. There was an anxious pause, a very long anxious pause. "Very much." The poor boy was doing his best, in the absence of his mother and older siblings, to entertain their guest.

George nodded. He felt sorry for him but was numbed himself. Not so much over the death of The Bishop, though that was terrible enough, no, he was also plagued by the tousled four poster and Mags's state of undress, and the bloody bus ticket. He wished sincerely that he did have a car, then he could get in it and drive home, to Palmers Green, to safety and sanity. He dredged up a nugget, "I expect when you're older you'll have a car."

"Yes," Freddy drummed his heels against the faded chintz frill on his chair, "I expect I will."

"Like Mags'."

"Mmm," he nodded. There was something about Freddy, or rather, there was nothing about him, nothing odd. He looked, sounded and behaved like a normal twelve-year-old boy and it was very disturbing. "I'm going back to school soon."

"Ah. Do you like it?" Then George remembered hearing that he didn't and puffed out his cheeks, he'd put his foot in it again.

"Yes. I've made lots of friends."

"Oh, have you? That's good."

"Yes." He brightened, his mouth twitched, "Tony Cheevers has said I can go and stay with his people at half term. They've got one of the best shooting estates in the country."

"You'll enjoy that."

"Yes, if- if- mother lets me go."

"Ah, well."

The double doors opened, both looked up, hoping for rescue, but it was only the twins. They sidled in, dressed completely and identically in deep mourning, their white-blond hair sleeked back in matching buns fastened with black, feathered clips. Holding hands, heads down, they shuffled across the room, giggling as they passed George and Freddy, hurrying towards the window seat and hiding themselves behind the curtains, tucking their skinny legs under their full skirts, still giggling.

"Creeps," muttered Freddy into his stiff collar. George thought it best to offer no opinion. He looked in the opposite direction from the window and his gaze stalled upon a gaudy oil painting of a young man in regimental red, his cap at a cheeky angle and a swagger stick under his arm. A gold plaque under the painting announced, 'Captain Howard Berenger, BGC'. So, this was the much-mourned husband, supposed father of all Lady Lydia's children. None of them looked the slightest bit like him; he had buck teeth and a squint. George checked his watch, seven-thirty. He wondered what Mags was doing. "I think," he got up, "I think I'll just..." he gestured towards the doors.

"Mmm?" Freddy's nose was reddening.

He couldn't leave him so sat down again and

blurted, "I suppose that's your father?"

Freddy looked at the painting, then back at George and nodded.

"He looks... um.   BGC, what does that mean, some sort of medal or order...?"

"It stands for 'Bloody Good Chap'."

"Ah. Right, never heard of that one." In the ensuing few minutes of silence George could hear the unsynchronised ticking of two or three clocks, the twins whispering and Freddie sniffing. "Look," he stood, "I won't be long."
Freddy looked up at him, his mouth trembling and nodded again. "Here," George took his best linen hanky, for display purposes only, from his dress jacket top pocket, and handed it to him.

"Thanks."

As he left the room, he heard young Freddy blowing loudly.

Out in the hall a deeper silence pressed about him. The famous arras, faintly lit by the various oil lamps which were perched on every available flat surface, billowed ocherously in the constant breezes that scurried through the corridors. George pulled up his jacket collar and wondered how to find his fiancée in the sprawling mass that was her home. Then he remembered Ethel and her assurance that he would always be able to find her in her room. He didn't want her getting the wrong idea; he was not interested in Ethel, but she had been kind, and she seemed quite normal, so he began to climb the stairs.

He might very well have thigh and calf muscles strong enough to arouse Lady Lydia, but after five minutes his lauded limbs were quivering. The lamps got fewer, the draughts quite vicious and the stair carpet more worn. He paused for breath in the very centre of the monstrous and silent house, seemingly the only living soul in it. Above, only darkness. Below, a spiral of shallow steps and sinuous banister whirling away into a vortex of yellow-green light. He steadied himself, one hand on the split panelling.

Oh, Christ, The Bish was trying to reach that ticket. He died trying to reach for a ten-a-penny, tuppeny-ha'penny stub of a ticket that a child might throw away any day of the week. His legs gave way and he sank onto his haunches, hid his face in his hands and tried not to laugh.

Of course, he knew where the ticket had come from.

"Hello. Coming to find me?"

The cheery voice made him look up. Ethel, in white mob cap and frilly apron, a black band round her black and white striped sleeve, was coming down towards him.

"Yes," he levered himself up using the banister, which wobbled, "I wanted to know where Mags' room was."

"Oh." She folded her hands at her waist and pursed her lips.

"I didn't know if she was coming down for dinner, or not."

"Not, I'm afraid. Nanny has given all the ladies of the family sedatives."

"I see," he frowned, "But, I saw the twins earlier..."

"Oh, they had them too, but nothing works on them. Have to crack their skulls with a hammer to get them to lie down." She began to step past him.

"Ethel?"

"Yes?"

"I feel very out of place here."

"Well, you are. You're a bus conductor and they're all county nobs."

"Yes." He could see she was about to leave him there on the stairs, no help or succour in sight so he grabbed her arm, clasped her to him and kissed her hard on the lips.

After a moment she pushed him away, he toppled and nearly fell but she grabbed him back. He kissed her again, not knowing what else to do. She struggled free and wiped her lips. They stood panting on the stairs, staring at each other for several seconds, then she said,

"Come down and have a cuppa tea then."

Hurrying down that same dreadful staircase with Ethel made him feel quite light-headed with happiness. He flew down, her capped head bobbing at his side. Once in the still-deserted hall she led him through a green baize door under the stairs and below, into a different world. A row of bare bulbs marched down the centre of the ceiling illuminating a wide corridor with many doors off it. Worn paved slabs of stone on the floor, buttery-yellow walls, green painted wood-work and people, lots of them. George took the last few steps slowly, gazing around. Two footmen were playing catch with what looked like a silver tea pot, a maid was pinning up her hair in a mirror tacked to the wall and surrounded by brightly coloured postcards from seaside resorts. Smears rushed out from one door, across the corridor, dodging the tea pot, and disappeared into another door, his waistcoat undone, a bottle in his hand. Someone bellowed in a foreign tongue. Something crashed. A saucepan lid rolled out into the corridor, spiralled round and round on itself and landed flat with a hollow clang. A skivvy ran out to collect it.

"Oh, dear," Ethel turned to him apologetically, "I'm afraid Cook's a bit upset today. Never mind, follow me." They wove their way down the corridor, avoiding staff in variously smart and informal dress and nobody stared at him or made him feel out of place. He was in his place, he saw that, and for the first time at Leatherboys Hall, he relaxed.

She sat him down in a tiny sitting room complete with kettle on the hob, a lace covered table with an aspidistra in a highly glazed brown bowl and bookshelves full of colourful romances. "This is my little room," she told him, spooning out leaf tea into a floral tea pot.

"It's very nice."

"It's cosy."

He decided not to query the fact of an upstairs maid having the use of her own sitting room. This was an odd house, it made its own rules and he was comfortable in his Windsor chair. Raindrops sparkled at a high window, sparkling against the indigo blue evening sky and the kettle began to whistle.

"I'm sorry about that, on the stairs," he began.

"Don't be. It was all right, I didn't mind. I have been kissed before. It wasn't my first time or anything, and I am sixteen now." She poured the steaming water into the pot.

"Sixteen?"

"Just." She reddened.

"I thought you were older."

"That's not very gallant." She popped the lid on and put the pot to draw on the grate.

"No, I'm sorry, I didn't mean it like that. You don't look older, now I can see you properly," her cheeks darkened "but you are very grown up in your manner."

"Well, I've had to be, haven't I? Phew, it's hot in here, isn't it?" She fanned her face with her hand and stood up to open her little window with a hooked pole.

"Here, let me do that for you." He took the pole from her and flicked the latch open.

"You're very nifty with that."

"I have to change the numbers on the buses." He flexed his wrist, aware that Mags would have turned this whole conversation into an innuendo ridden jest. He sat down again. She put pretty gold rimmed cups and saucers out on her lace cloth and he noticed her hands, small, neat, chapped. She offered a biscuit from a tin with kittens on it, he picked one out. "You're the only person here I feel comfortable with, Ethel." And he realised that, in a disconcerting way, she reminded him of his Mum.

"I don't think any of us is comfortable at the moment. With poor Bish gone it's like... I dunno, it's like we've got no direction. You heard what Cookie was like. Of course, he's taken it so hard. He's been with the family over thirty years." She poured out the tea.

He watched her, nibbling his biscuit. "I know it's not really any of my business, although it might be, one day, if Mags and I..."

She bit her lower lip and handed him his cup, "If Mags and you what?"

"Marry."

"Marry!?"

"Yes, well, whatever. But, they cannot all be Lady Lydia's husband's children, can they?"

"I don't know what you're talking about."

"He died around thirty years ago."

"It's private family business. Nothing to do with outsiders." She turned slightly away, sat down and raised her cup to her lip like a duchess.

"I'm sorry again, Ethel. It's just all so very odd here."

"Not so very odd."

"Have you ever lived anywhere else?"

"No."

"Then how can you tell? Surely, when you lived with your family you had a more normal life.

"I am living with my family, if you must know."

"Are you parents in service here, then?"

She pursed her lips and her cup and saucer shook, "One is."

"Well, if you've never lived outside in the real world then you won't know how unreal this house is. Everything is extreme, nothing's normal, except you. I don't know how to behave."

"Dinner's about to be served upstairs, sir," Smears popped his head round the door for an instant.

"Right, thank you." George put down his cup and stood, looking down at Ethel, "Thanks for tea, thanks for rescuing me."

"Back upstairs to the nobs now, are you?"

"For now. But I'd like to come back down here to see you again, may I?"

"If you like," she bent her head to her tea, "then I could put a bandage on your cut hand, if you want."

"No, its fine," he'd forgotten all about it but appreciated that she'd noticed. "Thank you." he patted her cap and left.

Smears led him the back way, directly to the dining room, "Members of the family don't know this route exists," he told George as they walked smartly between lead lined doors and dark cells, where the glinting rings of wine bottle ends were stacked up as far as the low vaulted ceilings. Smears' hair was newly oiled, his waistcoat buttoned, his black jacket spotless and he smelled of peppermints. "Nice little girl, Ethel," he remarked.

"Very nice."

"I won't have her trifled with."

"Of course not."

"Do what you like with them upstairs, but keep your trousers buttoned round my staff."

"Of course."

"Thish way, shir." He opened a baize door and ushered George into the dining room. Those already seated turned to stare at the newcomer, Smears explained, "Mr Pender got losht."

"Easily done," agreed Harry. "Come and join our far from merry crew, George." He pointed him to a chair opposite himself, next to Freddy. "Mother insists on coming down. We'll just wait for her Smears, then you can serve."

"Yesh shir." He bowed himself into a corner by the service door.

George sat and fingered his cutlery until he caught Smears' frowning tut, so he sat on his hands and cleared his throat, "I was wondering if I ought to go home, after this."

"After dinner? It'll be rather late." Harry wrinkled his nose and his glasses rose.

"No, I meant after the accident. Well, perhaps in the morning I could-. I mean, you don't want me here while the family are in mourning, because of the death. I feel I'm intruding."

"Nonsense," Harry, shook his head, "Mags will need you now more than ever; she's already said so. My sister has appetites, as you must be aware, and death always sharpens them."

"Does it?"

"It's happened before. We've had her seen to by the most eminent men in their field. They all say it's a form of life affirmation after the sudden and tragically early death of our father. She still goes to see some of the specialists and they no longer charge, it's very decent of them. In fact, I think that's what she was doing when she met you, wasn't it?"

"I don't know."

"She doesn't talk about it, much. It's the cross she has to bear."

"Ah." George nodded, weakly.

The main doors flew open and Lady Lydia marched in, her black sequinned dress cut low over her bosom, her lips very red. The three remaining males at the table stood and she paused to stared at them al while Smears closed the doors behind her,

"And these are all my men." She spoke as if quoting, but George couldn't place the words. "Well." She tossed her head and went to her place at the top of the table. Smears moved her chair in and, George was sure, stroked her arm as she sat. "Still no sign of Hilda?"

"No, My Lady," Smears shook out her napkin and made a to-do of placing it in her lap, "but I did hear that she went to the woodsh to find mushroomsh for chef. She took her wicker bashket with her."

George fell backwards into his chair, but his distress was missed, as The Beautiful Child chose this moment to rush in - hair wild, pyjamas, with pink elephants on, unbuttoned over her lacey vest - yelling "Blood, blood, blood!"

CHAPTER 3

"What?" Over the line, my mother's voice is quivery with shock. I'm quivery too,

"It's all right," I calm her, hoping to calm myself as well, "I haven't lost the baby, the doctor says he's fine."

"Thank God. What caused it, did he say?"

"Carrying something heavy," I fudge.

"Carrying what heavy? Clover, have you been silly?"

"No, I wasn't aware of it being heavy at all."

"What was it?"

I don't want her to know I've got the picture. That I was trying to hang it all by myself, out of spite. I want to keep it all secret. "I moved an armchair."

"An armchair?"

"Well, the leather sofa actually."

"Why, Clover? Why on earth didn't you wait for James?"

Why, why, why? Because, mother dear, we've had a flaming row and James won't be coming round anymore to move sofas, have meals, paint the window frames, wash my little car, use my bed. "Because I wanted to lie on it and have a nice view out of the window."

"You need your head seeing to, my girl."

Yes, I do. "I'm sorry, Mum."

"Don't 'sorry' me, I'm coming round."

"OK." I turn the phone off and lie back, relieved; Mummy's coming round.

I try to cry but I cried so much last night that I don't think I can have any tears left in my ducts. I knew, as soon as James got himself closeted in the kitchen with his sneaky sister, that there was going to be trouble. Everything had been going so well. I had managed to get Aunty's picture into the back of my car and then put my car away in the garage as soon as I got home, so that James didn't see it. I knew he wouldn't like having the painting around; he hates old things – antiques - says their maudlin. That's one good thing that's come out of all this, he no longer has any say in what I do or don't do, have or don't have. He didn't object to driving to his sister's in his car, he was very chatty - about work or something - and I thought, foolishly, this is going well for a change. I should have known...

The meal started promisingly, goat's cheese and red onion tartlets, Amber had made a real effort. However, the main course pasta was overcooked. I didn't say anything, but I must have made a face, a moue. James caught me and gave me one of his looks, his hard stares. I used to joke that they were like Paddington Bear's 'hard stares', and he used to laugh. Amber picked up on it. She must have seen his look rather than mine and asked,

'What's wrong with it?'

She has a thing about my cooking. I'm very good, it's no vain boast, everyone acknowledges the fact. It tends to make friends and family anxious whenever they have me over for a meal. And anyway, Amber is fairly anxious all the time, I maintain it's because James has always been so demanding of her. He is such a perfectionist. That's why he liked me, originally, because I was such a 'perfect cook'. So, I simply said,

'Perhaps the pasta is a little soft,' that's all and she was off, crying in the kitchen. He went to placate her and they were in there for such a long time that it was awkward. The rest of us tried to carry on but when your hostess is weeping audibly in the next room it is hard.

I did feel bad, I suppose. Simon, Amber's partner, said it was her time of the month and I made some remark about every moment being time of the month when you're pregnant, and we laughed. It went all quiet in the kitchen, for quite a while, then James's voice was raised and I knew. I knew just what that little bitch had done and cursed myself for admitting it to her. My weakness with secrets. Eventually they both came out; her all red-eyed, him all compressed lips and the rest of the evening, all ten minutes of it, was a disaster. I couldn't eat or speak, I was so nervous. Everyone else frizzled in the tension, knocking over a glass of red wine, dropping a fork on the wood strip flooring, banging their head on the table while retrieving it. Jumping when James suddenly scraped his chair back and announced we were leaving.

He shouted at me all the way home, driving like a maniac and left me on the wet pavement outside my flat, at half past ten, speeding away with squealing tyres and his parting words, 'conniving cunt', ringing in the night air.

Funnily enough, all I thought at the time was, 'Mmm, clever alliteration.'

The front doorbell is ringing, "It's on the latch, Mum!" I call from my bed. I shall have to tell her, I suppose.

"How are you?" She's all bustle, all righteous and smug. "What did the doctor say, exactly? Your father dropped me off because he's on his way to have his blood pressure checked, though God knows what it'll be with this little bombshell landing on his lap this morning. And you're sure you haven't lost it?"

"Quite sure."

"I'll make us a cup of tea and then you can tell me all about it. Where's James, mm?" Her coat is off, her handbag stowed, her sleeves rolled and she's off to create havoc in my kitchen. "You have told him, I suppose?"

"I did ring, I got his answer phone." Yes, and then he rang back and accused me of cheap tricks to get him over and me with blood running down my legs and gripping pains in my bowels. Bastard.

"Perhaps he'll be over soon."

"Perhaps."

"So, what did the doctor say?" She's moving things, clashing plates and saucepans.

"Leave it, Mum."

"I'll just do a bit of clearing away."

"I don't want it cleared away."

"These metal containers all over the work surface, where do you keep them usually?"

"On the work surface - to hand. Leave them there."

"They'll just gather dust and grease and be a bother to clean. I like a totally free work surface, myself."

"Well, I don't!"

"I'll just-"

"Mum!" I am screaming, being over dramatic it's so silly but - her face appears at my bedroom door,

"No need to get strident with me, Clover."

"Why not? I feel bloody strident."

She comes into the room, arms folded, "What did the doctor say?"

"He said to rest for a couple of days, keep my feet up," I indicate my feet under the duvet, raised on two pillows, "Then I'm to go and see him on Monday."

Her face softens, I must look pathetic. "You make it so hard for yourself, dear. So hard for us to be kind to you."

"How? I don't know what you mean."

She comes to sit down on the bed and takes my hand. I shall cry. She sighs; she's going to cry. "Is James ever going to be a proper father to this child?"

Oh, Christ.

*****

Harry looked aghast at George and shut the library door on the continued blood-curdling screams coming from The Beautiful Child, "You mean you think Hilda's been out there in the wood all day, perhaps ill, perhaps... Oh, Christ."

"I didn't see her fall or anything, just put her hands to her chest, like this," he demonstrated, unconsciously copying the exact look of shock on the old lady's face. "Then I just ran and I'm afraid I didn't think, or connect her with this missing Hilda, until Smears said about the basket and the woods and- Oh, Christ, I'm so sorry."

Harry wrung his hands together for a moment in thought, then said, "Well, we must go and look. I'll get a torch."

"Yes, yes. I'll come with you and show you where I saw her, if I can remember. Oh God, I'm so sorry, Harry."

"Yes. Can't be helped. She shouldn't have gone out alone, she's been told often enough. Heart." He tapped his own chest, opened the door and went out.

George hung back a while before following. The Beautiful Child's distant screams, growing ever fainter, echoed around the house and in his head.

He ran a hand over his hair and looked up, coming face to face with the huge raddled head of a buffalo, hanging low over the doorway. The glazed bulbous eye and the pink plaster tongue, poking between the balding folds of the lips, gave the creature a mocking, knowing appearance. "Sod off," George told it and, as he opened the door, he thrust a fist up into the bristly lower jaw.

The last person he wanted to see was Lady Lydia, unfortunately she was standing in the hall, watching Harry run upstairs. George tried to shrink back into the shadows of the study door but she spotted him and beckoned,

"Mr Pender, come. Harry's going to hunt for Hilda, will you go with him?"

"Yes, of course." What had Harry said to her? Did she know about his part in Hilda's possible - accident? One son dead over a bus ticket and now an ancient aunt with a dickey heart shocked in a clearing more than - he checked his watch - twelve hours ago.

"It's only just gone eight. We're not keeping you up, are we? It's pouring, take a mackintosh from the porch, we can't have you catching pneumonia." Her words were sharp, her eyes impatient. "If only Alphonse were here...."

"Alphonse?"

"The dear Bishop. I must go and see Cookie." She strode across the hall, wrenched open the green baize door and disappeared.

George went out to the porch and chose a

long, rubbery smelling mac from the assortment hanging there; he also found a pair of wellingtons which fitted and then waited, dejectedly for Harry, while the rain splatted down from a broken gutter just outside....

"You've got a very nice profile, you know," Harry shone the torch right into George's face making him blink and shy away from its glare.

"Thanks."

They were resting under an oak, both soaked and miserable having searched the woods uselessly for nearly half an hour. George's stomach rumbled - he'd only had breakfast and two tiny crab sandwiches all day.

"I'd like to paint you," Harry informed him, "if you've got time tomorrow. Just a few pencil sketches to get the feel of flesh on bone, then a quick oil sketch."

"Well, we'll see."

"I've done all the family hundreds of times. It gets a bit boring, for them and me. I need a new challenge. I'd be very grateful if you could oblige."

"Yes, well, yes of course." What else could he say?

"Come up to the studio about eleven thirty."

"Alright. Perhaps we should get on...?"

"Mmm?" Harry was squinting at him in a very piercing manner.

"Looking for Hilda?"

"Yes, of course," he flashed the torch around

the clearing in front of them. "Does any of this look familiar?"

"No, it all looks the same."

"Shame Mags is still comatose, she'd be a great help. She knows these woods intimately."

"Mmm," George began to pick his way through a prickly patch of briars. His fiancée seemed to be on intimate terms with quite a lot of places and people. It was confusing and upsetting; he always liked to know where he stood and here, in this crazy house, in this sodden wood he was completely lost.

Harry cleared his throat, "You did say, I believe, that you liked art?" His torch beam highlighted the diamond scatter of falling rain drops against the darkness beyond as he followed close behind. "I am extremely excited by it," he confided, "by the possibilities of what oil paint can do on canvas, or graphite on paper. I've ordered some pastels for something new to try. I've done frescos too. I frescoed the wall of my studio, you'll see it tomorrow. I'd like your opinion. I do firmly believe that anyone can paint, I think too much training can ruin a native talent and that's why I've always refused lessons. What I have learnt, only I have had any influence on. I regard myself as a 'Naive Surrealist', if you want to put a label on me. Which is what people do, isn't it, put labels on you? What is it, exactly, that you actually like about art – paintings - I presume you mean painting, do you?"

"Yes, I suppose I mean painting. Bugger," a

snag of sharp thorns ripped the side of George's hand just where he had hurt it the previous evening on the French windows and he wished he had taken up Ethel's offer of a bandage.

"So, what is it that you like?"

"Er..." he sucked his hand, "beauty, and talent. I admire talent."

"Talent - that goes without saying. But what is beauty to you?" Harry probed further.

"Um," he flipped his dripping hair back from his eyes and an image of Jane's face came to him. He paused.

"What do you feel when you see something beautiful?" prodded Harry, breathing down his neck in the confines of the thicket they had blundered into.

"I feel, joy- Ow! Uplifted, you know." George response was testy, as he ploughed into a fallen stump and barked his shin.

"Well no, I don't, that's why I'm asking. You see I don't think I've ever seen anything really beautiful."

"That's ridiculous."

"It's not, it's very sad, I think - tragic really."

George stopped and Harry bumped into him. "Don't you feel overcome when you look at a Rembrandt?"

"Rembrandt?" Harry sounded defensive.

"Or a Murillo, or a Vermeer?"

"I have heard of them all, of course."

Now it was George's turn to peer into Harry's

face, but all he could see was the reflection of his own torch in his companion's rain blurred glasses. "Haven't you ever seen one, then? Gone to a gallery and stood in front of a great painting?"

"Not as such. Just seen books, you know, black and white pictures." A gust of cold wind blew a spatter of rain into their faces and Harry shivered, "Shall we get on?" He pushed his way carelessly out of the thicket and George was able to pass relatively easily in his wake and catch him up back on the path.

"Have you never been to the National?"

"The National what?" Harry was busy dancing his torch light over the surrounding bushes and trees far too quickly to be of any use.

"The National Gallery."

"Well that would be difficult." He hurried on.

"Why?" George asked, as they squelched single file, playing their torches to either side.

"Because I've never been to London, that's why. Do you go to the National?"

"Yes, it's free, they'll let anyone in, even bus conductors." Harry's tone had annoyed him.

"I didn't know that. You see, we're not a very artistic family. Mother hates London and, of course, being in mourning still, makes it difficult for her to go. The Bish is – was - only interested in the buses there and Mags only goes up for her consultations."

"Jane goes," George reminded him, "to the dentist."

"Ah, yes, well," he scoffed. "Waste of time that

is, and money too. Aunt Suzy seems to think that getting her teeth seen to will make her half present-able."

George pulled him back by his coat sleeve, "You asked me what I think beauty is? Well I think Jane is beauty. Fixing her teeth, calling her 'plain', it's all rubbish and you know it is. Jane is the most beautiful girl I have ever seen, and I've seen quite a few in my line of work, so what is all this about?"

"All right," Harry wrenched his arm free, "no need to get aggressive. Beauty is in the eye of the be-holder, I suppose. But while you're fucking my sis-ter do you think you should be taking such an inter-est in her cousin?"

"I didn't say I was taking an interest, just that no-one could help noticing her, that's all." As George turned away his torch beam flashed across a mound of pink. He refocussed on the object and swallowed, "Look, there she is."

"Jane?" Harry asked, confused.

"No, Hilda."

George's footsteps dragged through the leaf litter as he approached the dead woman. Harry was on his knees at her side, her wrist in his fingers.

"Quite dead," he glanced up, "we'll have to move her."

"Pick her up?"

"We can't leave her here."

George stared down at the corpse, her face bluish in the spotlight, her glasses pushed to one side of her nose, her cheek on her hand as if it was only sleep that had detained her here in a forest clearing all day and half the night.

"I don't think I can touch…"

Harry tutted, "Take my torch then, light the way." He got his arms underneath her and hoisted her up into his lap. She didn't seem to be heavy, but she was rigid. "Rigamortis," Harry noted with interest and stood. "Lead on."

"I don't actually know the way." George reminded him.

"Head east."

"Yes, but which way is east?"

"It's a west wind brings rain, keep the wind behind you. Don't you know anything?"

"Apparently not," he muttered and held a finger up to gauge the direction of the wind, he turned away from it and set off, Harry crashing and cursing behind him.

George lay in his second hot bath of the day until his shivering stopped and his bones felt warm. His pyjamas were neatly folded over the massively decorated radiator and his dinner jacket hung crookedly on the back of the door. The shoulders and back were sodden where the rubberised mac had let the rain through, his trousers were mud-drenched up to the knee and dripping dirtily on to the marble tiled floor. It was a hired suit, two guineas for the four days with a one guinea refund if the suit was in perfect condition on its return, otherwise the money was forfeit with an extra ten-shilling liability clause, depending on the extent of the damage. He mentally waved goodbye to £2 12s. A week's wage.

He laid back in the water, hearing it gurgle in his ears and shook his head about, trying to shake the worries away. His eyes were shut, so it was the sudden cold draught that alerted him to another presence in the bathroom. He opened them and saw one of the twins, immobile in the doorway- eyes wide, mouth agape and one hand on the doorknob. George sat up, groped for his flannel and braced himself for the scream. None came, and by the time he had found the tartan square, covered himself and forced his lips into a lopsided smile the door was closing again, very slowly.

At the sound of the click he puffed out his cheeks, "Oh, bugger it," hoisted himself up and out, dripped across the floor, turned the key in the lock and slithered back to the deep, hot comfort of the bath. At least she hadn't screamed or had a heart attack like her aunt. His stomach rumbled and he sat up to soap himself. He had never been so clean - two baths in one day. A giant yawn cracked his jaw as there was a tap-tap on the door. His shoulders sagged, had she come back to apologise, or to have another look? "Yes?"

Smears walked in. George hadn't expected anyone to actually come in, having locked the door, so he covered his groin quickly with the soap and flannel and hoped he looked affronted.

Smears pocketed his set of keys and frowned

down at him, "I'm cleaning Mr Harry's suit, sir, I thought I might do yours at the same time," he had obviously decided that George did not merit the famous 'Smears lisp'. "Is this it?" he flicked the lapel.

"Yes, thank you, Smears, I would appreciate that."

"How much?"

"Pardon?"

"How much would you appreciate my cleaning of your suit, sir?"

"Oh, er, I'll give you two shillings."

"That is not what I meant, sir."

"I'm sorry."

"But I will accept the tip and thank you. No, I meant what will you do for me if I clean your suit?"

"I don't know. What do you want me to do?"

"Just that, sir."

"What?" His shoulders and chest were getting cold and he was confused again.

"Ask that question of me, sir."

"Wh- what question? Look, Smears, I'm getting bloody freezing here and I don't understand how to play your games."

"Simply ask me what you can do for me, sir, when the time is right. That's all I ask," he unhooked the suit from the door, winked exaggeratedly at George and bowed out.

George threw himself back in the bath sending a whoosh of water out all over the tiles and groaned.

Dressed in his pyjamas, George padded along the darkened corridor to his room and found Ethel there feeding the fire. She glanced round at him and smiled,

"I've brought you a tray of sandwiches."

"Oh, thank you."

"On that little table there."

"I'm starving."

"All that fresh air," she straightened from the grate and put her hands behind her, watching as he sat on the edge of the sofa and lifted a corner of the tray cloth to peer beneath. "Cookie was going to give you the leftovers from tea, but I made you some fresh."

"Thank you, they look lovely," thick, crusty rounds with flaps of beef and frills of lettuce escaping from them.

"There's tea here by the fire, shall I pour you a cup?"

"That would be nice." He took a bite of sandwich and pickle trickled out and down his chin, he trapped the flow with his finger and redirected it, "Mmm, delicious."

She blushed over the tea pot as she handed him his cup. "How's your hand?"

He glanced at the pinkly clean wound, "It'll be alright."

"Are you warm now?"

"Yes, but it's been a bit of a day, hasn't it?"

"Very unfortunate."

"To say the least. Is everyone very upset about Aunt Hilda?"

"Oh, yes."

"Where exactly did she fit into the family? Was she Lady Lydia's sister?"

"No! Sir Howard Berenger's aunt, along with the other two, Grace and Matilda. They were all born here, at Leatherboys Hall, over eighty years ago." She smiled wistfully.

"Were you born here, Ethel?" he sipped his tea.

"Yes."

"Only sixteen years ago."

"Yes."

"I expect you hope you won't still be stuck in this mausoleum seventy odd years from now."

"Oh, no," her smile faded suddenly, "I don't ever want to leave here, ever." Her mouth turned down and a sob made her bosom jump.

"I'm sorry. I thought-"

"No, you didn't think at all," she accused and hurried from the room.

George puffed out his cheeks, let the air go with a 'pop' and finished his sandwich.

Another night on the hard sofa, but he was so exhausted that he slept right through and woke with a startled snore as a bang and a thud outside his room made the door shake. "Wha- what?"

"Is that you?" a little voice asked. The door-knob turned excruciatingly slowly but the door never opened.

He got up, "Who's there?" and shuffled over to the door, his steps and mind still fuddled with sleep. There was an answering giggle, high and affected, another thump and, as he opened the door, the cool draught of someone passing at speed, but in the daylight gloom, unaided by lamp light he could only sense a presence receding.

He shrugged, shivered and returned to the sofa to snuggle under the ragged eiderdown in search of some fleeting warmth. As his mind cleared, and he failed to get warm again, he remembered all that had happened yesterday. There was only one thing for it, he must leave now, or as soon as he had eaten breakfast, because he was still hungry, despite everything. He checked his watch and sat up. Ten to ten. Where was everyone? Yesterday Smears had woken him, or rather relieved his discomfort, with a cup of tea at eight. Perhaps they had allowed him to sleep in. Mum had sometimes let him do that, after a late night at the 'Hole and Ferret'.

He decided to get up, dress and go in search of breakfast and Mags, to tell her that he wanted to go home.

It was like the bloody Marie Celeste. No-one about upstairs or down. He opened all the doors on the first floor, The Bishop's included. A nasty part of him had hoped to find Mags in there, on the big four poster bed mourning her brother, so that he could face her with his suspicions. But the bed was empty - neatly made - and the curtains were open, allowing a watery sun to light up the collection of church plate on the mantle and the bus posters and paintings on the facing wall. The other bedrooms were equally neat and equally empty. He wondered which was Jane's.

He walked down the final flight of stairs to the ground floor hall and called firmly, "Hello?" The echo was very effective, "Lo..lo..lo..?" No-one replied. He tried again, louder "HELLO!? LO..LO..LO..?"

Perhaps the entire family had piled into cars and left him. He wouldn't blame them; perhaps they were terrified he was going to finish them all off, one by one. He opened the drawing room door, to find that the only moving thing in there was the pendulum swing-tick of the brass and marble clock, on its red marble tripod by the fireplace. He tried the study door, remembered the buffalo head and merely ducked his own head round to check that it was as empty as everywhere else.

In the dining room there was no sign that any-one had eaten there this morning. A thick, dusty silence prevailed behind the long holland blinds. He remembered Smears' short cut and hurried the polished length of the table to open the secret panelled door in the corner, gaining access to below stairs. But here it was just as quiet and deserted. The busy corridors of yesterday stood wide and bare. He peered into rooms full of scrubbed tables, vegetable baskets half empty, sinks, wooden tubs with dollies waiting, washing hanging in waves and flat irons up-ended; cupboards stacked with china, flour bins, chamber pots, brooms and mops. In the main kitchen he did find, thank goodness, a tray with an empty tea pot ready for the water bubbling on the range and a caddy unlocked, bread waiting to be toasted, jam in a dish, butter in curls on a plate and an egg cup with a silver spoon attached by a silver chain to its splayed base.

He poured in the water, cut some bread and spread on the butter and jam. As he ate greedily, in relative comfort and ease by the hot range, he became aware of a distant humming, uneven and booming. He stopped chewing and listened more intently. The noise ceased, he waited a moment then took another mouthful of bread, but it started up again, breathy and very sad. He got up to investigate and discovered, beside the copper jelly-mould loaded dresser, behind a wooden screen, a door left ajar. It led into a corridor, similar to the one he had followed to the kitchen from the dining room, but narrower, darker. The shadows of half open doors, the play of light from unseen windows, striped the uneven stone floor which glowed from the polish of a thousand footfalls. The noise eased again to a whisper.

"Hello?" He asked into the tunnelled silence.

A shuffling patter was the only response and he immediately thought of rats. Since an episode in the coal hole at home he had conceived a morbid fear of large, whip-tailed vermin. He shivered and wondered about going back upstairs, packing and trying to walk back to the station. It was eight miles but someone might pass and offer him a lift. No, it would be rude to leave without saying anything or thanking Lady Lydia for her hospitality, especially in the circumstances. Trying to forget the rats, he buttoned his jacket and began to walk down the passage.

Not wanting anything, i.e. rats, to come out behind him as he went and perhaps surprise him by skittering about his feet and biting his ankles, wrapping their tails about his legs and bringing him down to nibble at his face and eyes, he bravely peered behind each and every open or half open door, asked, "Hello?" into the variously dark or gloomy spaces, and then shut the door after him.

The sudden resumption of the breathy humming made him jump, but then relax. It was an organ, like the one in the church on the green at Palmers Green, and it was playing, rather badly, 'Abide With Me'. As voices took up the refrain and drowned out the organ, it suddenly dawned on him that it was Sunday. They were all at church and this passage way led to the family chapel. Big houses always had their own chapel, he'd read that somewhere, especially if they were Catholic. He remembered Mags' punishment of twelve Hail Marys and the largeness of the family was suddenly explained, though not the fatherhood.

Smiling at his recent fears, he hurried on and

climbed an iron spiral staircase at the end of the corridor, coming up into a well-lit, white panelled lobby at the back of the chapel. A tall painted screen blocked his view and then took all his attention. It was covered with very realistic and brightly coloured depictions of various forms of horrible death. Groups of naked women screamed soundlessly from the midst of flesh-charring flames, men were spread-eagled on wheels of hot iron as hooded figures thrust pokers into their orifices. Eyes were being gouged, breasts and penis's severed, testicles toasted, hearts extracted from living chest cavities, whilst their owners gazed down in agony and terror. It made him feel sick, made his own heart leap against his ribs. He spun away and peered round the screen as the singing ended.

The chapel was quite large and richly decorated. Light from high, stained glass windows patterned the many flags and pennants hanging beneath them. The altar shimmered with what must be real gold decoration and layers of elaborate lace. About fifty people, all dressed entirely in black, stood in the pews with their backs to him. At first, he didn't see anyone he recognised, then, as he edged nearer, saw two that he did. The Bishop and Aunt Hilda were both propped up, dressed in their best, on velvet covered boards against the altar rail.

He was sure he only muttered "Christ!" ...but, in the absolute silence, as the organ echo faded, the sibilance whispered loudly round the swirling stone columns and several draped crosses.

Everyone turned round.

"Sorry, sorry," he backed off, crashing a heel into the screen, "sorry. I'll just, sorry…"

A black-veiled woman detached herself from the end of a pew and swept towards him. He was sure it was Lady Lydia, about to hit him or haul him up to face the dead - his dead, his awful accidents, but it was Mags. She raised her veil,

"Darling…" she held out her arms to him.

He paused in his flight, straightened and almost smiled with relief, "Mags…"

"Quick, quick," she took his arm as she passed, pulled him back into the lobby and pressed him up against the nightmare screen. "I've been waiting for you to come. Quick. "She began to undo his jacket, his fly.

"What? Mags, no-"

"Yes. Now." She spun him round so her back was to the screen and his view was all of the horrors there and hooked one black-stockinged leg over his hip.

"Not here!" He hissed, aware, above their urgent whisperings, of the silence in the chapel.

"Take me, now!" She pulled open her dress, ripping off a fusillade of bead buttons which bounced all over the red and white tiled floor and revealed herself to be, of course, naked underneath.

"I can't!"

"You can," her black, silk gloved hand slid easily down inside his underpants.

Yes, he could.

While they heaved and grunted, her head banging hollowly against the screen, the man having his testicles roasted screaming into George's rapt face, the organ started up again and the congregation sang, 'Lead Us, Heavenly Father, Lead Us.'

CHAPTER 4

I don't usually watch Songs of Praise - I'm not in the least religious - but as the last strains of the hymn die away in the airy vaulting on the screen, I feel strangely calm and placid. I was hoping to see Antiques Roadshow to get some idea of how much this painting might be worth, but it's not on. Songs of Praise will be followed by golf from Lytham St Annes, I'm told by the announcer. But not by me. I turn it off and sigh. My great aunt is up on the wall beside the TV. Derek, my neighbour, put her up for me after he knocked to say that my mother had told him I wasn't well, and could he help out in any way. Derek is about fifty, divorced and needy, plus he fancies me. He doesn't know I'm pregnant and have nearly had a miscarriage, he just thinks I've got flu or something.

"You look poorly," he told me when I shuffled to open the door to him.

"Thank you, I'm supposed to stay lying down." Not keep getting up to open doors for people.

"Well, you go and do that, and I'll make you a cup of tea."

"No, thanks, Derek." Why do people always think you need a cup of tea if you're feeling ill?

"Well, is there anything else I can do?"

"Yes please, actually, I need a picture putting up." Clever me!

"Well, I'll do that then." He seems so pleased to be of use it makes me feel even more pleased for asking him.

I know he'd do anything I asked, poor Derek. Before his marriage broke up he was always doing DIY, so he told me. He'd made bookshelves and cabinets and built a barbeque in the back garden, apparently, so I had expected quite a professional job. But the picture, as I lay and look at it, is crooked and hung far too low. No wonder his wife got rid of him (and for a younger man).

"Who is it?" he'd asked, standing back to admire his workmanship. "Anyone famous?"

"Not really, no, it's my great aunt."

"Ah yes," he nodded and looked from me to the painting, "you can see the family likeness."

Aunty is not a blood relation, but I didn't enlighten him. It's nice to be flattered when you feel like a limp rag, when your face is as white as marble on a tomb, when you are clenching up every inner muscle to hang on to the precious life inside you and your legs wobble, jelly-like, if you stand for too long. I smiled and nodded and let him make me a cup of tea before he left to watch golf on the telly.

Bloody golf, it's ruined all the schedules. James liked golf; He used to watch it eagerly and go off for long weekends with 'some guys', to Scotland or Portugal. I begin to wonder now, about those weekends... I found a cute card once, at his flat, it said, 'Jimbo, thanks for a lovely time, Jill.' 'Lovely', underlined three times in mauve. Jimbo? Makes him sound like an elephant. I asked James later, apropos of nothing, who Jill was. 'Work colleague,' he replied, not missing a beat, but never asked me why I wanted to know. Changed the subject bloody quickly - I noticed that. Weekends with some guys; I doubt it. Maybe he was already looking for an excuse to get rid of me and go off with Jill. Jimbo and Jill went up the hill, I bet she'll always stay on the pill.

Mum says I've done a wicked thing, I didn't tell her; I've learnt my lesson with Amber. Never confide, especially when drunk or vulnerable. But, being Mum, she jumped to all the right conclusions.

"Wasn't it planned?"

"Yes."

"I mean by both of you, Clover,"

"I thought you wanted a grandchild."

"Not like this! You've done some silly things in your time, but I never thought you'd do anything... I can't tell your father- he'd be horrified."

"Why? What is all the fuss? Women do it all the time, take their own destiny into their own hands. We don't all need a man to bolster us up."

"And what about the poor child, Clover?"

"He'll be fine."

"I can't talk to you about it. I'm- I'm actually

ashamed of you."

"Don't be so silly, Mum."

Ashamed of me? Now she'll know how I felt every time I saw her with her beige mac, her beige baggy jumpers and matching beige skirts gaily waving, as she met me from school or when we bumped into friends whilst shopping. Shopping with your Mum. 'Let's go down the High Street, Clover, do some shopping.'

Oh, I don't mean it. I'm not ashamed of her now. I've got over all that and she'll get over this. When he's born, she'll be so happy, she'll smile and hug him and cry again. Only another four months; four months all alone...

Crying is good. It gets rid of toxins, I read that. I must be totally de-toxified. I bet Aunty never went through all this, with her slim hips and tapering hands, her smile and gently knowing eyes. Great Uncle George must have really loved this painting. He did like Art, he gave me a book once, for Christmas, 'Great Artists of the Modern World.' He never tried to paint himself, he once told me, because he thought it took 'a certain kind of temperament', and he didn't have it; 'But I can appreciate art and admire talent in others.'

*****

"Can you? That's a gift too, you know George." Harry patted him on the shoulder. "Come on up, if you're not too tired after Mags..."

"Don't. I feel so awful about that," his cheeks

flamed and he bent his head to follow Harry up the narrow stairs to his turret top studio.

"Don't worry about it old boy, I told you she'd be needing you."

"But I really should leave."

"What's the point? You'll be going home tomorrow anyway."

"I suppose so."

Harry stopped at a small metal bound door and turned to face him conspiratorially, "Now, this is quite an honour you know. You're the only non-family member I've ever allowed in here."

"Right," George attempted an appreciative smile as Harry lifted the latch.

George had never been in an artist's studio before and didn't know quite what to expect; an easel presumably, some paints and brushes, a few finished works. But he had been in several butcher's shops, and that is what Harry's studio reminded him of. The smell of blood and none too fresh flesh, the sawdust on the floor, the feathered partridges and pheasants hanging from the wall, the bones in a pile in one of the eight corners, the flayed tiger and zebra skins folded in another.

"Phew, Harry..."

"A bit stuffy, I've not been up here for a day or two. Wait, don't go, I'll open a window."

There was an easel, a table with paint tubes writhing on it, their petrified guts oozing out, and a few stubby brushes in a jar. The canvases were stacked under the table and he didn't like to disturb them, so there was nothing for George to look at while the air cleared, but dead birds and Harry's brightly frescoed walls. The turret was an octagon, barely fifteen feet across, and every wall was covered with figures. The style and content of the frescoes had obviously been heavily influenced by the screen in the chapel; the talent was missing but the imagination was just as lurid.

"Ah, yes," Harry came up behind him, "what do you think?"

"It's, er, very interesting. This is the house." It was easier to state bare facts than to point out the various near-naked members of the family in awkward, lascivious poses, or to criticise the amateurish brushwork. "And this is the woods where we were last night; it's all in the right place."

"Yes, isn't it. See here, I've depicted Mummy as the Virgin, washing Jesus' feet on the terrace, but do you see who Jesus is? It's Daddy, so Mummy is also Martha, over here washing his-"

"Yes, I see." Both depictions seemed to necessitate the models baring more flesh than was strictly necessary, George thought. The hollow chested young man with the moustache and halo did bear a passing resemblance to the painting in the long gallery, however, the leer distorting his mouth, the huge erection and the swagger stick ruined any reference to Jesus Christ. But that was nothing compared to the image of Mags, squatting on the edge of a manger and giving birth to a chain of babies, linked like sausages, issuing from her vagina, all bluish, all dead. "That's rather..." words failed him. He wanted to get out.

"Yes. It's unfinished, of course, I add to it as and when."

"You mean she's had all these babies!?"

"No, of course not. And that's where Bish was so useful. God knows what she'll do now he's dead."

"Harry, I think I have to go. Get some air, you know, the smell..."

"Ah, the smell. Yes, you have to get used to it. You haven't seen the canvases yet. But you do like my work, don't you? I so rely on encouragement and criticism and you are the first outsider to see this."

"You're very talented. It's very realistic," George opened the door and slid out.

"Yes," Harry called after him, "but is it beautiful?"

George ran down the turret stairs, along a corridor, any corridor and found an open window to lean out of. His head swam as he gulped cool, untainted air and his legs threatened to crumple. He hung on to the sill and slowly calmed himself by breathing deeply and not thinking. When he finally raised his head, he saw he was overlooking a rear service yard with a pump and a black dog asleep in a slant of sunlight. A man came out of a doorway to the left below him, lit up his pipe and clicked his fingers to the dog who got stiffly onto his feet, stretched, head down and followed the man round a corner and out of sight. It was the same man George had seen on his first afternoon. The man he had been told didn't exist.

He genuinely wished that the whole family, the actual house, did not exist. It was bizarre, they were all weird and he just wanted to go home. Then he heard footsteps on the cobbles below and Ethel came out with a bowl of water, she emptied it down a drain, stood for a moment to breathe in the air, repositioned a hair pin holding on her cap and went back inside. He would go and see Ethel. He had upset her last time with some thoughtless remark and needed to apologise, to speak to someone relatively sane.

As he was making his way down another set of stairs into another gloomy hallway, thinking that he must get used to carrying a torch around with him, he bumped into Jane, quite literally. She was all in black, with a veil over her illuminating face, so he just hadn't seen her.

"Sorry, I didn't hear you."

"I've taken my shoes off," she told him.

They stood for a moment at the foot of the stairs, on a draughty corner, with nothing to say. She smelled of lavender. Her breath moved her veil slightly, rhythmically as she waited for him to do something.

"I've just been up to Harry's studio," he told her.

"Was it awful?"

"Vile. I mean that, absolutely vile."

"It would be. I wouldn't go even if he asked

me."

"He wants to know what beauty is. He wants me to tell him. He says he's never seen it."

"Of course he hasn't."

"But you have." Every morning in her mirror.

"Yes," she agreed, shyly.

He had to ask, to dare her reply. "What do you think is beautiful?

"So many things, trees, flowers, the sky, babies..."

George controlled a shudder,

"- kittens and puppies, your bus."

"My bus?" He laughed, "What do you know about my bus?"

"I've been on it."

"You have? When?" Surely, he would have noticed her?

"Whenever I go up to the dentist."

"But I've never seen you."

"I wear a veil. I never go out without a veil."

"Why?"

"I think its best."

He wanted to touch her but put his hands in his pockets instead while he digested this, explored possibilities and wondered if he dared ask something else. She wasn't going anywhere, she'd made that clear. He had the time. "Let me get this straight; you come up to London to go to the dentist, you ride on my bus in your veil, you've seen me before but I've never seen you?"

"You're always polite."

"I am," he agreed.

"So, I told Margaret about you. I knew what would happen."

George let himself fall softly against the panelled wall in what he hoped was a nonchalant way, in case she could see him through her veil, in the half light. "Why..." he breathed, staring at where he knew her face was, "why didn't you say anything?"

"I knew I wouldn't stand a chance and besides, I wouldn't have known what to say to you."

"How about, 'You've got nice hands, the kind I wouldn't mind being touched by'?"

"Oh," she puffed, her veil billowed out towards him, "is that what she said?"

"Yes."

"Those were my words!"

"Then say them, Jane."

"I can't! I can't!"

His hands were out of his pockets, attempting to find a part of her but only flailing in empty air. "Jane? Jane, come back!" Nothing. "Shit! Shit!" He fell back against the wall again and leant there for a while.

When he eventually found himself back in a part of the house he knew, he made his way to the baize door in the main hall and opened it. The comforting smell of cooked cabbage and polish, an aura of steam and laundry soap cheered him. He ran down the wooden stairs and along the wide, well-lit corridor, dodging a scullery maid who was carrying a basin of dripping. He slowed to a fast walk to pass a man in a chef's hat sitting on a chair in a doorway, chequered legs splayed, pale waxy face drawn and somehow familiar; and so along to Ethel's sitting room, where a kettle was singing on the hob and she was just in the act of lifting it as he knocked on the open door.

"Oh, that's good timing. I expect you're dry." She pursed her pretty mouth and concentrated on pouring the boiling water into the flowered china pot.

The memory of the incident in the chapel came back at him with a rush, all the servants, filing past him as he tried to re-button his fly and close up his jacket. The shame of it all!

"I'm being used," he blurted.

"Yes." She answered as if she had always known, as if everyone had always known and only he - the dim ignorant peasant - was blundering in the dark.

He dropped into the armchair he had occupied before, "What is everyone saying?"

"They're all remarking on your stamina and your readiness."

"Oh, Christ," he covered his face with both hands and rested his head against the crochet chair back. "I feel that everyone here is mad, that only you and I and Jane..."

"Ah, its Jane now, is it?"

He sat up, "She's been to London. She's seen the outside world."

"You want to watch Jane."

'A pleasure'. The words almost slipped out as he took his cup and saucer from Ethel, instead he asked, "Why?"

"She wants something."

"What?" After all, everyone here seemed to want something.

"Not for me to say."

"Oh, now don't start that. I can't stand that. Smears was doing the same thing to me last night. If you want to say something say it, straight out." He sipped his tea and Ethel sat down opposite him with hers. She cocked her head, pursed her lips but said nothing, so he had to ask again, "Do you want to tell me something about Jane?"

"No. But I would like to know what Mr Smears said to you last night."

"I'd tell you his exact words if I could make them out but the jist of it was he wanted me to be in his debt. Not monetary, you understand, just to be beholden to him."

"I wonder why?" she sighed.

"So do I."

They drank their tea in companionable silence for a while and George relished the undemanding normalness of it, he liked normal, he liked ordinary and this family were neither. Yes, of course he was being used; what Harry and Jane had told him made sense. Mags was a nymphomaniac and he had been brought along for the weekend to fulfil her needs. He was no more her fiancée than

Smears was. He was just another menial servant. So, it followed that Harry, in spite of showing him his awful studio, didn't like him, and that Mags, in spite of all the sex, didn't like him. He'd rather hoped that Jane might like him, but she'd run off. The only person here who might like him for himself was sitting opposite him now. He smiled at her and she blushed but he was below even Ethel, the upstairs maid.

"I must go," he put down his cup. "I can't sit here in this room with you drinking tea."

"Oh," she bristled, "getting used to being with all them upstairs, are you?"

"No, just the opposite. I like it below stairs, with you, but I feel low and brutish and you're so nice and respectable."

"How'd you know I'm respectable?"

"You are, Ethel - I can see it. You're wholesome and kind, I'm not worthy enough to sit here."

"That's rubbish. You came here in good faith."

"I did."

"You thought you were coming to meet your fiancée's family."

"I did."

"You were the innocent one."

"I was."

"And you're still wholesome and kind, I can see that too." She lowered her lids, "Too kind, you mustn't let yourself be put upon."

Her words reminded him of something Mags had whispered to him, that first evening in the long gallery. "I try not to," he protested, "but it just happens. Oh, Ethel," he slipped to one knee and put his hands over hers. "You do seem to understand me."

Her bosom heaved just inches from his nose, her sigh blew his hair off his forehead, her lips parted in an 'oooh'. And her starched, doughy plumpness seemed, at that moment, far more enticing than Mags' slim, silky undulations and Jane's throat-catchingly beautiful face and he wondered - why can't they all be united in one perfect girl?

"Ahemm! I hope I have interrupted something?" Smears' triumphant voice brought George smartly back on to his seat. "Ethel?"

"Mr Pender's upset, Pa."

"Pa?" George spun round. "Pa?!"

"Mmn. Upset about what, sir?" The voice reverted to the usual downstairs monotone.

"Ethel's your daughter?"

"I like to think of all the staff as my children, sir."

"But she really is your daughter, isn't she?" He got up to face the butler. "Hence your little remark the other day," he raised an eyebrow, hoping Smears would take the hint and that he wouldn't have to repeat it in front of Ethel. He turned back to Ethel, all pink confusion after her slip and looking delightful. "And that's why you never want to leave because of your father. You said one of your parents was in service here."

"It seems Miss Ethel has been saying rather a lot."

"I'm sorry, Pa."

"Don't worry," George told them both, "your secret's safe with me."

"Oh, it's not a sec-"

"Ethel would you like to go and help search the upstairs rooms," her father suggested.

"Search for what, Pa?"

"Gaye has gone missing."

"Oh, all right," she didn't sound too worried and left him with a shy smile.

But George sank back into his chair and racked his memory for a trace of what he might have done to one of the weird twins. He could find nothing. He couldn't even remember the last time he had seen them. Ah, yes - before dinner last night, and then, the startled face in the open door of the bathroom. "When was she last seen, Smears?"

"This morning sir, before chapel."

"Ahh," he breathed easy. He could have absolutely nothing to do with this latest disappearance. "Can I help in the search at all?"

"Kind of you to offer sir, but you're more likely to get lost than she is. This often happens, the twins like to play hide-and-go-seek, sir. Such is their childish nature that games are more interesting to them than chapel. Especially now that the poor Bishop is not around to take the services. He always made them so very interesting with his jokes and witticisms."

"Really? It's such a shame I never got to hear him."

"Indeed sir, and now I understand that the police are to be called."

"The police?!"

"Yes. Miss Mags thinks he might have been murdered."

"But he wasn't murdered. We all saw him - you saw him, Smears. He just leaned forwards and fell."

"They suspect poison, sir."

"But who would...?"

"Who indeed. Now, I would suggest you go back to your room until luncheon."

"My room?" he felt like a disgraced child.

"Or a walk around the gardens, it's stopped raining."

"I might get some air. I need to think."

"Yes indeed. Think very carefully about your next move, Mr Pender. I'll show you the way to the gardens."

George gave him an exasperated glance as Smears preceded him into the passage. He had been on the point of admitting his part in the deaths of both The Bishop and Aunt Hilda to Ethel when her father had barged in. Thank God Smears had come in but not that he had jumped to the wrong conclusion. George glanced at Smears' smug face as they walked, a conclusion which would soon be fudged and confused by George's subsequent total lack of interest in his daughter. He was leaving tomorrow anyway; he need never see Ethel again and looked forward to the time he could look back on all this and laugh. In the meantime, all he had to do was tell the police truthfully all he had seen and not even mention the bus ticket.

At the end of the passage, down some steps and into a brick floored scullery, Smears showed him out into the same little yard he had glimpsed earlier from the corridor window. The angle of sunlight had increased and steam was rising from the low roofs opposite to where the dog had been sitting. Before he could close the door on him George turned and asked Smears, "Is there a man here, with a pipe and a dog?"

"A pipe and a dog?" He drew his head back in somewhat exaggerated amazement.

"Yes, I've seen him twice now. The last time about an hour ago, from that window up there," he pointed vaguely, there were so many windows. "He came out of this door and lit his pipe and called the dog and..."

"No-one like that here, sir," Smears informed him and closed the door firmly.

George blew out his cheeks, remembered he wasn't supposed to and took a deep breath of fresh, damp air.

*****

Mmm, it's so nice to be outside again after three days stuck in the flat! The doctor has given me the all clear so I'm going to work. I feel light-hearted and happy, though I don't know why, but nothing is going to depress me today; I'm wearing my new shoes. I have this thing about shoes, high heels, low, sandals, boots, blue alligator, pink sued, leopard skin, embroidered satin and especially anything in red. These are red, kitten heel, killer toes with little leather bows on the outer instep. I got them in a sale, so that's OK. They go particularly well with my black handkerchief point, low-waisted skirt (the only type I can wear comfortably now – thank goodness they're in fashion), my beige scoop necked tee and black leather jacket, I have my cherry red pashmina in case it turns colder tonight and my dear little red leather, pencil case handbag.

Oops nearly turned an ankle. These pavements are terrible, especially with me in this condition and being so 'fragile', that was the doc's word. I don't feel fragile, but I do feel quite fat this morning. Baby is hanging out a little above my skirt, below my tee, but my tum is still brown from the summer-from our fantastic two weeks in Mexico. But I'm not thinking about that sort of thing today. Nothing is going to depress me. I didn't get depressed about having to park two blocks from the agency, partly because it gave me an excuse to walk in my new shoes and strut my stuff a bit past the plate glass windows of 'Coffee Train', where there are always a few late starters grabbing an espresso to go on the way to the office. But not today- the shop is empty-never mind.

Sometimes I wish I did work in an office, although I always swore I never would, at least you meet people there. By 'people' I mean men. You don't meet many men in a dress agency. Bibby and I set the agency up when we couldn't get jobs as store buyers up in town. It's going very well. We have our regulars and a fairly constant drizzle of callers, it's all down to location. We have a very good location just down from the tube station, opposite a string of usual High Street retailers, three doors along from Coffee Train and with a nice little bistro four doors along the other way.

The bell welcomes me in, 'bing-bong'. I insisted on the bell, Bibby says it's naff. "Hi, Bibs."

"Hi. You made it. You look frazzled. Was it awful?"

"What?"

"Nearly losing the baby."

"Oh, the baby."

"Why, what else has happened?" Bibby is very perceptive.

"Nothing."

She doesn't believe me. "Mmh. So, have you been for a check at the doc's? Don't want you voiding all over the limed oak."

"I'm fine." I hang up my jacket and drape my pashmina over the coat stand behind our beautiful steel and wood counter. "Been busy?"

"Not really. Someone came in and tried to offload a bag of tat. Thought we were the other type of dress agency. Clover, you look shifty."

"Shifty?" I've never been accused of that before. I'll tell her so that she can assimilate the news about James and me, ring a few people to gossip about us and get it out of her system. "If you must know..."

"Ah,""

"James and I have..."

"Oh, my God! I wondered if that was it. I thought you hadn't been your normal happy self recently. I put it down to the baby, that's enough to make anyone a bit snappy,"

"Snappy, too? Shifty and snappy, mmm."

"Only shifty today. So," she leans her elbows on the glass counter top, "tell me what happened."

"We argued."

"Over what?"

"Food." That was what started it after all.

"Food," she nods sagely, "I knew that would be the rock upon which your relationship floundered." Sometimes Bibby sounds just like her mother. I suppose that's all of our fates. "So, are you going to carry on with it?"

"With what?"

"Honestly, Clover, wake up. The baby."

"Carry on with the baby? Of course."

"Oh," she nods again, sadly this time.

I am shocked. Shocked that a close friend of mine, someone I've known all of seven years could even think that I'd get rid of it just because the father has dumped me.

"It's not like a dress, Bibby! Not something you can bring back here if the date is cancelled. It's a little human being with arms and legs and its sex all worked out."

"I know, I know. I just thought you might... that's all."

The bell rings, Mrs Brabhams comes in to return her gown from Friday's night at the opera and I let Bibby go and deal with her. She is one of Bibby's mother's friends after all and I need a cup of mint tea and a moment to gather my thoughts in the back room.

Did Bibby seriously think I could terminate my baby just because James is no longer on the scene? Does James think that about me? Do other friends admittedly mostly his friends but those of mine I still see - do they expect me to get rid of it now? I fondle my bare tum, cool from the street but I know my baby is safe and warm inside. Do I come across as that shallow? I sit down while the kettle boils. Kill my little son?

I curl forward over my belly, protecting my child from harm. I nearly lost him! I will never get rid of him. Who are these people I thought were my friends? They have no idea what it's like. How could she even suggest that to me? Though I have joked, in the past, about 'flushing it down the loo', making that appointment at the clinic or taking something, when gossiping about someone else's little mistake. That little reminder of the time they forgot to take the pill or use a condom or had a fling with a– a brickie or something.

"What's the matter?"

"Nothing."

"You're crying. Oh, Clover, I didn't mean it,"

113

she puts her skinny arms round me and I smell Armani. "It was very stupid of me to say anything. Of course you're going to keep your baby. I'm so sorry about James but you know, I never really liked him, did I?"

All I can do is shake my head. She'd always said he was selfish and cold.

"I can't wait for your baby to come and I shall love it to bits, I promise."

"I know."

"I've already bought him something, actually."

"Bought him something?" I raise my hot wet face from her bony shoulder.

"I'll show you," she wrinkles her nose in excitement. "I saw them last week and I thought, 'Clover's baby'." She goes to the desk, opens up the bottom drawer where she keeps her bag and lunch, brings out a tiny carrier bag, Armani. Well, it is her favourite shop and I smile now, because I know whatever it is will be in wonderfully good taste. "Look." She hands me the bag and I peer inside.

"Ohhh!" The dearest, most perfect little fur bootees with tiny buckles and straps.

"They'll keep his feet nice and warm, won't they?"

*****

George's feet were freezing. The grass was sodden and his shoes had let in water. He was worrying about his feet and catching pneumonia

114

when he should have been worrying about the police. He was aware of this and concentrated even harder on the dramatic scenario; his mother, father, brother gathered round his bed, his enfeebled hand raised as if to confer a blessing on them all. But no, that reminded him of The Bishop and took him off track.

In all honesty he was innocent, wasn't he? He had never intended to harm The Bishop or Aunt Hilda. He had never even spoken to Aunt Hilda. No-one could connect him to either unfortunate death. The only clue to The Bishop's fall was in his pocket right now. Perhaps he should try to dispose of it but that was ridiculous because the bus ticket had been in his pocket originally and him trying to get rid of it had caused The Bishop's death in the first place. He could not throw it away; it must remain in his possession otherwise something else terrible might happen.

He might catch pneumonia.

Death bed scene, harrowing funeral - would Mags turn up, or Jane or, for that matter, Ethel? He tried to imagine it, his parents, hunched and dowdy, beside Mags and Jane, exotic black birds in their funeral outfits, all feathers and lace veils. Mags would have to get all those buttons sewn back on again. But Ethel would fit in with his family, they could never be intimidated by her.

What a surprise for Mum and Dad, discovering his association with three women, two of them extraordinarily lovely. It would certainly make them see him in a new light. Good old reliable, sensible George, not like his younger brother, fly-by-night Reggie, always getting into scrapes with girls.

George had only ever really been in one scrape, with Alice Todman. A back row of the cinema, behind the bus garage kind of scrape, which had resulted in tears and tantrums when he refused to marry her. He had heard that she was anybody's, that the baby could be anybody's and had been proved right when she gave birth far too early for him to have been blamed. Thank God he had never told his parents; he could have ruined his life, marrying her.

He looked up. Leatherboys Hall rose from its damp lawns, turrets and gables proud against the blue autumn sky. The walls were washed with sunlight and deep shade, the windows blinked, innocently. Houses are like people, he thought, all show on the outside, all murky horrors within. This profound discovery made him straighten his shoulders. He was growing up.

"Admiring the house?" Lady Lydia's voice, so close behind him, made his heart leap and she saw his flinch. "Did I startle you? I've been watching you from my little hidey hole, the thatched summer house, over there," she pointed with her umbrella at a tumble down shed with a falling straw roof, almost hidden from view by sweeping tree branches. "Manfully striding about, deep in thought. I was thinking how terribly attractive a man deep in thought looks. When a woman thinks, she frowns and makes herself ugly. I try never to think too deeply about anything. I leave it all to you men, you do it so well. What were you thinking?"

George had known that was coming but still fell into her trap, "I was thinking about my wet feet."

"And you got so wet last night too, hunting for poor Hilda. We must take more care of you," she linked her arm in his and began to steer him towards the summer house. "I think it so propitious, you being here at this time- this awful time. I take great strength from it. Young men are born to be heroes and you are our hero now. Adolphus is gone, in every sense – they came and took the bodies away half an hour ago – and Harry is not cut in the heroic mould. I think it's something to do with him wearing glasses. I tried to make him do without but he refuses, he says he cannot see without them! Ridiculous. Come and sit here, beside me," they had reached the summer house and she manoeuvred him onto the rustic bench beside her. "Show me your shoes."

He raised both legs out straight in front of him. They both looked down at them and she shuddered.

"The sight of your legs there, under that rough- what is it," she fingered the fabric of his trousers, "gabardine? The mere thought of them makes me feel," she gazed into his face, "very close to you."

"Ah, yes, you like inner thighs, don't you," he sighed, almost prepared for the worst.

"Inner thighs, lower backs and just here," she ran her finger from his ear lobe down his jawbone and turned his face to meet her lips full on. Kissing Lady Lydia was like having your innards sucked out by a vacuum pump. She seemed to be trying to get most of her face inside his mouth. His initial slight surprise gave way to a burst of devil-may-care lustfulness which involved his hands and her bosoms and widening his thighs to accommodate her hand at his groin. She was insatiable, much like her daughter, and succeeded on flattening him under her along the length of the uncomfortable bench. He banged his head on the bark covered arm rest, she rolled off him onto the floor and he followed, his fall cushioned by her plump body. She tasted of face powder and lipstick. She felt soft and agreeably slack under his hands and she was admirably able and competent. Like her daughter, she wore no under-wear so it was an easily manageable and very satisfying coupling.

She sat up afterwards, straightened her tweed skirt and cradled his head and shoulders upon her bosom. "I knew you were a hero, from the first moment I saw you," she told him through lipstick smeared lips. "Best not to tell Mags about this, my little darling. She gets very jealous, though she has enough men herself. It's a mother and daughter thing, I think. She sees me as old, but I don't see myself as old. Do you think I'm old?"

"Older than her, but not old, no."

"I was married at sixteen, widowed a year

118

later. I've been without a man in my life for thirty years and I'm a woman who needs a man."

"Lady Lydia-"

"Call me Lydia, darling," she stroked his hair fondly.

"It has occurred to me that-"

"Don't let anything occur to you. It would spoil you completely. Just let things happen to you," she pulled up his shirt, had a good look at his stomach and ran her hand over it, massaging gently, edging lower. "I've always let things happen to me. Given into my slightest whim and it's never done me any harm. I've had, on the whole, a very happy life."

"But you cry, every evening Mags says."

"For my lost youth and husband and all that might have been. I cry whenever I see his face, I can't help it. He is still young, you see, still vibrant."

"I thought he was dead."

"He is, but vibrant in memory."

"You seem pretty vibrant yourself, ahh..." Her hand had reached its destination.

"And how about you?"

CHAPTER 5

So, he had compounded all his other excesses in this house by fucking his hostess, who also happened to be his fiancée's mother. Did he feel as 'low' as he should? He probably was very low and venal, sitting in his room in a dishevelled and sticky state and wondering about asking for another bath. If the luncheon gong had not rung out across the sun kissed, sparkling hummocks of grass he would probably still be in the summer house with Lady Lydia being hero-worshipped to a state of exhaustion. As it was, when the gong had sounded, very loudly and suspiciously close by, she had instructed him to help her up, then dusted herself down and set off across the lawns; umbrella in one hand, her gloves in the other, leaving him to follow,

"A few minutes behind, my darling, so as not to arouse Mags' ire."

No, he did not feel low, he felt, rejuvenated. Lady Lydia's faith in him had renewed his faith in himself, he would not get pneumonia. He would not be arrested for murder. He had nothing to feel guilty about and certainly not where Mags was concerned. By all accounts, even her mother's, she was what his own mother would call a 'tart'. So was Lady Lydia, mind you but she was a tart with a heart, he'd decided, because she seemed to genuinely like him. Unlike her daughter who seemed only interested in what he could do for her. Pondering this he washed himself quickly and hurried down to the dining room where the unexpected aroma of fried bacon greeted him.

"Ah, George," Mags greeted him and signalled him to sit beside her, "where have you been all morning?"

"Out in the gardens, getting some exercise." He flicked open his napkin with a flourish and pointedly did not look up towards the head of the table, but he was aware of Lady Lydia there, looking splendid. Mags, however, did not look splendid. He hadn't seen much of her since The Bishop's fall, her face had been shrouded by veils in the chapel, but she had definitely lost some of her sparkle. Her nose was pink and her eyes luminous. He felt sorry for her and put a hand over her's on the damask cloth. But she was not in the mood to be consoled. She moved her hand tetchily and tutted.

Soup was being served, something green and glutinous dribbling from the ladle wielded by the footman and splatting into the plates. As he bent to serve Mags she straightened suddenly, waving her hand, knocking the green stuff out of the ladle all over the footman and asked shrilly,

"How can we all sit here and eat without the dear, darling Bish? He's barely cold and about to be all cut up, his flesh invaded and we are going to sit here and eat soup?"

"You suggested the autopsy, dear," her mother said reasonably, "you are the one who suspected poison."

"This soup could be poisoned, too; did you ever think of that? Well, you can all stay and eat it but I won't." She got up, pushed back her chair, winding the poor footman who was probably already burnt, and strode out.

George offered the footman Mags' discarded napkin to wipe himself down with and looked around at everyone else. Lady Lydia closed her eyes for a moment then opened them and instructed,

"Serve what's left of the soup, Charles, then go and change."

Those left at the table made an effort to pretend that all was as normal, Harry was very deliberately breaking up his roll and dropping the pieces carefully into his soup. Aunt Suzy was patting her mouth with her napkin, very pink about the cheeks.

"There's Hilda too," one of the remaining old aunts reminded them.

"Yes, she forgets poor Hilda," added the other, both then nodded and fussed about with handkerchiefs.

The twin who was not lost had put the tablecloth over her head, disturbing all her china and cutlery, Freddy was nudging her and hissing 'Creep', and Jane... well, Jane was looking straight at him, her expression pained and sad.

Jane's gaze held his and at last George did feel low, base, carnal... even guilty and surprisingly felt better for it.

The door opened, Mags put her head round and called, "George, come with me, I want you."

Now, everyone stared at him, even the twin and he wished he could hide his head under the tablecloth too. He was hungry, his green soup awaited. "No, I think I'll have some lunch-"

"I think not, George," Mags told him. "I think you will come with me."

"No. I'll have my lunch." He insisted quietly.

Mags came in and marched up to him, taking hold of his chair back and trying to dislodge him from its seat, "Don't be so bloody silly. Come up-stairs with me now."

"I'm not being silly. I'm sorry for your loss but life must go on." It was hard to keep his voice level whilst being violently jiggled but he held on to his seat and maintained an appearance of calm.

"Why? Why must it go on? He was so much better than you, than a stupid bus conductor. Why didn't you die instead?"

"Margaret!"

She ignored her mother's voice and went on, "Think you're engaged to me, do you? Think you can become part of all this? Well, you're wrong. I only ever wanted one thing from-"

George stood up. The chair, now free of his weight came up in her hands and she tumbled under it.

"I know I'm not engaged to you," he told her as she sat up on the floor, the chair between her legs. "I'm not a complete fool." He took the chair from her, put it back in its place and offered her his hand. "Get up, sit down at the table and have some lunch."

She glowered at him, ignored his hand, scrambled clumsily to her feet and ran out of the room.

"Carry on with your lunch, I'll go to her," Lady Lydia told them and, as she passed him, muttered for his ears only, "I knew you were a hero."

George took a deep breath, picked up his napkin, sat down and scanned the rest of the diners. Once again, Jane held his eye, but this time because she was smiling; a close, secretive, triumphant smile.

Lady Lydia did not return to the dining room and after a rather silent luncheon of pea soup, bacon and eggs and custard, everyone got up and left, intent on their own business, but George was intent upon Jane and followed her out of the dining room.

He touched her elbow as she began to mount the stairs, "Rather an odd meal."

She paused, "The chef is ill."

"Oh, I'm sorry. What are you going to do now?"

"I suppose I must carry on looking for Gaye, no-one else is."

"Not been found yet, then?"

"No," she turned to face him. "She often does this, or Joye does. I think its attention seeking."

"Do you? Yes, they do seem to be very strange

girls."

"Freddy says they should be locked up, but then he's only twelve." Her voice suggested that, even so, he was probably right.

"Shall I come with you to look for Gaye?"

She put her head on one side, "Shouldn't you go to Mags?"

"I think her mother is with her."

"Yes, but she wanted you."

"Then she's got to learn that she can't always have what she wants."

"Yes," she nodded, "it's about time she learnt that. And that you should be the one to teach her, how strange. It's almost as if you are taking over a fatherly role where she is concerned, isn't it?"

"Well, hardly, I…" he narrowed his eyes at her. What was she getting at? "No, I don't think I can fill that void. How about your father? He is her uncle, after all, shouldn't he take on that-?"

"That's none of your business."

"Does your father smoke a pipe?"

"No." She turned to continue her climb but he caught hold of her arm.

"I'm coming with you, remember?"

"I wish you wouldn't."

"Why?"

"I don't trust you."

"Oh."

The doorbell rang but Smears was already halfway across the hall, a looming figure in the shadowed gloom. The door groaned as he hauled it open and daylight bounced off the chequered floor except where two male silhouettes shadowed it.

"Come in, shirsh; I heard your car on the drive."

"Thank you, er...?"

"Shmearsh, the butler."

"Ah, the one's who's always 'dunnit', eh?" The owner of the voice laughed heartily at his own joke then sobered, "Inspector Fowey to see Lady Berenger, and this is my constable, Bacon."

"Ah, we've jusht had bacon for luncheon. Come in, gentlemen."

George looked up into Jane's wonderful face, so close, and illuminated by the afternoon light. As the door closed with an echoing thud and her face faded back into shadow, the constable piped up,

"Blimey sir, it's like a bloody morgue in here."

"Come with me," Jane hissed and grasped his lapel, "quickly."

And George stumbled up the stairs after her.

"We'll start looking along this corridor." After the urgency on the stairs Jane was matter of fact again. "You take this side, I'll take the other. And remember, just ask quite calmly? 'Is that you Gaye? Don't you want lunch?' otherwise she'll pretend to be frightened of you and won't answer."

"OK."

As they worked their way along the corridor, repeating their trite little questions with controlled friendliness, George noticed that, as well as having the most beautiful face, Jane had shapely legs, well modelled hips and a pert bust. Her well-cut black dress draped around her much as he found himself wishing he could. Her skirt flounced at the hem as she swung half into each room, issued her enticing invitation, waited and swung out again, her hips swivelling, her back supple, her ankles so firm and slim above her neat black court shoes. He hardly noticed what was in the rooms on his side at all and when they got to the end asked,

"Is this the west wing?"

"No."

"Only I saw dust sheets in one room and I heard that the west wing was being decorated, your mother said."

"Gaye could be under any of those dust sheets - which room, do you remember?"

"No."

"Well, we'll have to go back along your side and look for it."

He followed her, willingly, "How many rooms are there?"

"Over eighty - more than a hundred if you count servant's rooms and service rooms."

"Oh, there are more than twenty of those."

"How do you know?" she stopped and faced him. "Have you been down there?" She sounded amazed.

"Yes. Haven't you?" He echoed her amazement and, he felt, with more reason.

"Never. Why would I go there? Why did you?"

"Ethel took me there for a cup of tea."

"Ethel?"

"The upstairs-"

"I know who Ethel is," sometimes she sounded just like Mags. "I just wondered why she should do such a thing."

"I was lost, she took pity on me."

"Are you so pitiful? It seems to me we are the ones to be pitied."

"Why?" Had she guessed, did she know about the bus ticket and the naked fright?

"You seem to have an unusual effect on all the women of this family."

"Do I?"

"You know you do and you're revelling in it. I had hoped... I had hoped that once you got here, once we'd met that...Then I saw you in the summer house!" Her eyes shone, her mouth puckered. "Mags I could understand, but her mother? And now the servants."

"Now, hang on, I've never touched Ethel." It was a lie but he reckoned she didn't know about the kiss on the stairs. Then he met her hopeful gaze and suddenly it was all too real. He felt panicked and put his hand to his head, raking it through his hair.

"You swear?" She insisted.

"I swear!" The repeated lie made his heart contract and he swallowed hard, she was crying. "Don't cry." He begged, lamely. "Here," he handed her his handkerchief, his last one.

"How could it all go so wrong?" She sniffed.

"And I was the first one to ever see you, too."

"Jane, oh don't cry. Why can't anyone say what they mean?"

"You know what I mean. You just want me to say it, to swell your head even more."

"My head isn't swelled, it's confused."

"I have such feelings for you! All right? Is that enough?" She blew her nose loudly. "Now you've got us all, apart from my mother," except she said 'mudder' because her nose was blocked. It sounded sweet and he stroked her hair. "Don't do that! I can't have you touching me; you're soiled. I know that but I almost don't care!"

He stood in the corridor and gazed at her, lit up by the sunlight glancing in from a turret window and reflecting off a mirror in the room behind her.

"I wish I was pure," he groaned, "more than anything in the world I wish I was pure enough for you."

"Ohhh, you've made me so unhappy!"

He had, he really had, he could tell, and now he was unhappy because she was and he could have made both their dreams come true if only he'd resisted in the summer house. Why hadn't he resisted? "She seduced me."

"Who did? Which one? Or did they both and you succumbed both times because you're weak?"

"I'm not weak."

"You have been. But," she swallowed, "you were strong with Mags at dinner."

"I was, I can do it. I can do it for you, Jane."

"But it was only because you were hungry!"

"No. Well- yes, I was hungry. I'd also seen your look. That look you gave me and I felt unclean and venal."

"Venal?"

"Yes, it means-"

"I know what it means. I'm just surprised you do."

"Ah! I'm only a bus conductor. I don't know about art. I don't know what venal means! You're all alike. What exactly is it that you like about me then? Why do you have 'such strong feelings' for me if you think I'm soiled and stupid? And what does strong feelings mean anyway? You can have strong feelings about a...a cake-" He broke off and ran his hand through his hair again. "Do you mean... I mean, do you love me? Is that why you're so upset? Do you Jane? Is that... Am I even mad to suggest that?!"

'No." She blinked at him, a teary blink that sent drops of water from her long, dark lashes on to her smooth, flushed cheeks. Her lips parted, she sighed, "Oh, I love the unexpectedness of you. I love your mouth and your nose and your eyes and the way the hair grows at the nape of your neck. I love the way you cheer up the old ladies on the bus, and tousle the children's hair, and help the elderly on and off, and the way you say, 'thank you', with a little lilt to your voice. I love the curve of your legs in your uniform trousers, and the way you run up the first few stairs to collect fares on the top of your bus. I love your hands, the way you operate your machine, your fingers and knuckles, and the way that your collar fits round your neck." She stopped, breathless, but George got the impression that she could go on. She pressed his slimy wet handkerchief into his hands to push past him.

He didn't stop her; he was too stunned.

Gaye completely forgotten, after the revelation of Jane's love, George wandered back down through the house, alone but not lonely. He was loved! And by the most beautiful girl he had ever seen. Mags was definitely in the past; he would not be seeking her out again, or her mother. Why, oh why had he given in to the mother? Poor Jane, to have seen the unelevating sight of her loved one pumping away on top of her fat, old aunt. He was disgusted with himself.

Soiled. It was her word and it suited him admirably. He found himself on a landing, halfway up - or down - a flight of back stairs, he sat and rubbed his hands over his face. But how could he get clean again? A dim window, covered with cobwebs, allowed enough light into the stair-well for him to see his own 'beloved' but filthy hands. He looked at them, turning them this way and that. They looked ordinary enough hands to him but to Jane- Jane had wanted to be touched by them, once.

A door opened somewhere above him and heavy footsteps began to descend, then a voice said, "Well, we must think of a motive, Bacon. Motive and means, that's where we'll find our killer."

A new panic filled his gut. His thoughts in turmoil over Jane, his guilt about The Bish and Aunt Hilda, (would anyone believe his story?) he was not ready to face the police. George stood up quickly and began to run as silently as he could down into the darker depths. After two turns he came to a blackened dead end and bumped into the wall. The sound of his hollow thud spiralled upwards and Bacon's voice answered,

"There's someone down there, sir."

"The house is full of people, constable, fifty-three at the last count, according to Lady Lydia, mostly servants. Bound to be people going about their business all over the place." The footsteps stopped. "Are we getting anywhere, Bacon?"

"Early days yet, sir."

"No, I mean, with this bloody staircase?"

"It must lead somewhere, if there's people below."

"But is it somewhere we want to be? That Lady Lydia, Bacon..."

"You think she did it? Poisoned her own son?"

"We don't know if poison was used yet, never jump to conclusions."

"No, sir."

"No, I was er.... Handsome woman, would you say?"

"Handsome is as handsome does, sir."

"Don't spout clichés at me, constable."

"No, sir. Sorry, sir."

Silence ensued; George strained his ears as he

felt around the walls for some sign of an exit. The stairs must lead somewhere.

"These stairs must lead somewhere, otherwise why build them. Let's carry on down, constable."

"Yes, sir." The steady advance of the two pairs of footsteps resumed and George's frantic fingers fumbled against what felt like a latch. Using both hands he pressed down and pulled, then pushed, the door gave with a terrific grating which halted the footsteps above once again. George slid into the wonderfully lighted space revealed and shut the door noisily behind him. He took a deep breath of fresh air and looked around.

He was in a tiny courtyard, surrounded by stone and brick walls, at least five stories high, and tapering away above to a square of bluish sky, which was filtered by what looked like netting. On the walls surrounding him were rows and rows of iron hooks and from them hung the corpses of birds, rabbits, foxes, and at least one half rotted deer. The air he had a moment before thought was fresh, now seemed thick with decomposing flesh. The sawdust beneath his feet was soaked in puddles of blood, dried and drying, littered with desiccated claws and fragile bird skulls. Two rooks, tied together at the feet and slung over the rusting hook nearest his head, eyed him suspiciously through flat, enamelled eyeballs. Foxes gaped, suspended by their lower jaws, staring at the distant sky, rabbits just folded their neat front paws and looked down sadly at the floor.

George spun towards the door to make his escape just as it opened out to him, "Ahhh!"

"Ahhh!"

"Ahhh!"

Three cries of alarm rang out, round and round the walls, as if all the creatures were venting their agony.

George was the first to regain his composure, after all, he knew who the two newcomers were. He put his hands in his pockets fingering the wretched ticket and remarked, "I'm afraid you won't get out this way, gents."

The inspector twisted his scrawny throat against his stiff collar and adjusted his shoulders, "Thank you. Mr...?"

"Pender. George Pender."

"Notebook, Bacon."

"Yes sir," Bacon finished straightening his helmet, got his notebook out of his top pocket and flicked through the pages, perusing one at length. "No mention of a Mr Pender, sir."

"I'm a guest." George told them.

"Are you indeed?"

"A friend of the Honourable Margaret's."

"Put that down, Bacon."

Bacon scribbled.

"Shall we find our way back upstairs?" George suggested, his stomach tightening "This isn't a very salubrious hole."

"So, what are you doing in it, Mr Pender?"

"Getting lost, like you." He led the way back into the stairwell and, once the door was closed behind them, began to mount the stairs blind, with the policemen close at his heels. Each man stumbled at some point; swearing, muttering, clutching hold of the cold, plaster walls or one another, until they came to the cobwebbed window. Here the inspector elbowed his way to the front of the line, sandwiching George as if he was the accused, and continued the ascent to the first door they came to.

"Right, what's this then?" The inspector halted, having opened the door and George peered over his grey serge shoulder.

"Looks like an armoury." He suggested.

"Bloody hell you could equip a regiment with this lot," constable Bacon's breath was hot in George's ear.

The inspector walked into the room allowing George and Bacon to follow. "I think we need to make a list of this lot, constable, make sure they've got licenses for these guns."

"I don't think they'd need licenses," George remarked, gazing round at the circles and fans of guns, spears, swords, rifles and daggers fixed to the oak panelled walls, "most of it looks pretty ancient. This is a flintlock."

"Don't touch! There might be finger prints," inspector Fowey instructed, walking to the window and glancing out.

"But no-one's been shot, have they?" Asked George.

"Ah, no, but you never know, sir, in cases like this." He narrowed his eyes at him and George felt impelled to assure him,

"I'm pretty sure it was an accident, you know. I was there, on the lawn, he just leaned forwards and fell."

"Not now sir, we'll take statements when we know we have a crime to investigate. Our main task at the moment is to find our way back into the habitable zones of this place. We seem to be on the northern side on the building, judging from the shadows on the lawn. I'd ask you to be our guide, sir, but you seem as unfamiliar with the place as we are."

"Yes. In fact I've decided I'll go home."

"Not just yet, sir. I don't want to lose sight of any of my suspects"

The word tolled in George's panic ridden belly, "But I'm on the evening shift tomorrow. I could lose my job."

"Which is?"

"Bus conductor."

"Bus conduc-""

"Bacon. I've warned you before, haven't I?"

"Yes, sir, sorry, sir."

"Just carry on getting down all these firing pieces in your notebook and keep your trap shut." He tapped his nose twice.

"Yes sir," Bacon grinned.

"He's new," Fowey hissed out of the side of his mouth as he fingered a red and green tassel hanging from an eight-foot lance which was angled against the window frame. "Bus conductor, mmm. Are you sure you're Miss Berenger's guest?"

"Quite sure."

"And not the deceased's?"

"Who, The Bishop?"

"Alphonse Berenger was very interested in buses; I wonder if he wasn't equally interested in their conductors as well?" He seemed totally involved with the tassel.

"Well, yes he was. He pounced on me as soon as he found out what I did."

"Pounced on you? An unwelcome advance was it, Mr Pender?"

"Well, I don't mind talking about buses with those who are interested in them but he was a bit... strange," he was gabbling, couldn't stop gabbling. "They're all a bit strange, have you noticed?" George saw a flicker of communication pass between the inspector and his constable, "You must have noticed," he pressed.

"They seem a perfectly normal family to me, sir."

"Well, you haven't been here very long, I suppose."

"This 'pouncing'," Fowey pursed his lips and finally dropped the tassel, "what form did it take?"

"Well, you know, wanting me to tell him the number of my machine, the make, all that. He knew all the bus routes off by heart and has got pictures of them all over his room."

"You've been in his room, have you, sir?"

"Yes. When he fell Mags was up there on the balcony, screaming her head off, in a dreadful state, so I ran upstairs, found the room and ran in to comfort her. While I was comforting her, I noticed all the pictures and the pulpit and everything."

"You hadn't been in there before, for any reason?"

"No, why should I?"

"So, Miss Margaret, Mags as you call her, was in the room when he fell?"

"She was in the room; he was on the balcony. She didn't push him or anything, we'd have seen her."

"So, there wasn't anything of an intimate physical nature between you and Mr Alphonse Berenger?"

"What?!" He had an awful urge to fart. He controlled it. "Why on earth should you think that?"

"I don't know, sir, why I should have thought that. Perhaps your use of the word 'pounce' brought to mind a vivid picture of the moment which was purely a figment of my imagination."

"Well, I'm sorry if I misled you, inspector," he tightened his sphincter even more, "but you certainly have a very vivid imagination."

"One of the requirements of the job, sir."

George had heard something like that before; he frowned in concentration and Bacon nodded over his notebook,

"Got most of it down, sir."

"Well, done Bacon. I don't think we need speak to Mr Pender again on the matter. Other than to ask you, sir, if you could draw me a rough sketch map of the position of everyone, as you remember it, yesterday afternoon in the garden when the fall occurred?"

"Oh, yes, yes, I can do that." He was too eager, they would see his eagerness and suspect it, surely.

"Very well, we shall continue, Bacon." The inspector signalled him to open a door in the far wall.

"Yes sir," he did so and stood aside as the inspector walked into a cupboard and smartly out again. "Sorry, sir." The constable ran round and opened another door which led into a corridor and they both hurried out to the right.

George breathed a sigh of relief, expelled the tension in his gut and sank onto the window seat. Had he been interviewed then, and dismissed as a suspect? Was that the conclusion he should draw from his interrogation? His heart was scattering beats all over his chest and he needed a good few minutes before he got up and followed them out into the corridor. As he closed the door behind him the two policemen passed, heading left, and ignored him completely.

CHAPTER 6

"Clover?"

"What is it, Aunty?" Her voice sounds weak and quavery on the phone, alerting me and my stomach sinks.

"I've done a silly thing."

"Well, we all do silly things." Some more often than others.

"I came down this morning and noticed that the picture had gone and thought I'd been burgled and rang the police."

"The police?"

"So, if a nice man with a moustache and silly beard comes to arrest you, I didn't mean it."

"Oh, Aunty, didn't you explain that you'd given it to me to return to Leatherboys Hall?"

"I did tell him that, after I'd made him some tea and given him some of that fruit cake. You know, I'm not half-way through that cake yet, do you think it will have gone off? I don't want to be suspected of poisoning a policeman."

"I'm sure you won't be accused of that."

"I've only ever had one other experience of the police. A nasty, skinny little man who thought

George had murdered The Bishop. Well, I thought he had as well for a while, in a fit of jealous rage. But he hadn't, of course."

"No, of course. So, just tell me again; you rang the police because you thought you had been burgled and they'd taken the painting?"

"Yes. That's right, how did you know?"

"You just rang me and told me. Aunty, should I come round to see you? Do you want the picture back?"

"I don't want it back, have you taken it to the Hall yet?"

"Not yet, no. I've been a bit ill."

"Was it- was it the cake?"

"No, nothing to do with the cake."

"Thank goodness for that. And you're well now?"

"Very well, thank you. Now, don't worry about the police; they've probably realised that you just got a bit confused and forgotten-" The door bell has just rung, "-forgotten all about it. I have to go someone's at the door. I'll ring you back, take care."

"Alright dear."

Aunty is losing it, so sad, but she is pretty old. I open the front door and a nice, rather plump young man with a goatee smiles and me and flashes his identity card.

"Miss Berrow?"

I nod.

"Nick Middlecott, I'm a detective sergeant at Palmers Green."

"I know who you are, my great aunt has just been on the phone. Come in."

"Thank you. I was coming this way anyway and just thought I'd follow up her complaint, even thought she withdrew it."

I lead the way into the sitting room and kick a few magazines under the sofa, "There's the picture."

He glances at it and nods.

"She gave me the painting a couple of weeks ago and asked me to take it back to her family home in Norfolk for her. She says it reminds her of things she'd rather forget, and if I'd looked like that when I was young and was Aunty's age now, I think I'd feel the same."

"That's her, is it?" He's impressed, "Quite a looker. And I can see the family likeness," he tries it on.

"No you can't, we are not related by blood at all."

"It was worth a try."

"Anyway, I can't haul it about at the moment," I stick out my belly a bit more, "and I love the painting and just thought I'd enjoy it until I'm capable of getting it to Norfolk. Are you going to arrest me?"

"No," he grins, "old people get muddled and confused all the time. It's just we've got a knocker doing the rounds at the moment and I thought he might have got his hands on her portrait... you know."

"Well, it's good to know our bobbies are doing

their jobs."

"Yeah," he grins again then his mouth twists in discomfort. "Would you mind if I used your..."

"Aunty's cake?"

"I thought it tasted a bit off."

"First door on the right in the hall."

"Thanks."

While he's in there I ring Aunty back to let her know it's all sorted, "The policeman is here now."

"Are you arrested?"

"No, no. Not at all, he just wanted to make sure I did have the painting because they've had some men going round fiddling old people out of their antiques. You've heard about knockers, I expect?"

"They're breasts, aren't they?"

"No, darling, in this case they're dealers in antiques who try to sweet talk people out of their heirlooms. You mustn't let them into your house. Promise me, not to let strangers into the house."

"I promise. And you promise that you're all right, Clover?"

"Yes, everything is fine, Aunty," I hear Detective Sergeant Middlecott groan loudly from the loo. "Nothing to worry about at all."

*****

Giddy with relief after his interrogation, George set about finding his room. Fortunately, he recognised a particular suit of armour, with a rivetingly large cod-piece, from a former excursion down the corridor and was soon able to let himself into his room and lock the door. His dear little room. He was quite fond of it by now; it offered safety and seclusion from a crazy world. He almost sank onto the bed, remembered in time, swivelled on his heel and flumped onto the sofa instead.

As was his wont, lying prone, his hands dangling on the floor to either side, he let his mind meander round the meaningless, rather than concentrate on the important particulars. What on earth would it be like to wear a suit of armour? Heavy, obviously, hot and sweaty, probably. You'd cook in it during sunny weather and it would probably chafe. He grimaced at the thought of the chafing. And cod pieces, what were they for, exactly? Proclaim your manhood? Protect same manhood? He puffed out his cheeks and tilted his head. Something was squeaking nearby, mice or rats? He sat up straight and listened more intently. The squeaking stopped and a scuffling followed. Too big for rats, unless they were whoppers and there was a gang of them.

Trying to pin-point the source he got up and tiptoed slowly round the room. There had been a noise this morning and something - someone - at the door had woken him, but this particular disturbance was coming from his cavernous carved wardrobe. He searched for a weapon to defend himself with, kill the little buggers with, and grabbed a poker from the fireplace. Poker aloft and at the ready he positioned himself and flung open the wardrobe door. It was dark inside and the hangers were strangely bare. He looked down and The Beautiful Child smirked up at him, a pair of scissors in her hand, his newly cleaned, hired dress suit in tatters across her lap.

"Hello."

"What the hell d'you think you're doing?!" He lowered the poker, though the urge to pop her one was strong.

"I was bored."

"So you decided to cut up my clothes?" His pyjamas were in a similarly scattered state, and his clean shirt. "Get out of there!"

"Don't shout at me. It's not allowed."

"I'll shout at you if I want. Now get out and give me those scissors."

"Shan't, they're Nanny's scissors," she retreated further into the dusty corner of the wardrobe.

"Give me the scissors and I'll give them back to Nanny."

"No." She had an evil little face, not beautiful at all. High forehead, beaky nose and thin brown hair pulled back tightly into braids.

"Then I'll lock you in there and forget about you," he made to do so and she scrambled out, scissors in her fist. "I'm going to tell your mother what you've done," he bent to pick up his tatters of jacket.

"Sneak."

"You need a good hiding."

"I shan't get one. I'm the favourite."

"Favourite what?"

"Child, of course."

"I can't think why."

"I don't like you."

"The feeling's mutual."

Her face twitched, she smoothed her gauzy lilac dress, "What does that mean? Moochal?"

"I don't like you either."

She actually gasped - flinched as if slapped. George tried to remember that she was just a little girl, who had lost her eldest brother the previous day and an ancient aunty too. He should be kind and compassionate but she had left him with no clothes to wear.

"I've got my best dress on," she said suddenly. "Because I'm allowed down for Sunday tea. And look," she stuck out one skinny, dust besmirched leg, "I've got matching socks on too."

"And I've got nothing left to wear except what I'm standing up in, thanks to you."

"Nanny says I'm a prodigy and mustn't be upset."

"Nanny must be mad."

Her lower lip trembled, "I'm The Beautiful Child."

"You're a bloody nuisance."

Her face contracted into hard little lines, "I hate you!"

"Good, now get out of my room." He went to open the door for her, so her subsequent screams echoed loud and ringing into the corridor,

"He's raped me!! He's raped me!!"

George folded his arms and watched her.

"The nasty man's raped me!" She cupped her hands round her mouth for added volume and frowned at George, like a little weasel, he thought.

"I don't think anyone's coming," he told her during a lull in her performance. "Maybe no-one cares, certainly no-one will believe you."

She stared at him, opened her mouth to scream again and Mags swept into the room.

"What is all this racket? Why are you in George's room? Where's George?" She spun round and saw him, "Darling, where have you been, I've been looking everywhere for you since luncheon?"

"Have you? This little brat has just cut up all my clothes," he pointed at the wardrobe.

"Sybella?" Mags made a lunge for her but she writhed free and ran off, screaming resumed. "Little sick bucket. She's been told about this before. Oh well," she shrugged and stroked his cheek.

"No, it's not 'Oh well'," he backed away. "That was a hired suit and now I've got no clothes left- no shirt, no pyjamas!"

"I'm sure she didn't mean any harm, darling."

"I'm not. That suit cost two guineas to hire."

"Well, buy a new one."

"That's one week's wage, Mags."

"Oh, I do wish you wouldn't keep on being so common, talking about money all the time." She sighed but forced a smile.

"I thought you liked me being common, I thought that was part of my attraction." George was seriously affronted; he had tried all his life not to be common. He had read widely, visited museums and attended elocution classes as a boy. Mags was stroking the bed cover,

"Only part, darling," she was about to sit down.

"I wouldn't do that if I were you, the bed springs are bare under that cover. I think you could at least make sure your guests are properly housed, I have to sleep on the sofa."

"But I told you darling, the west wing is being decorated." She patted the lumpy bed and raised an eyebrow, "Like making love on a bed of nails," she laughed, her throaty laugh, "could be interesting."

George ignored her, returned the poker to the fireplace and went to the wardrobe, crouching down to sort through the remains of his clothes, "What am I going to wear tonight?"

She was suddenly behind him, arms round his neck, the soft wool of her jumper tickling his jaw. "I'm sure we'll be able to find you something but you know how I like you best."

"Mags," he disentangled himself and stood up, "I'd leave here right now but the police want me to stay until they've decided if a crime has been committed."

"Poor Bish!"

"You don't really care about me, you don't love me and as far as I'm concerned, we're not engaged, so leave me alone."

"Oh, you're so proper. I love that." She advanced, "I do love you darling, I was under pressure at lunch; unhinged by grief. I said some silly things."

"Maybe, but you've made me realise the truth. I'm just here to fuck you and keep you quiet."

She was quiet, for a moment. Her cheeks pink, her eyes moist and her mouth in her seductive pout. She was lovely, her dark plum suit of jumper and skirt fitted her so perfectly. Her body was a ripe flesh ready to burst through the thin wool. George knew he was faltering. He tried to look away but she knew how to draw him in,

"Georgie," a voice so soft and husky, her lips so meltingly soft, "there have been others, but you're the one I need forever..."

"Not your brother?" he blurted.

"My brother?"

"What were you doing in his room when he fell?"

"Oh, Georgie, you think we were lovers? Oh, never!" she fell on him, pressing her firm body into the curves of his. "I was telling him about you, how I love you. He wanted to tell you how much he liked you, that's why he went out on to the balcony to call down to you - he couldn't wait. He said, didn't he, 'You are a Christian gentleman'? His last words were about you darling. Because I'd told him all about you and how good you were for me and how happy I was."

"But the bed - it was rumpled." He would hold out, though it was hard. Everything was hard.

"I'd been bouncing on it, in my excitement."

She wriggled against him, "You know how I like bouncing."

He did. She often bounced on hotel beds, very noisily. "You had nothing on under your dressing gown," he persisted.

"I'd had a bath, after the woods. And then ran along to dear Bish's room to talk to him, to tell him."

"You told everyone about us."

"Why not? When you're in love you want to tell the world," she flung her right arm wide and beamed up at him, a snapshot, "Don't you?"

"You don't tell everyone all the details," his hand flickered at her waist.

"There you go, being proper again. Darling, you might not but I do." She brought her right hand down slowly and caressed his groin area. She gave a little private laugh and nuzzled his neck. "Come and fuck your Magsie." hanging on him she tried to drag him to the floor.

George found it impossible to bring Jane's face to mind. He told himself later that had he been able to do so he would never have succumbed.

Later Mags led him into the drawing room like a prize bull. He held back, scowling, not daring to raise his eyes and see Jane. The sound of tinkling teaspoons ceased as Mags announced,

"We're reconciled! Soulmates once again."

"Bravo," Lady Lydia boomed out and someone clapped.

George dropped into an armchair, folded his

hands and stared at the highly patterned rug.

"Topping," Harry laughed, "he really is a good chap and he loved my paintings."

"You've shown Georgie your paintings?" Mags sounded genuinely amazed.

"Well, only the fresco and he liked that, didn't you, old chap?"

George nodded, eyes still lowered. Mags came to sit on the arm of his chair, to enfold him in an embrace, "See how everyone here loves you?"

Wretchedness welled up in George's abdomen; he thought he would choke on it.

"Well I don't like him," The Beautiful Child announced.

"Silly girl," cooed her mother.

"And he said he hated me."

"Well, Sybella, you did cut up all his clothes," Mags defended him. "What do you expect him to do, make love to you?"

Sybella screamed, one short burst, and waited for the response.

"Sybella, is this true?" Lady Lydia's voice held a hint of reproach. "Poor Mr Pender. What is he to wear? Did you think of that?"

George squinted up at the room to gauge Sybella's silence. She was sitting on the floor at her mother's feet, cutting pictures out of a book. A leather-bound book that looked as if it might be an antique. Her face was turned away from him, towards her mother, so he was not prepared for the next shriek. He jumped. Mags jumped.

"Now stop that, Sybella," a hint more firmness in the mother's voice. One might almost call this a telling off. Mags drew in a breath; the room was so quiet George could hear the blood rushing in his ears.

"He raped me!"

"Rubbish!"

"Don't shout at me, Mother!" There was actual menace in the shrill childish voice, in the stiffness of her plaits.

"Go to your room!"

"Shan't!" But she dropped the book, its pages crumpling, and got up, then made a sudden lurch towards her mother, scissors raised.

Mags screamed, Lady Lydia screamed. George pushed Mags to the floor in his urgency and reached Sybella as the scissors were about to descend into her mother's soft, warm and welcoming bosom. He snatched the scissors from her. She kicked his shins and ran screaming from the room.

"My own child!" Lady Lydia held out her arms in despair.

George, hopping on one leg, nursing the other, over balanced and fell into her embrace. From the muffling softness, George hardly heard the last scream and the resounding thud that quickly followed it. No-one else paid much attention. Lady Lydia was near to a faint, Mags was fanning her with a cushion, Harry was hauling George out of his mother's lap; Aunt Suzy was ringing for brandy and the two old aunts were fluttering at the back of the sofa, patting Lady Lydia's dark, artfully waved hair.

George straightened and searched for Jane in the melee. She was standing back, her hands pressed together, eyes wide with shock, he hobbled towards her,

"I'm sorry, I'm sorry…"

She focussed on him and her lovely mouth tightened on the word, "Weak."

"Where's my hero?" Lady Lydia called from her sofa. "I knew you would be good for this family as soon as I saw you. I said so, didn't I Margaret?"

"Yes, Mummy. Don't talk Mummy, have some brandy."

"I say!" Freddy piped up, his voice gaining attention as he entered the room, "Did you know the bison head has fallen? And I think there's someone underneath."

"Christ!" George skip-hopped across the room out into the hall and, Freddy keeping up with him, gained the library before the two policemen, who were issuing from beneath the stairs. The huge fallen head blocked the library doorway, one horn hung awkwardly across the shaggy dome of the skull. George braced himself against the door frame and peered over the moth-eaten mound. Amid the sawdust a small foot in a white satin shoe and lilac sock poked out from under the pitted leather nose, twitching for just a moment. "Christ!"

"I don't see why it should be me," George complained as he followed Smears's broad back down an interminably long passageway in the half dark. His shins still hurt and he was feeling pretty jittery, it wasn't often one witnessed the squashing to death of a child. "She won't know who I am and how am I supposed to break the news? Her favourite child, her prodigy."

"Oh, she tells them all that. She believes in instilling total confidence in her charges. To my way of thinking she ruins them." Smears stopped and flicked on his lighter, "It gets quite dark along here, mind your feet."

George focussed on the willowing flame. He must leave Leatherboys Hall; escape was the only answer. If he didn't go soon, he'd knock off the entire family.

'It looks to me' Inspector Fowey had called down from the top of the step ladder in the Library, 'that the head had been loosened in some way. The nail in the panelling is bent and the rust is cracked. Take notes Bacon.'

'Yessir.'

'This is what years of experience can do for you. Do you think anyone else would have noticed that? The cracked rust? A trained eye,' he tapped his own eye with the end of his screwdriver and winced. 'Yes. A trained eye. This head was just waiting to fall. The tragedy is that it chose to fall on the one member of the family too small to withstand the impact.'

Lady Lydia had fainted at this point and George had been forgotten for a while as they dealt with her. Then Mags had rounded on him and cried,

'You must go and tell Nanny!'

So here he was, going to tell Nanny. Surely his feeble attack on the head, his punch the previous evening, had not caused the nail to bend so? Who would be so foolish as to hang a huge bison head up by one four-inch nail? They were ultimately to blame, weren't they?

"Here we are sir," Smears frowned at him in the yellow stutter of his lighter. They had stopped outside a door with what looked like a list of rules pinned to it. From the other side of the solid oak a weak but not unpleasant voice was trilling, 'Who is Sylvia?' "Just stand your ground and don't let her bully you," He knocked softly on the door and hurried away.

Left alone in the dark, the weedy notes undisturbed by the knock, George rubbed his lumpy shins, groaned and knocked again, loudly. The singing stopped. A chair scraped. Footsteps, familiar somehow, pattered away. A door slammed. Silence. Since he didn't know the way back to the hall, George had no option but to knock again. He raised his hand and the door shot open.

"Who are you?"

He blinked in the sudden light, saw a parrot on a stand over the burly shoulder of his inquisitor and shaded his eyes, "George Pender."

"We meet at last. Come in."

George shut the door behind him and, his eyes now adjusted to the brightness of the room, watched with interest as Nanny rolled away from him on obviously bandy legs and turned to sit in a high-backed Windsor chair by the window. She was built like a prize fighter, massive bosom encased in a starched white apron, dull, grey hair pulled up into a ridiculously small bun on top of her fleshy head and sensible brown brogues peeking out from under her navy serge skirts.

"I've heard all about you," the voice was crisply Scots with a throaty growl. "Come and sit here, so I can look at you. Why are you limping?"

"Sybella kicked my shins," he sat as directed on a low three-legged stool in front of her, the cushion of which was still warm.

"She's a child of spirit. Do you need some arnica?"

"Some what?" He hoped it might be something liquid, possibly alcoholic, he was parched.

"For your bruises. Have you not heard of it? What did your mother put on your childhood sprains?"

"A plaster."

"Tch. Show me your shins?"

George was somewhat loath, the last time he had shown someone in this house his legs it had resulted in fornication and he had no wish to fuck the mighty Nanny. He began to raise his trouser hems but she lost patience and was on her knees before him, her capable, square hands on his bare calves before he had time to protest.

"She has not broken the skin, at least. What

shoes had she on? Oh, yes, I remember, her white kid, they'll do you no lasting damage. Sit there, I'll get the Better Box."

"The what?"

"It's the name young Master Howie gave the first aid box," she got up, her knees cracking, her skirts giving off a whiff of mothballs and talc.

'Howie'? Was this another posthumous child he had yet to meet? Then he remembered that Lady Lydia's husband had been a Howard. Nanny must have been with them for years yet she had a vigour about her which belied her age.

"You wouldn't happen to have a glass of water, would you? I didn't manage to get any tea."

"Missed your tea, did you?" she bent to look in a cupboard under a sink in the far corner of the room.

"Missed your tea, need a pee!" squawked the parrot.

"Be quiet, Stewart, Master George is not used to your rough ways."

The parrot side stepped along his perch, muttering.

"That's quite a bird," George remarked, watching the beady eye and the black beak, he wasn't fond of birds.

"A macaw. They live for years, you know," Nanny sat down in her chair again, a red and white first aid box on her lap. Her mouth folded into a comfortable hum as she searched through it. How could he tell her about her youngest charge? What words could he use? "Here we are. A dab or two of this will work wonders. I've used it on all the children over the years," she squeezed a worm of white cream onto the fingers of her right hand, "Allez-up."

George lifted first one then the other foot into her large lap and she applied the cream with infinite gentleness while he took in the oddities of the nursery. He was getting used to this house now and what would once have shocked, now only mildly amused. The large diagram of a pinkly naked person, the flesh peeled back to reveal the innards, on the wall above the sink did not make him blink. Nor did the stuffed dogs, three of them; a poodle with a top-knot bow, a droopy eared beagle and a large, lean wolf hound, all in glass cases beside the bookshelves. It seemed entirely in keeping that the books on those shelves should include titles such as; Lady Chatterley's Lover', surely a pirated edition, Huxley's Chrome Yellow and Antic Hay alongside Treasure Island and a full set of Beatrix Potter. However, a glass display case filled with pieces of what looked like wood, each one annotated, did pique his interest. Nanny noticed,

"I see you've homed in upon Master Larry's collection of knot-holes." She wiped her hands on a piece of towelling and motioned him to remove his foot from her lap.

"Is that what they are?"

"He was a very tactile child, unlike his brother Howie, he loved to fondle and suck them, and of course, being knot-holes, there were no splinters to worry about. I firmly believe that every child should have a hobby." She got up to return the first aid kit and George went over to the case. It was lined with ancient green velvet, bare in patches, faded and moth-eaten and each mounted knot-hole had its own label with thick black ink lettering, 'Floorboard, main hall', 'Staircase skirting, second landing.' 'Library panelling, beside fireplace.'

George sighed, "Nanny, I have to tell you something and I think you should sit down."

"Very well, but first I'll get you that drink of water you were asking for."

"Water, water everywhere! Mine's a double!"

"Please excuse Stewart, he was brought up in a barracks." She ran the tap, the pipes clanked above their heads. "I've tried over the years to modify his language, but I've come to believe that children benefit from exposure to all forms of communication."

"Fornication?! Well fuck me!" The parrot chipped in.

"Yes, all forms, however crude. None of my children swear now, they've got it out of their systems, you see. Here," the deluded woman handed him his drink and sat. "Now what did you have to tell me, young man."

George gulped his drink.

"You'll get wind," she warned.

He wiped his mouth with the back of his hand and she tutted. He began with, "It's very bad news, I'm afraid."

"Well out with it then, I hate a ditherer."

"Sybella is dead, she was squashed by a bison."

"Now there's an example of what I call lazy speech. Swear if you want but enunciate properly. We don't say 'bison', we say 'basin'."

"No, you didn't hear me..."

"Excuse me I did. I heard you quite clearly and you said 'bison'."

"Yes, it was a bison..."

"Now let's not get silly about this, Master George. I'm sure we're getting on far to well to argue over one little word."

George tried another tack, "You know the library?"

"I do indeed, little Sybella has been having lessons in there recently and-"

"And you know-"

"Don't interrupt your elders. You know I've told you that so many times."

"Yes, all right, I'm sorry. But you know the stuffed head in there; the bison?"

"Yes," she brightened, "shot by young Master Howie on a trip to America. Straight between the eyes, like a true Berenger. I remember him bringing it home in a big wooden case and it being unpacked in the hall. I can see him now arranging for it to be hung, so excited."

"Well, it's fallen."

"Fallen? Oh dear."

"Yes. On top of Sybella."

She digested this for a moment, still smiling,

until the words sank in and her smile faded and her mouth opened in horror. She pressed her hands to her chest. The action was too similar and George was at her side in a moment, "Is it your heart?"

"Broken... Broken..."

"Can I get you anything?"

"My little beauty. Dead, you say?" She looked up at him, grey eyes, watering. "Did she suffer?"

"It was instantaneous."

"Thank God for that," she sat up and waved him away. "I think I need something from the Better Box."

"Yes, I'll get it for you."

"Good boy."

He went to the cupboard, removed the box, remarking the many bottles of caustic fluids also kept there and returned to her with it.

"Thank you," she opened the lid, reached straight in and brought out a bottle of transparent liquid, unscrewed the top, put it to her mouth and swigged it dry.

"Gin?" he asked.

"Rum." She looked up at him, her eyes filmed. "Master Alphonse yesterday, Miss Sybella today; the oldest and the youngest. Tragic, tragic..."

"Yes, indeed."

"Fetch me the caustic soda from under the sink."

"Ah, no, now you mustn't-" he put a hand on her solid shoulder.

"It's more rum, silly boy."

"Are you sure?"

"Test it yourself if you don't believe me. Go on, go on," she gave him a hearty shove in the side.

He went to the sink, found the caustic soda, the blue, ridge-backed bottle half full and unscrewed the top. One sniff was enough to convince him, but he took a tentative swig as well, it made him cough.

"You're not used to it," Nanny told him, "you try bringing up eight children without it."

George handed her the bottle, "Should you go and lie down?"

"I can handle my booze." She upended the bottle.

"But wouldn't a cup of tea be better for you?"

"No." She dropped the bottle to the floor and stared very hard at the little three-legged stool. "How is Lady Lydia?"

"In a faint, the last time I saw her."

"Poor Lady."

"In fact, Sybella had tried to stab her," there was no response so he added, "with your scissors."

"Mmm," Nanny nodded, "she would."

George stood at a loss beside the immobile bulk of Nanny. Had he done enough? Was it safe to leave her now? And, if he did could he find his way back to the main hall again?

"Nanny?" There was no reply, so he bent to look into her face. The eyes were glazed, the mouth slack but she was still breathing. He supposed he should go and find a servant to stay with her. "Nanny, I'm just going to try and find a servant or someone to stay with you, alright? Will you be alright if I leave you for a while?" There was no response, even to his hand, waved inches from her nose. "Right, well I'll just go and find someone... Don't do anything silly, will you?" The giant bosom rose and fell rhythmically, her face had sunk into the folds of her jowls. "I'm going now..."

A titter made him straighten and look round. Nanny had not moved and anyway, the sound could never have issued from her rather bristly lips. Stewart seemed to be involved with a spot of claw nipping. So, was someone else in the room, hiding? Of course,

"Is that you, Gaye?" he eyed the nursery brightly, searching for a scrap of movement.

"Gaye?" Came back the question, and the voice was hers, high and thin. The voice he had heard when he arrived.

"Yes Gaye, do you want some tea?"

"Want some tea, have a pee!"

"Shut up, Stewart," he told the parrot then spun slowly on his heel to scan the room. A cupboard door, under the run of windows, juddered open and a twin appeared, unfolding her bony length and brushing down her black silk skirts. George smiled encouragingly at her, "Gaye, is that you? We've all been looking for you. Do you want some tea?" Noticing the girl's pale-eyed glance of worry towards the stunned woman in the chair he explained, "Nanny's having a rest, shall we leave her to it?" He held out a hand and, amazingly, Gaye hop-skipped across to him and took it, shyly. He was so relieved and pleased to have found her safe and well that he gave her fingers a little squeeze and raised them to his lips. She watched in wonder and blushed fiercely. "Now, you'll have to be a very clever girl and show me the way back to the front hall. Can you do that?"

She nodded vigorously and smiled. She was quite pretty, in a vacuous, pallid way. She led him towards the door, he opened it for her and as they slipped through, a telephone began to ring from somewhere back in the nursery. George paused, wanting to go back and answer it but she urged him on and whispered,

"It's only Stewart."

CHAPTER 7

"It's me - James."

Goodness I know that, it's only been a few weeks, "Hello James." I must maintain my cool.

"I'm ringing to apologise."

My heart leaps but my 'cool' restrains it, "Really, for what?"

"For doubting you the last time we spoke."

"Which was when? Remind me."

"Come off it Clover. You know bloody well when. When you rang to say you were losing the baby."

"Well, I was."

"I know that now. I've seen Bibby."

"Have you? Where?"

"It doesn't matter where; what matters is that I behaved appallingly. Even if I didn't believe you at the time, I said some terrible things and I'm ringing to say I'm sorry and to see how you are." He pauses, but my cool is holding out. "Are you OK now?"

"Yes, thank you. And I didn't lose the baby - I don't know whether you'd regard that as good news or bad."

"Don't be childish, Clover. Of course it's good news, one can't be flippant about a human life."

He's right, I'm being childish and flippant. "So, how are you?"

"I'm fine, busy as usual with work."

"But finding time for golf?"

"Yes. I want you to know, Clover, that what you've done is, in my view, pretty immoral."

"Immoral? What, you mean sleeping with you 'out of wedlock'? That's the phrase, isn't it?"

"That's not what I-"

"Because if I've been immoral by doing that so have you."

He takes a deep breath, now I can see him as if he was here in front of me not miles away down the Northern Line, "You know that's not what I mean. I'm talking about you taking the unilateral decision to become pregnant."

"Unilateral? Isn't that word usually associated with arms agreements?"

"D'you think what you've done isn't explosive in its own way? That it won't have repercussions?"

See how we talk to each other? It's not love, is it? "James - I'm tired, I've had a hard day, on my feet all the time..."

"Well get used to it, once that baby is born, you'll know what a hard day really is."

"And you'd know that I suppose? What do you know about being pregnant?"

"It was your decision, Clover; yours alone."

I fell into that one, no wonder he sounds smug. "I was going to offer you access, but now-"

"Access? The child's not a car parking space. You stole my sperm, my DNA, my identity. That's what it comes down to and if I want to see him after he's born - and I haven't made up my mind yet about that - there are others to take into account."

"Others? Other babies?"

"Other people. As I was saying, I haven't decided if I want to see him yet. He's my son, after all..." His voice goes funny, sort of twisted. "But if I do, I hope you'll be grown up enough to allow us to have a relationship."

"If you decide you want to?"

"Yes."

"I'll see. Is that all, James?"

He sighs, "Clover..."

"Yes?"

There is silence for quite a long time. I wait, my stomach churning. Is he going to ask me if we still have a chance? Will I say no? Am I that cool? Who are these "others" he's got to consider? Why isn't he telling me he loves me, forgives me for this supposed "theft of his sperm" and wants to be with me? If he did, would I say, yes? I always loved his decisiveness, his broad shoulders and strong legs and the way he would stretch his arms way above his head every morning and grin at me across the pillows. I sigh to let him know I am still here, I daren't actually speak.

"Never mind, it doesn't matter. Goodbye

Clover, take care."

*****

"Watch out for the step." Gaye had taken charge of George and was manoeuvring him along the corridors as if he was an ancient relative.

He allowed it to happen and did as she said because he was so overjoyed that she was safe. Deep in the doubting depths of his mind he had begun to think that in some terrible but perfectly innocent way, he had caused a disaster to befall her too. But here she was, alive and well and talking to him in an almost friendly way.

"We never get lost."

"No, well you've lived here all your lives. Was that you I heard singing when I knocked?"

"Yes, I've got a good voice."

"You certainly have."

"Nanny says so. No-one else knows. No-one else cares. Our only way out is to run away and we're scared to do that, but then we could go on the stage."

"Would you like that?"

"Oh, yes, it's what we've always wanted! Although if we got stage-door Jonnies after us, they would have to be brothers to take us both on, because we'd never be parted."

"I see." He did, partly, and felt a surge of pity for the twins. "Have you asked if you can go on the stage?"

"Who would we ask?"

"Well, your mother, for a start."

"She wouldn't let us. She doesn't like people leaving here, leaving her all alone with her sorrow."

"Is that what she says?"

"She always says that." She stopped, let go of his arm and opened a door into violet, early evening light. "This is our favourite place." She led him into a small, walled garden with a raised flowerbed at one end. Odd planks of wood had been laid across the straggling weeds and bushes in the bed to make an uneven, but fairly level, stage. Gaye ran to it and jumped up, spreading her skirts wide and striking a pose. "Shall I sing?"

"Please do."

She smiled and hunched her shoulders in excitement then tossed her neat blonde head and began;

"I am a fair young maid you see,

A picture of propriety,

But when I sit on someone's knee,

I just don't know what gets in to me..." she held the high note for his admiration, her eyebrows raised, then picked up her skirts and began to dance, kicking and crossing her skinny legs:

"I love to kiss and cuddle,

To get into a huddle.

Young men all laugh and call my name,

They want to know if I'm on the game..."

"Yes," George held up a hand to halt her in mid top-note, "very nice, but shouldn't we be getting back to the others? It's nearly dark."

"Oh. All right then." She stepped down, rather deflated and pouted up at him, "Didn't you like my song?"

"Do you understand it?"

"It's just a jolly song - Mags taught it to us."

"Ah, right, well I preferred 'Who Is Sylvia?'"

"Did you? Then I shall always sing that for you."

"Thank you."

She took his hand again and led him back inside. They weren't far from the main hall and, hearing the sound of a rhythmic rasping and male voices up ahead, George prepared for his grand entry with the missing twin.

To his surprise they came into the hall from the other side of the main staircase. Across the expanse of parquet, by the light of several oil lamps, Smears and the two footmen were in the process of sawing up the bison head to clear it from the library door. They had their jackets off and there were copious amounts of sawdust all over the polished floor; thankfully the crumpled little body of The Beautiful Child had been removed.

"Smears?" George squeezed Gaye's hand.

"Shir," the butler straightened, a saw in his hand, "how did Nanny take the awful newsh?"

"She's in some kind of shocked alcoholic daze."

"I'll shend Ethel to her."

"I think that would be a good idea and look who I've found," he drew Gaye forward, she giggled and hid her face behind her free hand.

"Good evening Mish Joye."

"Joye?" George slumped and dropped her hand, she tried to slide her fingers into his again but he turned on her. "You told me you were Gaye." She pouted and shrugged, so he appealed to the butler, "Are you sure it's her?"

"Oh, yesh, shir, Mish Joye is the shorter of the two."

"But how can you tell?"

"I am shorter," Joye told him, "by one inch."

"Oh, I give up."

"Now don't deshpair, shir. Mish Margaret hash shaved shome tea for you in the drawing room."

Shaking the clinging Joye off, he strode into the drawing room and shut the door on her hopeful face. He felt immediately churlish and opened it again, but she had run off. Smears was putting on his jacket and the footmen were back at their task. He closed the door again and turned to find Mags, draped across the sofa nearest the fire, waiting for him, her clothes a disordered pile upon the hearthrug, a cup and saucer balanced jauntily upon her naked stomach.

"Oh, God..."

She smiled slowly and beckoned him forward, "Come and have some tea, Georgie."

"I don't want any tea, Mags." He leant back against the door.

"Why not?" She wasn't annoyed, yet.

"I have had a very trying day."

"So have we all. I've just lost a sister, remember."

"Yes, so should you be thinking of 'tea' when she's hardly cold? Where is she anyway?"

"Mother has had her taken up to her room, she wants to weep over her in private. Now, come here because this tea is still hot."

"Harry told me about you, how death sharpens your appetites. These specialists you go to see in London, are they treating you for nymphomania, by any chance?"

"Oh, some name like that, I'm a special case, apparently. They have to study me in detail. Now come here."

"Mags, take the teacup off your belly and put some clothes on, you look ridiculous."

"What?" Her snappiness reminded him of her late sister.

"I said, you look-"

"Ridiculous?" She sat up, the teacup tumbled and tea went everywhere. "Is that what you said?"

"Here," he patted his pockets for a hankie, "dry yourself off," but didn't find one.

"I am never ridiculous," her voice was very level, but worrying.

"Perhaps I used the wrong word."

"It was the word you used, therefore it was the word you thought most appropriate for your fiancée's appearance."

"Mags. Just calm down."

"I am perfectly in control."

"You're using longer words than usual, you're getting angry."

"So would you be angry if your fiancée had just called you ridiculous."

"You've called me enough names in the past."

"Such as?"

"Common; you're always accusing me of being common."

"Well, so you are, but I love you in spite of that. I think that shows me to be a very forgiving person, don't you?"

"I don't know. I don't know what to think of you."

"Yes, you do. I am, apparently, ridiculous."

"Lying there starkers with a teacup on your belly, at this moment and after all that has gone on over the last two days, you did look ridiculous!"

"And how do I look now?" She held his gaze, eyes glittering, hair dishevelled, legs elegantly spread across the cushions, hands on the back and arm of the sofa, breasts thrust forward, she looked magnificent.

George swallowed hard and ran from the room straight into Inspector Fowey.

"Ah, Mr Pender, fleeing the scene of yet another crime?" He laughed at his little quip and Bacon smirked.

"Hardly a time for jokes, inspector." George closed the door firmly, amazed at his own audacity.

"You're quite right sir, I'm sorry. I had

wanted to have a word with you about this latest atrocity but I was informed that you were in the nursery breaking the news to the child's nanny."

"That's right."

"You must be held in pretty high esteem here sir, to be given that sort of mission, and yet you say you only arrived on Friday evening?"

"Yes. I was only asked to go and tell her because I only arrived here on Friday afternoon and Nanny didn't know me; no-one else could bear the thought of her shock and misery."

"Very good of you, sir. And how did the old lady take it?"

"She was very shocked and miserable."

"To be expected, I suppose," The inspector made as if to open the drawing room door. George blocked him. "Excuse me, Mr Pender, is there some problem?"

"No, but Miss Berenger is in there, grieving."

"I see. Then where shall we have our little interview? The library is out of bounds; the dining room is being laid up for supper and now you tell me the drawing room is-"

At this moment the door behind George opened and Mags, fully dressed but holding her stockings and shoes, slipped passed, patting his cheek and blowing a kiss as she went.

"Grieving?" The inspector queried.

Bacon snorted behind his hand.

The inspector frowned at his sergeant, then at George, "I believe the room is vacant now, shall we...?" Fowey led the way in, George followed, Bacon closed the door behind him and stood guard at it. "Now, sit yourself down Mr Pender, you must be quite tired after the day's exertions."

George sat in the armchair he had occupied earlier and the inspector sank into Mags' vacated place on the sofa.

"I know what you're thinking," George closed his eyes briefly.

"Well, yes, you might at that," Fowey agreed.

"I arrived here on Friday evening and since then there have been three unusual deaths."

"Ahh. Was I thinking that, Bacon?"

"I don't know sir, but I was."

"Indeed," Fowey turned to look at his constable with another, more questioning, frown. "So," he focussed on George again, "you think that your presence here is suspicious?"

"No, I don't think that, but I thought you might."

"Right," Fowey shifted on the sofa. "Let me put your mind at rest. It had never occurred to me that you might be implicated in these deaths until now."

"Oh."

"But you're right; it is very odd." He shifted again and patted the seat and George, even through his distress, remembered the spilt tea. "Let's go through them one by one." He counted off on his fingers, "One - the old lady had a heart attack in the woods; she had a dickey heart, she'd been told not to go off alone. I think you come out of that one alright. Two - Adolphus Berenger falls from a balcony in full sight of a dozen people and you are at least one hundred feet from him when it happens. As yet we don't have the autopsy report, it being the weekend and the morgue being closed, but even if poison is involved, we have it on good authority that there were others more likely to wish him dead than a bus conductor he had only met the evening before. So, you are not number one suspect there either. Three - a child of nine is tragically squashed by the falling head of a stuffed bison. True, she had apparently cut up all your clothes…"

"Who told you about that?"

"Her mother, poor lady. But you were in the room with said mother, another sister, a brother, three aunts and a cousin, and you had in fact just saved Lady Lydia's life when the child, in a fit of anger, ran from the room into the library and her death. Now, even if you had known that the child would have a temper tantrum, you could not have known that she would run into the library, so why would you have tampered with the bison head? Too many coincidences, Mr Pender. So, unless you have anything to confess to me, I think I and," he empathised the next two words, "my constable, will have to delete you from our enquiries."

George blew out his hot cheeks.

Fowey patted the sofa cushions to his left and moved slightly along, easing his trousers out at the back of his thigh.

"Oh, Miss Berenger spilt some tea on the sofa, inspector. I'm sorry - I should have said earlier."

"Ah, hence the removed hosiery," he nodded. "I'm afraid I jumped to an entirely different conclusion, Mr Pender, my apologies."

"It's perfectly all right. I'm so relieved that you don't suspect me. I thought it looked so odd, me turning up, all these deaths." Shut up now, you're off the hook. George cleared his throat.

"Listen, Mr Pender, Bacon and I were here during the last death, weren't we? And we're obviously not responsible, are we? Maybe it was just a terrible accident, maybe they have all just been terrible accidents."

"But you said, I think, that there were people who might wish The Bishop - Mr Berenger - dead?"

"Ah Mr Pender, we can't tell you all about that, that's a police matter."

"Of course, sorry. Can I go now? I have to go and change for dinner, although I have nothing left to change into..."

"Off you go. We're eating with the staff. That's where we get all our-"

"Sir." Bacon warned from the door.

"Yes. That's where we get all the best food, I was about to say, Bacon."

"Yes sir."

"Also," George rose slowly, "I was wondering if I could go home now?"

"Not yet, sir - not 'til we've had the autopsy report."

"And that will be...?"

"Maybe Tuesday, sir."

"But if I'm-"

"I'm sorry, sir."

George sighed, "I'll probably lose my job."

Fowey shrugged and shook his head, and then Bacon stared hard at him and winked as George left the room.

To his surprise George discovered his wardrobe full of clothes. Very smart and expensive looking clothes which smelled of perfumed smoke and hung on padded hangers. He took out a sports jacket and held it up in front of him; it looked promising, so he took off his own jacket and slipped it on. The sleeves were a bit long - the leather binding the cuffs coming to mid finger - but otherwise it was a good fit and flattered his colouring. Next, he tried on a navy pin-striped suit; again the sleeves and also the trousers were slightly too long but he didn't look ridiculous.... Why on earth had he said that to Mags? It had been cruel. He had shut the door on Joye's eager little face and that also had been unkind, after her opening up to him. Harry had said that the twins never talked to men, yet she had sung to him. He sat down on the bed, yelped and jumped up again. He was in a dreadful fix. He no longer seemed to be in control of his actions and emotions. He was sure old friends would not recognise him now, especially in these classy clothes. He was a misfit in every sense. He was becoming more and more convinced that he had a terrible power over everyone in the house, their futures and safety were in his hands. But he never knew which of his seemingly innocent actions was likely to cause distress or death and as long as he stayed in this house, the rest of the family were in danger from him, of this he had no doubt. He had arrived in that little red car on Friday so full of expectation, and had turned into a dreadful...nemesis - was that the word?

There was only one thing he could do and to do it he needed help from Ethel. So he washed, got himself up in the new dinner suit and hurried along to her cosy sitting room.

"Mr Pender!"

"Ethel," he had barged in on her without knocking and now averted his eyes as she fluffed down the skirts of her navy serge uniform. Imprinted on the inside of his eyelids was a vision of shapely black-stockinged legs and flounces of white lace petticoat. "I'm sorry, I should have knocked."

"Yes, you should," her cheeks were hotly pink her mouth puckered.

"Ethel, you have to help me."

"Does the suit fit, sir?"

"The suit? Yes. Did you-? Of course it was you, who else would it be? You are so kind to me."

"Lady Lydia told me to sort out some of The Bishop's things for you."

"Oh, they're his...?"

"Dead men's clothes. Does it make you feel squeamish?"

"A bit."

"You're too sensitive. So, what did you want?"

"Ethel," he sat down unasked and grabbed hold of her clasped hands. "Can you help me leave? I'm meant to report for duty at Victoria bus station at four tomorrow afternoon, I'll lose my job if I don't. You understand how important that is, don't you? I've spoken to the inspector, he doesn't believe I have had anything to do with any of these awful deaths, even though they've all happened since I've arrived. I'm not a suspect or anything, so it wouldn't be breaking any laws to leave now, would it?"

"Has he said you can go?"

He dropped her hands, "No."

"Then you can't. If you do it'll look so suspicious."

"Will it?"

"Yes. So, you'll have to stay here. Get Lady Lydia to write to your employers, she writes a very good letter."

"Oh, Ethel," he sunk his face into his hands and it was very nice, a moment later to feel her hand stroking the back of his head. Then she asked,

"Why don't you get Mags or Jane to help you?"

"Help me what, leave? They won't do that. Jane hates me for being so weak and giving in to Mags and I've spoilt it with Mags by calling her ridiculous."

"Did you?" She sounded pleased, he looked up. She smiled brightly at him, "Really, you said that to her? What happened?"

"She got cross. I ran away. I am weak."

"Wise, I'd call it. So, you came to me."

"I trust you."

"Do you?" she put her hand to her bosom and backed into her other armchair, sitting suddenly. "That makes me feel so grown up."

They sat and looked at each other for a while and George became aware of his heart beating harder. "Ethel...." But he had no other words.

"Yes, George?" She prompted after a moment.

"Ethel. I wish I could stay down here with you. I feel safe here. Upstairs I'm terrified I'm going to do someone harm. I mean, I've never meant to do anything to any of them, they've been terribly kind but I feel responsible."

"For what?"

"For all these accidents."

"But you're not."

"Well, I am in a way... Aunt Hilda-"

"Yes?"

"She saw me naked in the woods. It probably proved too much for her heart."

"Oh. I see."

"You won't tell anyone?"

"Of course not. Oh, you poor thing, you must feel so bad."

"I do, I do. I feel terrible."

"But that wasn't your fault, was it? Mags got you to strip off, you didn't want to, did you? You said it was too cold and wet."

"I did, yes. I did say that, how do you know?"

"Well, it got around."

"Does everything get around?"

"It does if she wants it to. The footmen are awfully pleased you've come. They find it very hard to keep on running up to her room and do all their other duties."

"The footmen too?"

"It's everyone, George, she can't help it."

"She's a nymphomaniac."

"She's worse than that." Ethel put both hands over her mouth and shook her head, "I'll say too much, I always do."

"Ethel, you are so sweet. I wish I'd never met any of these bloody Berengers, and just met you." His words did not have the desired affect. Her mouth turned down with misery and her eyes filled. "Oh God, what have I said now?"

*****

I'm always putting my foot in it, perhaps it's my hormones. Ever since James' call I've had one thing on my mind- he said he'd seen Bibby, but he wouldn't say where. You know how a thing gnaws at you, eats away all the good and positive thoughts in your head to replace them with just one? Suspicion or doubt, feelings of betrayal maybe. Well that simple little remark, and the refusal to elaborate on it, has ruined my night's sleep. And I need my sleep.

James and Bibby do not move in the same social circles and it's very unlikely that they would meet casually, so did she call him on my behalf? I know Bibby; if she'd done that then she would have told me to prove what a good friend she is. Or did he ring her to check up on me? Wishful thinking, I'm afraid. They've seen each other, not phoned, that was his word: 'I've seen Bibby'.

They're going out.

There's no other explanation.

My best friend is cheating on me with my ex-fiancé.

So, when I got into work today, I accused her of it.

"Bibby, are you seeing James?"

"Seeing in what sense? I saw him, yes."

"Where and when?" I hadn't even got my jacket off or my handbag stowed under the counter. She looked at me, confused, guilty? I tried to discover, but then she turned away quickly, unable to stand my open, prying gaze.

"I didn't say anything because I didn't want to remind you of him."

"What?" I thrust my tum towards her and raise my tee-shirt, "This reminds me of him all the time."

"Calm down Clover, please. I saw him on the tube."

"On the tube?" Millions of people use the tube, how likely is it that they would bump into each other?

"We overlapped for one stop. I told him about you and the near miscarriage and he was terribly upset."

"He rang me last night. When did you see him?"

"Two days ago."

"He took his time, if he was so upset."

"He was on his way to Heathrow."

"To Portugal for golf?"

"No, to Paris on business. Clover sit down, I'll make you a cup of camomile tea and you can calm..."

"Don't patronise me. He didn't say anything about Paris. Was he with anyone, on the tube?"

"Don't you believe me?"

"I asked him but he wouldn't explain."

"Well, I am. And no - he was alone." She looked affronted and went to put the kettle on. Someone came in; I think I served them, I assume I was polite and friendly, I seem to remember them going out with one of our carrier bags. Then Bibby emerged with my camomile tea and her bag over her shoulder.

"Here's your tea. I'm going out. I may be a while. I'm very hurt, Clover. I don't think I can be here with you just now. I'll be back later."

And with that she was gone.

So now I'm alone in the shop and wish I could start today all over again. It must be hormones, mustn't it? I don't usually go around alienating people. Of course they could have met on the tube. Millions of people use the tube it's perfectly feasible for two of them to know each other vaguely.

I rearrange some hangers, fluff out a couple of tulle skirts, reposition the line of matching bags and shoes in the big window and there is Bibby, just outside The Coffee Train, on her mobile. Cup in one hand, phone in the other, long dark hair swinging as she strolls about in the sunshine on her three-inch heels, slim and alluring. Men look at her as they pass. Why wouldn't they? She's very attractive.

'Very attractive, your friend Bibby.' James said that, the first time they met. He said it in a cheeky way to upset me but it was all in fun. A joke to get me going and, I remember, I smiled and told him, 'She doesn't go for your type, you're too smooth for her, she likes a bit of rough.' And he grabbed me and rubbed his unshaven chin along my neck, 'Rough enough for you?' I can still feel the shivers he sent through my body.

I sit down on our stylish chrome and plastic chair and watch Bibby finish her call and her coffee and stride off towards the tube station.

CHAPTER 8

After upsetting Ethel yet again, George went upstairs to the long gallery. It was empty so he found himself a writing desk and sat down to draw out the plan of the tea-lawn for the inspector. Light-headed with relief to find he was not a suspect he overreached himself in the detailing of the house and the balcony, he even embellished the stick figures representing the family, servants and himself with hats and caps and trays, drew in a few flowers and the jellies on the trolley. Pleased with his effort he took a fresh sheet of paper, sighed, and began on his letter of explanation to his supervisor at Victoria bus station.

'Dear Mr Heavershedge,

I'm afraid I will not be reporting for duty this afternoon due to unforeseen circumstances. I am staying with friends in Norfolk and have been asked to remain here until Tuesday by the local police. I am not in any trouble myself but there has been a series of unfortunate accidents and no-one is allowed to leave the house.'

Would Heavershedge believe that? He was not a man of great imagination and he already had a slight aversion to George due to a lost cap badge the previous week. He had not believed the truth then; that a group of louts had knocked George's cap from his head, kicked it about as if it was a football and pulled the badge from the front as a trophy. So, was he very likely to believe that one of his conductors was staying with 'friends in Norfolk', and had got himself innocently involved with the police? It sounded a very upper-class thing to do- stay with friends in the country - and George was not upper-class, as Heavershedge - with his bicycle clips, meat paste sandwiches and Fisherman's Friend lozenges - well knew.

George screwed up the letter, and began again;

'Dear Mr Heavershedge,

I seem to have contracted a strange disease over the weekend. My lips have swollen to double their size and I have a temperature of 110 degrees. My doctor has forbidden me to leave the house until at least Tuesday. As I am also likely to be contageious he has advised me to tell everyone I come in to contact with to wash their hands. If I were you, I would burn this letter before doing just that. Yours sincerely, G Pender.'

He underlined his name with a flourish and a heavy hand came down on his shoulder; he jumped and the flourish shot off at an angle.

"George?"

"Ah! Lydia," he jumped up, "Lady Lydia I mean, how are you?"

"Correspondence?" Her eyes were red-rimmed, her face paler than usual under the rouge but her voice was steady. "Can I see?"

"I'd rather you didn't."

But she whisked the sheet of paper from under his hand and swept away to read it out loud, 'Dear Mr Heavershedge' do people actually have names like that? 'I seem to have contracted a strange disease over the weekend. My lips have swollen to double their size and I have a temperature of 110...'"

"He wouldn't believe the truth. I did write the truth the first time, here," he smoothed out the first draft and handed it up to her, "but he might believe I'm ill. He hates illness you see; germs, people sneezing all over him..."

"My dear little Georgie, of course your second attempt is better and far more believable, although you have spelt contagious wrongly. Never be ashamed of lying, I never am and I do it all the time. If you start telling people the truth, they always expect it of you and it's not always convenient. People know I lie consistently and that makes me far more reliable than someone who tries to tell the truth most of the time." She smiled, then quickly sobered, "However, I hope you will believe me when I say that I am eternally grateful to you, darling, for saving me from Nanny's scissors." She squeezed his shoulder, "I've been down to the chapel and said a prayer for you. Your coming here this weekend has been the best thing that has happened to me, to the whole family, since... since I don't know when." She moved away, his letters still in her hand, and sat down in her usual armchair, "Life gets so dreary sometimes." She pulled her handkerchief from her sleeve, "I don't know how to carry on... but I must, for everyone's sake. I am their strength, you see," the crying began, gentle sobs and George felt that he had to show her some kindness.

He left the desk, knelt down beside her and patted her elbow. He was not expecting to be engulfed in an anguished embrace but he patted her back consolingly when he was, adjusting his position on his knees to come round rather more to her front. He did not return her kisses at first, then began to feel ungrateful and responded, in what he felt might be construed as a 'brotherly' way. She misconstrued him entirely and he was soon on his back on the floor with her on top of him.

Sex had become a way of life for George since arriving at the Hall; it was how he paid his way, appeased his guilt and, of course, he felt that to refuse would be taken as awfully bad manners. He knew from experience that Lady Lydia would not hang about, would soon be back on her chair, hair immaculate, only slightly out of breath and very pleased with him, and so it was... They had a full five minutes to kill with idle chit-chat about his daily routine and what he liked in his sandwiches for lunch, before Harry came in and Smears arrived with the sherry.

"You'll never guess what I've been doing,"

Harry sidled up to George, as he went to take a glass from the tray, and smirked.

"No, what?"

"I've been playing fast and loose with your profile." He hissed, "I've put you in the mural."

"Ahh, interesting."

"Yes, you must come and see."

"Stop whispering, boys." Lady Lydia swivelled round in her chair to stare at them. "What's going on?"

"I've put George in the mural, Mother."

"Ooooh," she wagged her finger at George, "see how important you are to us all? I was just telling George before you came in, how much I value his presence here at this time."

"Absolutely," Harry agreed, "you saved Mother's life this afternoon. You really have become one of us."

"Have I?" His eye was caught by a movement on the window seat, one of the twins emerged from behind the curtain.

"Come to Mummy, Joye." Lady Lydia called, waving her hanky and George's letters.

As the twin shuffled past him George hissed at her, "And how long have you been there?"

She sat on her mother's lap, rested her head on her shoulder and lisped, "Since you shut the door on me."

"She speaks," cried Harry, "and to you George, only to you!"

"I'm sorry about that Joye, I really did think

I'd found Gaye."

"Do you like Gaye better, then?" Her lower lip threatened a pout and he knew all about Berenger pouts.

"No, I like you better, I've never really spoken to Gaye, I don't think." He hardly had time to wonder what on earth Joye must have made of the grunting and puffing of a few minutes ago before Mags entered, teetered at speed down the width of the gallery to her mother's side and slid to her knees, with her black satin evening dress falling dramatically off one shoulder as she dropped.

"Mother darling, how are you? I've just been up to your room and found Nanny there, she is taking Sybella to the nursery to lay her out. I shall go and say my goodbyes after dinner."

"I told her to put the child into her communion dress."

"Very suitable." She kissed her mother, got up and sighed so deeply that the other strap fell to her elbows.

George went up to her, lifted both straps to their proper position and turned away again.

"See how very prim and correct he is? It's his upbringing," Mags caught hold of his hand and pulled him back to her, "Nanny was very impressed with you, although she said your speech was rather common."

"My speech is not common."

"Don't be so touchy, darling," Mags patted his cheek but there was a glint in her eye.

"And is there really no sign of Gaye?" Lady Lydia was stroking Joye's hair, pinching her cheek.

Joye shook her head and looked up at George from under her lashes. Mags saw the look and drew his face to hers, "What have you been up to?"

"Nothing. I thought I'd found Gaye, that's all. Only Jane and I have been bothering to look for her."

"Have you been making love to Joye?"

"No."

"Only to M-" The sound of the slap was quite loud. Joye started screaming immediately.

Lady Lydia muffled her against her bosom, "A fly on her cheek."

George could stand it no longer and headed for the door only to have it open in front of him to admit Aunt Suzy and Jane.

"Excuse me, excuse me," he squeezed between them and made his escape. He ran across the hall, opened the baize door and tore down the stairs to the relative safety and sanity of the service corridor.

A small knot of servants had gathered outside the butler's sitting room; maids, footmen and a boot boy. George slowed as he approached them and one of the footmen glanced round,

"Here," he called to George, "what d'you make of this?"

George only wanted to get to Ethel's room and peace, but he obliged, joined the crowd and peered over the heads and shoulders. Inspector Fowey, Bacon and Smears were in the latter's neat, overheated room, gathered round some items laid out on the olive-green, chenille-covered table in its centre.

Bacon was holding each item up for inspection; a pink silk slip, black stockings, a corset in pink and blue - the cups of which were stuffed with cotton wool which fell onto the table cloth - a pair of low-heeled black shoes, a black silk dress with white collar and lastly and most gruesomely, a hank of silvery blond hair tied up with a feathered bow.

"Gaye," George blurted the word and felt his face heat up as everyone turned to stare at him.

"Ah, Mr Pender," Fowey raised an eyebrow at him, "yes, as you surmised, all that remains of Miss Gaye."

"All that remains? Is she dead?!" George squeaked.

"Not that we know sir, this is all that we have found of her." Fowey beckoned him into the room. Smears stood and offered him his chair, which he sank into. Now he was so close to the pathetic remains his eyes were drawn to the two lumps of cotton wool, matted and grey.

"Where did you find these... things?"

"In the chapel passage, sir," Smears informed him, "in the dirty clothes room, behind a laundry basket."

"The chapel passage?" Memories of rats and scamperings flashed into George's mind.

"Everything's here but her panties," Bacon announced, to snorted giggles from the scullery maids.

"So, we must assume," Fowey nodded slowly, "that Miss Gaye is roaming the house or grounds naked, but for her panties."

"Well, no- surely..." All eyes turned to George. "I mean, if she took her clothes off by a laundry basket doesn't that suggest that she put on something from the laundry basket?" He appealed to Smears, "Doesn't it?"

Fowey and Bacon exchanged a pointed glance.

"Is that what happened, sir?" Fowey enquired.

"I've no idea. It just seems likely. Doesn't it? I mean, she's not going to wander around naked. She'd get cold for a start."

"It's a sensible suggestion," Smears remarked. "Miss Gaye was never one for taking off her clothes, even as a child, and that is remarkable for this house where, not to put too fine a point on it, nudity is never frowned upon."

There was general agreement to this. Fowey and Bacon both narrowed their eyes at the slippery pile of fabrics on the table.

George wondered if he should say anything else, betray Joye's confidence, mention the plans to run away. In his mind he was sure this was what had happened, but why would Gaye go without Joye? The deserted twin would be heartbroken.

"Are any items of clothing missing from the laundry?" Fowey demanded of Smears.

"I'll ask the laundry mistress, though until everything is ironed and put away it will be hard to tell. Someone should tell Lady Lydia." His eyes swivelled to come to rest on George's upturned face, "Sir?"

"Surely you would be better placed to...?"

"She sets a lot of store by you, since you saved her from Nanny's scissors, sir."

"Oh," he sighed and stood up, "very well."

"You certainly know how to make yourself useful here, Mr Pender," Fowey remarked, to more giggles.

The full family, or all that was left of it, was assembled in the long gallery, silent, sipping sherry and waiting for the gong. George shut the door behind him and leant against it for support. Joye, with one very red cheek and red eyes, was sitting on the fender playing cat's cradle, she glanced up at him then back at her skein of blue wool. The two old aunts were perched, like moth-eaten parrots, on a window seat. Harry and Mags were sprawled together on one sofa, Aunt Suzy and Jane sat very upright on another and Lady Lydia was writing at the desk. He went over to his hostess, aware of all the other eyes on him, leaned over her and whispered his news.

"Gaye's clothing and a length of her hair have been found behind a laundry basket off the chapel passage. No sign of her though, or of foul play."

"Oh," she put down her pen.

"I think you should be very careful how you

tell Joye..."

"Yes," she got up, one fluid motion and smiled at her daughter, "Joye, darling, come with Mummy I want to do your hair again, it's got rather messed up, hasn't it?"

Joye pocketed her blue wool, jumped up from the fender and took her mother's hand. Lady Lydia led her from the room, and George's gaze fell upon the letter she had been writing.

"Dear Sir,

This is to inform you of the delayed return of my house guest, Mr George Pender. He has been able to render me invaluable assistance this week-end. He saved my life this afternoon and I wish to show him some recompense. A quite extraordinary young man. How lucky you are to have him in your employ; brave, quick thinking and immeasurably kind. I thank God for the day I met him and do hope you will allow me to have my way over this. He will return as soon as possible and hopes desperately that his delay will cause you no annoyance, as do I, Lady Lydia Berenger."

The door clicked shut and Mags was at his side, "Georgie, what's happened?"

"They've found Gaye's clothes and her hair in a store-room, the dirty clothes room? But they haven't found her."

"Her hair?" Mags grimaced.

"Yes, it's odd, isn't it?"

"Bizarre."

"What ever could have happened to the poor

child?" Aunt Suzy pressed her handkerchief to her mouth.

"I looked in the dirty clothes room," Jane told her.

"When?" George asked her, grateful for the opportunity of a relatively bland question and hoping she would deign to notice him. But she didn't.

"This morning, but it was dark and I was looking for her, not a pile of clothes. Of course, the place is full of clothes, what a clever way of hiding them."

"I've never thought of Gaye as being clever." Harry sneered, "Both of them seem to me to have a screw loose."

"When have you ever spoken to them, Harry?" Mags countered.

"Not for want of trying on my part. Her few words to you this evening, George, are the first time I've ever seen Joye or Gaye converse with a man."

"Joye spoke to you?" Jane looked at him for the first time.

It was his chance to say something about the twins wanting to run away to go on the stage, but he dreaded parading their fragile dream in front of the rest of their family, so simply nodded. An expression passed across Jane's face, lighting it for an instance so that he thought he would faint from the excess of beauty there. He took a deep breath, the expression faded and she turned away.

Smears entered, "Shall I anounsh dinner, shir?"

"Oh, well, yes..."

"No," George cut across Harry, "we should wait for Lady Lydia..." he trailed off, amazed at his own affrontery. His mother would say he was getting above himself again but Harry agreed.

"Yes, what does Mother say? Should we start without her?"

"I will ashertain, shir," Smears bowed out.

"I'm so sorry, Harry, I shouldn't have..."

"Not at all. You seem to know far better than I do how to handle these things. I think you're keeping your head rather well, I'm afraid of losing mine. My family is diminishing before my eyes," he knocked back his sherry in one go.

"I know. I'm so sorry."

"Of course you are, one would expect nothing less from you," he grasped his forearm, squeezed it and went to stand by the fire.

George stood alone in the middle of the room. To one side Mags was regarding him steadily from her sofa, to the other Jane was flitting glances at him from another. Aunt Suzy and the ancient aunts were in conversation on the window seat. He wanted to go over to Jane, but instead went to sit beside Mags, she took his hand and placed it on her lap.

"Of course, on your bus you're in control, aren't you? You have to keep order, get people to pay up and not annoy the other passengers. It's this aura of quiet control and the knowledge that when you fuck you lose all control that I find so fascinating about you. I want you inside me now, can't we go behind the screen down there?"

"No."

"I am positively wet with desire."

"No."

"I can't go all through dinner like this."

"You'll have to."

She pressed his hand against her pubic bone, "Just a little...?"

"No," he snatched his hand away, got up and went over to Jane.

Mags shot up behind and, thinking she was following him, he braced himself for some form of assault, but she went on to the door and flung herself out through it. He sat. Jane moved further away from him to lean on the sofa arm but he could hear her breathing.

"I am in agony," he whispered.

"How do you think I feel? Watching you with her?"

"She makes demands. I try to withstand them."

"You don't always succeed."

"But I do sometimes. I am a guest here."

"Is that your excuse?"

"I am a misfit."

She turned to him now, "So am I." She gazed into his eyes and he could feel her scouring his soul. His belly lurched as he remembered a similar moment with Ethel and he closed his eyes, shutting off her connection. "See, you always do that," she accused him.

"What?"

"Pull back from me."

"I have no right to do anything else."

"What if I give you the right?"

"Will you?"

"Yes."

"And Mags?"

"Break off your engagement to her."

"I have tried."

"Try again."

"Then what?"

"Ask me."

"Will you say yes?"

"You'll have to wait and see."

He blew out his cheeks and stared at his hands. Out of the frying pan-his mother's saying came to mind. Mags was physically demanding, Jane might be an incredible emotional drain, he glanced up at her, but she was worth it.

Harry was sobbing into his third sherry and the aunts were out of sight. George put his hand over Jane's, she did not resist so he closed his fingers round hers and she watched amazed as he lifted her hand to his lips. She seemed pleased, so he chanced a kiss on her startled lips and sat back just as Mags burst through the door to shout,

"See, I don't need you!" her face red, her hair awry and a footman tottering behind her with the gong.

*****

A bell is ringing somewhere. It wakes me and

I thrash about for a while. It's the phone, of course but in my sleep-muddled mind I think it's a dinner gong - you know the kind - round, brass, hung on a wooden stand. I grab the phone, "Hello?"

"Clover, is that you? You sound odd."

"Aunty? It's.... half past four in the morning. Is something wrong?"

"Yes, most definitely. I can't sleep."

"Oh, poor you, have you a pain?" Oh God. I fall back on my pillows.

"It's worry- I'm so worried. Have you taken the painting back yet?"

"Um, no, actually. I've been rather busy."

"It must go back and soon. I've been having dreams about it, about them all and what happened back then. It's getting worse and I think it's all about returning the painting, we should never have had it, you see. Oh, I know it belongs to me, it all belongs to me but morally... Not a word we used much then... Strange days and it's nearly the anniversary, you see... It should be back there for the sixtieth anniversary. George went five years ago but he can't go this time."

"Look Aunty, this is obviously playing on your mind. I'll take it this weekend, if I can get help putting it in the car. Will there be people there to help me the other end?"

"People where?"

"At Leatherboys Hall."

"Oh yes, the whole family lives there still. I'll telephone and tell them you're coming, make sure they look after you properly. I'm sure they will, Ethel has always been very able."

"Ethel?"

"She's aged very badly; she thought I didn't see her at the funeral, but I did."

"So, when I get there I ask for Ethel. Have you a map?"

"Oh, you don't need a map. It's on all the signs. You go through the village and-"

"What village?"

"Leatherboys, of course, and you'll see the signs there. Oh, I feel so much better about this now, thank you darling, I think I can go to sleep." She puts down the phone and leaves me lying there, wide awake.

What is all this about? I try to go over what she was gabbling but quite honestly, I think she's going completely ga-ga. She was fine while Great Uncle George was alive; he must have been keeping her sane, although they were a pretty odd couple, come to think of it. Him sleeping on the floor all those years, going off for long fishing trips while she disappeared up to town for weeks on end, then back together again as right as rain. They were a loving old couple and always so kind to us children. I'd always accepted them for what they were, as children do, but now I have the time and inclination to think and wonder about them.... What exactly did happen sixty years ago and why is it so important that the painting go back now?

Hopefully I'll be able to get Derek to help me

put it in the car but I shall miss my lovely young aunt smiling down at me. How romantic things were then, not mundane and ugly like now. Fifty years is... 1936, a few years before the second world war started... Of course, they didn't know what was about to happen to them all; they must have been blissfully innocent, then.

*****

Jane was a complete innocent. The thought tingled at the back of George's mind all through dinner - only the second proper meal he had managed to eat since his arrival - six courses, all excellent. All exactly the same as his first meal on Friday evening but none the worse for the repetition; leek soup, grilled sole, lemon sorbet, roast beef and Yorkshire pud, spotted dick drowning in thick custard with cheese and biscuits to finish. He sat back sated and excited. Jane was a virgin and not just that, she was a blank sheet, unsoiled, pristine. A young man's dream. He'd had his fill of women like Mags and her mother, Jane would be his and only his. She would know only his love and they would be complete, together.

This was pretty powerful stuff on top of all that food and he had to excuse himself before the port and leave with the ladies to visit his bathroom.

"Don't be long," wailed Harry, deserted at the end of the long, ruined table. In fact, George saw him grab one of the discarded damask napkins and blow his nose loudly as he closed the door.

The women gathered for a while in the hall. He heard them below him saying goodnight to Aunts Grace and Mattie, before shutting themselves into the drawing room. He carried on upwards, turned at the first floor landing and bumped into Freddie.

They both yelped with shock.

"Ahhh!"

"Yikes!"

Much to George's shame he had forgotten all about young Freddie since the bison fell and now put an affectionate hand on his shoulder, "How are you, young chap? Haven't seen you around."

"I've been making plans," he hauled a large, bulging suitcase into view.

"Are you leaving?"

"Going to Tony Cheevers' first thing in the morning. Their chauffeur is coming to collect me, it's all arranged, I phoned in secret from father's office. But I've got to get this down into the porch without anyone seeing it or me."

"Doesn't your mother know you're going?"

"Not likely, she'd stop me, she hates anyone leaving here. If I were you, I'd get out tomorrow as well."

"I have to stay. The police have forbidden me to leave yet."

"Tough. I'm only a kid, so they haven't even noticed me."

"D'you want a hand with that?"

"I say, would you? That's awfully decent. I

was a bit worried about getting down the stairs with it, thought I might fall, break my neck, you know? We're not having much luck as a family at the moment - you've probably noticed," he managed a wry grin in the yellow lamp light and George suddenly wondered if he was wise to try and help. He might end up killing Freddie as well, which would be a real shame. He took hold of the leather strap and heaved. The case moved a few inches and the strap broke.

"Oh, sorry."

"Bugger," Freddie kicked the case and winced as its solidity damaged his toe.

"What on earth have you got in here?"

"Everything; clothes, toys, books, guns, the lot. I'm not coming back."

"Freddie, you're under-age, you'll have to."

"Look, could I come and live with you?"

"Um, no. I mean, I don't think-"

"I'd be no problem because I'm at school during term time and I can probably spend the vacs at Tony's."

"Well, Freddie, it's a nice idea but I don't really see how we could manage it. I'm still living with my Mum and Dad."

"But when you marry Mags, you'll have somewhere."

"I don't know if I'm going to marry Mags, really..."

Freddie slumped, "I thought you'd get wise, they always do. She's just too keen. It's because we all want to escape, I suppose. Don't go and marry Mags on my account," he allowed. "I'll manage something. It's funny, you know, before I went to school, I thought there could never be anywhere better than here." He shoved the case over on to its side in an excess of despair, then brightened. "Let's slide it down and hang the racket."

They lined up at the top of the stairs, linked arms and both put a foot to the edge of the case, pushing on Freddie's count of three. The case wobbled, toppled and began its accelerating descent of the stairs, jumping and jerking, thumping and banging as it went. It was accompanied, at the half landing, by the sound of a shot, which zinged across the hall, hit a suit of armour and ricocheted into a huge Chinese vase, smashing it.

"Oops, forgot to check all the guns were empty," Freddie grimaced.

Downstairs, both the drawing room and dining room doors burst open to cries of alarm. Upstairs, Freddie grabbed George's arm and dragged him back into the gloom, out of sight,

"Best to pretend you know nothing about this," he hissed and scarpered.

George raced on tiptoe up to his room, hurriedly relieved himself and ran back downstairs to join in the general amazement and confusion.

CHAPTER 9

Trust me to have arranged the removal of my aunt's precious portrait from my third floor flat on the very day that someone is moving out on the fifth. The lift is full of domestic appliances, so poor Derek is blindly manoeuvring the four-by-six foot canvas single-handedly down two flights of busy stairway.

"Clear the way," I call authoritatively down to a couple of women about to make an ascent.

"Uff," goes Derek, "ahh!" as he catches his fingers on the banister.

"I really appreciate this Derek."

"Mmm."

I go in front, not touching the painting but guarding it from the walls and banisters. I have wrapped it in various scraps of Christmas and birthday paper, to shield my aunt from the gaze of the modern world. The Hon. Miss Berenger has never been so gaudily dressed and I wonder now if I am protecting her or hiding her? The two women clatter past on high heels and stare at me, Derek and the painting. Their faces suggest that they think we might be burglars, I immediately feel guilty and then wonder why I should, cows. Never mind, only one more flight to go.

"Nearly there now." I chivvy Derek along, he is flagging, sweat on his brow. He can't have a heart attack here on the stairs, he'd pitch straight through the canvas. "Would you like a bit of a rest?"

"Well, maybe a moment to change my grip."

"This is awfully kind of you Derek, I hope you won't put your back out, or..." have a heart attack, I shrug.

"How on earth did you get it up here?"

"The lift was free and I got people to open doors for me and things."

"But still, it was a silly thing to do, in your condition."

"I know that now." How on earth did he find out? Mother.

We squeeze to one corner of the landing to let a removal man through with a pedal bin and a lamp stand. The idiot has put the lampshade on his head and he winks at me. Why do men think that women admire idiocy? James was never idiotic, he was just a bastard, that's all. I can't even think about Bibby, think about working with her every day and being pleasant. Normal relations are impossible.

"Right, last lap," Derek hoists the picture up again, he's a game old thing, I shall have to buy him a bottle of something nice to say thank you. "Uff. How far have you got to drive?"

"Oh, I don't know. Norfolk somewhere."

"Up the M11?"

"Yes." I'd thought I'd head north for the M25 and see what happened next. "The M11 is the best way, is it?"

"What?" He's feeling for the next step and I watch, my lip between my teeth.

"The best way to get to Norfolk?"

"Yes," he frowns at me round the painting. "You have looked at a map, haven't you?"

"Mm, last night." But I'd been looking at Norfolk, trying to find Leatherboys village, not at how to get to the county itself.

"Is your map in the car?" He lurches at the corner of the last flight.

"Yes. Oh, do be careful."

"I'm fine." He thinks I'm worried about him, which I am of course - I'm not completely without feelings. It's just that my feelings towards men in general are not very friendly at the moment. "When we get to the car, I'll have a look at the map and talk you through the route."

"Oh, thank you, Derek." I gush and clasp my hands like a girly, but I am truly touched, in spite of him being a man.

*****

"You're very strong," Mags glanced at George as she praised the manly efforts of Constable Bacon, "and brave. There might still be another bullet."

Bacon suddenly stopped hauling Freddie's heavy leather case across the hall and stood up. "Ahh, maybe we should clear the area just in case..."

"In case, the case, has another surprise in

store?" Harry was decidedly the worse for at least four sherrys, several glasses of wine at dinner and a brandy afterwards. He staggered and pretended to clutch at a wound in his chest.

"Harry, stop it," Aunt Suzy tutted. "I don't think I've ever spent a weekend like this. It's all quite horrid."

Inspector Fowey clack-clacked across the hall tiles, flushed from the excitement of examining a real bullet dent in a real suit of armour. "Now, whose case is this?"

Everyone shrugged and muttered, "Don't know." "Who can tell?"

"We have a store-room full of cases," Lady Lydia informed him, "all sizes all shapes. Anyone can go in there, choose a case, trunk or holdall and use it."

"Ah," Fowey smiled at her, "so we will have to open it to ascertain who is using it this time."

"But it could be booby trapped, sir," Bacon informed him.

Mags sidled round to take George's arm and hiss conspiratorially, "Where were you when the shot was fired?"

"Using the facilities."

"I doubt that very much constable, flip it over and let's open it up." Fowey's instruction caused everyone to take a step back and the effect was like a dark stain spreading across the chequered floor.

Mags squeezed George's arm and shivered; he

saw Jane move her mother closer to the drawing room door, Harry giggled. Only Lady Lydia stood her ground as Bacon hitched his trousers, crouched and slipped the catches. He paused a moment, then let the case fall open.

Inside was an awful mess of charred clothing, books and cardboard boxes. There were two hand-guns, a pair of boxing gloves, a machete and a hunting rifle, broken and laid across a surprised teddy bear with a scorched tummy. A wisp of grey smoke idled up into the yellow gloom and the smell of cordite tickled the back of George's nose.

"Freddie's things," his mother remarked. "He must have thought it was start of term, silly boy. Well that explains the shot, he's always so careless about unloading his guns. Where is the boy?"

"Have we met this Freddie?" asked the Inspector and Bacon rifled through his notebook.

"My youngest son," Lady Lydia sighed. "He's just a child, one of the few I have left." She gave a little totter and Aunt Suzy rushed to take her arm, she righted herself and asked, "Harry, how many have I got left?"

"Umm," Harry was not the best person to ask at that moment, he had sunk on to the lowest stair and was leaning against the newel post, "Um, are we counting both twins?"

"Most definitely."

"Then, um, six."

George did a quick calculation, "No, old chap, only five."

"Five?"

"Five?"

The smaller number seemed to give them all a shock. "Yes," he counted up on his fingers, "Harry, Mags, Joye and Gaye and Freddie. Five," and held up his hand in proof.

"And Ethel," Harry assured him.

"Ethel?!"

"Oh, yes, Ethel," Lady Lydia nodded, "I always forget Ethel."

"Ethel?" George turned to Mags.

"Mmm, she comes between me and Freddie."

"Ethel?"

"Darling stop saying Ethel like that, it's very silly."

"But she's the upstairs..."

"Someone must go and find Freddie," Lady Lydia cut in.

"Who saw him last?" asked the Inspector.

George sighed, stunned and weary but doomed to tell the truth, "I did, when I went upstairs."

"Then perhaps, Mr Pender, you'd like to go and find the young man, so that we can assure ourselves that he is still in the house and still... um-just go and find him, eh?"

Mags released his arm. He stood for a moment, still unable to take in this latest revelation. "Ethel?"

"Oh George, for God's sake!" Mag's sharp rebuke brought him round; he put back his shoulders, turned on his heel and ran up the stairs past the now comatosed Harry.

George had no idea where to look for Freddie. He did not know his room, there was no-one to ask and he was not really interested, knowing already why the case had been packed and why it had cannoned into the hall so explosively. Instead, he climbed up and up into the servant's attics and tried to remember what Ethel had said about the position of her room. Second door on the left, was it? He reached the top floor gasping for breath and shivering with the cold. It was darker up here than down below, very few oil lamps had been lit and by their faint light he could see his own breath. How on earth could Lady Lydia allow her own daughter to live in such conditions? And when would he learn not to be surprised by anything that this house and the family in it could throw at him?

So, Lady Lydia was Ethel's mother too. He seemed fated to become entangled with these Berenger girls, amongst whom he must include Lady Lydia. What a woman she was, urgent sex on the floor one minute, dominating matriarch the next. Was she fit to be a mother? Well no, she wasn't. He contrasted her with his own Mum; always washing, ironing and cooking, to keep him clean and fed, wanting to know how his day had been, fretting about his sore throats, chilblained hands in the winter, clean socks in the summer, boasting about him to her friends, scolding him with love in her voice when he forgot his lunch or stayed out late. He could never imagine his own Mum behaving as Lady Lydia did.

Shivering he felt his way along the wall and tapped at the second door, hardly hoping for a reply.

"Come in."

He twisted the door-knob and entered. Ethel sat by a blazing fire in a chintz armchair, she was wearing a pale blue twin set and matching pleated skirt. A magazine lay across her lap, a glass of something tawny was in her hand and her feet were drawn up underneath her. The room was freshly papered with roses and hung with pictures of children and puppies. The bed had a rose madder silk counterpane, the carpets were Persian and on the mahogany chest of drawers was a brand-new phonograph. She looked up at him; her cheeks pink, her hair in a long plait over her shoulder and waited for him to speak.

All he could say was, "You're a Berenger."

"Oh, yes," she bit her lip and nodded.

"Why didn't you tell me?"

"I sort of forget."

"I'm not surprised."

"Would you like a sherry? It's my little weakness I'm afraid."

"Er...no thanks." He came in and shut the door.

"It's not the stuff they have downstairs, it's premium amontillado."

"Oh, well..."

"Sit down, I'll get you one." She uncurled her stockinged legs and got up shyly. "I'm in civvies tonight as it's my evening off." She padded to her night-stand, opened the cupboard and took out a bottle and glass.

"But you don't have to work, do you?"

"I don't but I do, else I'd go off my head. I can't sit around all day like some of them, I need to be busy." She poured his drink and padded back to give it to him, "Sit." She repeated, so he did, in the matching chair to hers.

The fire crackled, she fed in two more logs and sat back in her armchair facing him, hurriedly hiding her legs from his view.

"Ethel, I can't make head nor tail of this place. Something bizarre is always happening. Did you hear the gunshot?"

"Gunshot? Is everyone alright?"

"Yes. It was Freddie. He'd packed a loaded gun in his bag by mistake, he was trying to escape to his friend's house. I've been sent to find him - I don't know why."

"It's because you've taken over."

"Taken over what?"

"Alphonse used to do it all, but now he's gone and you're in his clothes, they sort of expect you to tell them all what to do."

"But I have no real authority here. Lady Lydia- your mother is really in charge, isn't she?"

"Oh, yes, but she likes to have a man to hide behind."

"What about your dad, Smears?"

"He's in charge 'backstage', as he calls it. He runs all the finances and farms, the bottling plant and the tanning factory."

"Tanning factory?"

"Well the money to keep all this lot going has to come from somewhere. Dad does all of that."

"Is your dad the father of all her children?"

"Oh, no."

"So, who are the fathers of the others, your half brothers and sisters?"

"Let me see. Alphonse was Cookie's boy, of course."

"The cook?"

"Yes, that's why he's been so cut up. Then Harry's dad was a travelling photographer. The twins' father is still on the estate, so I can't divulge that little secret, in case you tell the twins, it would confuse them dreadfully."

"Did you hear about Gaye?"

"Yes and I'm not surprised, it's been on the cards for years."

"She has run away then?"

"Nanny is bereft, losing two of her charges in one day."

"It must be very hard for her" he agreed. "And Mags' father?"

"Ah, well that's where things get sticky," she bit her lower lip. "Are you going to marry her?'"

"I don't think I can."

"Then I can't tell you, because there are

others here who don't know and might be affected." She finished her sherry, "Now, my dad you know, and Freddie's dad was an electrician employed to re-do the electrics. Nice man. Unlike Sybella's dad who was a slimy little insurance man who came to do a valuation on the place and stayed for four months. We all hated him."

"And do they all know who their fathers were?"

"They must do, although they all claim that idiot Howard as a father."

Not the time to ask her what she thought of her mother's idiocies, he felt. So he stretched out his legs, revelling in the warmth of the fire, the sherry and her company, "Ethel, you know this place is quite mad, don't you?"

"Its home George and I'm happy here with Dad. I'll never leave, not for anyone," she blushed and lowered her gaze.

George busied himself with his excellent sherry, aware of his growing responsibilities and that the glass in his hand was beautiful, the stem twisted and filled with fine bubbles. But then everything in the room was of the finest, even the chocolate box pictures on the wall were all original oils. Squirreled away in the attic, Ethel lived well. Her father was the business brains; her mother a 'Lady' of peculiar morals and desires, her half brothers and sisters were variously warped by their upbringing, and they all carried on this charade under the name of a grinning, pop-eyed youth whose portrait hung in a place of honour in the long gallery. "So, how was Howard Berenger an idiot?"

"Oh, I think he fell off his horse on to his head as a boy."

"You mean he really was an idiot?"

"Quite loopy. They sent him to America soon after the accident, then - after an awful incident in a tepee - to the family cocoa farm in Africa. He spent his youth there killing everything in sight, including quite a few of the natives, so they thought they'd better put him in the army. Mother - Lydia Gervaise as she was then - had been promised to him in their childhoods. Grandfather Berenger wanted her family's bottling plant, you see, so he came to an agreement with Grandfather Gervaise; the bottling plant for the five-hundred-acre wood and mother as the seal on it all. Of course, the Gervaises didn't know Howard was dotty. Lawrence, his younger brother-"

"Jane's father?"

"Yes. He was very respectable and pleasant, so they had no idea about Howard, until he came back for the wedding."

"What happened?"

"A terrible row, apparently."

"But she married him?"

"Oh yes, then he was sent straight back out there and died. Down the aisle, out of the church, straight into a carriage and away to Dover," she waved a hand airily.

"How did he die?"

"We don't know." She got up quickly and went over to the phonograph on her chest of drawers, she selected a record and put it on the turntable, "Do you like jazz?"

"I do. Who've you got?"

"Mallory Pike and Duke Holland?"

"The best." George got up and joined her at the phonograph, as she set the needle down and turned the handle. As the first chords burst out she struck a pose and he took her hand in his, put his arm round her warm waist and they jitter bugged round the bed to the fire and back. "You dance wonderfully."

"So do you." She smiled up at him.

They moved so well together it gave George the confidence to try out some new steps. She read his mind, following his lead,

"Wizard!" and spun under his upraised arm.

They were still dancing twenty minutes later when a cold draught alerted them to the opening of the bedroom door. They stopped and turned as one to face Jane, her eyes were open very wide, she blinked a couple of times and asked quietly,

"What are you doing, George? We're all waiting for you downstairs."

"I couldn't find Freddie, sorry."

"You should have come and told us."

"I know, I'm sorry."

"Would you come now, please."

"Yes, right," he let Ethel go. "It's been lovely, Ethel. Thank you."

Jane held the door open for him and shut it when they were both in the corridor.

"I don't think it's right that you should ignore Ethel like that." He told her.

"Why, because she's a Berenger?"

"She's your cousin."

"She's chosen her place. I can't call her cousin sometimes and treat her like the upstairs maid at others. We have to stick with what we know." She led the way downstairs, "She understands."

He sighed, he supposed she did, she was happy here. Probably the only Berenger who was. "Jane, wait," he caught hold of her arm, "Freddie was trying to run away to Tony Cheevers'. I helped him push the case down the stairs... we didn't know the gun would go off."

"Why tell me? You'd best tell the inspector."

"Not in front of Lady Lydia, she'd be upset."

"Upset? Her whole family is dying and disappearing, I think upset is a rather useless word to describe that, don't you?" Her whole posture and voice spoke of her disappointment with him. He let his grip slide from her arm to her hand.

"Are you cross that I was dancing with Ethel?"

"No. Now you've discovered that she's a Berenger too, I suspected that you'd be interested in her. How do you think I knew where to look for you?"

"Don't be cross with me."

"I'm not cross. I accept you as you are."

"What am I, to you?"

"I think you're a gold digger."

"Huh!" he laughed and squeezed her hand. "After the Berenger millions? Is that what you think? I'm a poor sap who's got caught up with the most extraordinary people he's ever met and been bowled over by the beauty of one, the voracity of another and the kindness of yet another. Pity me, Jane. If you have any pity, use it all up on me."

She stood and stared at him, the lamp light playing across the soft moulded planes of her face, then she lifted her free hand and stroked his cheek, "Kiss me again and I'll try to do it better this time."

So he did, and she did. He felt like crying and when she begged,

"When you leave, please take me with you..."

He promised he would.

"So, young man, you were trying to run away from home, were you?" Fowey clasped his hands behind his back and rolled on his toes towards Freddie, who sat beside his mother.

"Not run away, no. I just wanted to go and see my friend, Tony Cheevers."

"It's still vacation time, darling, you spend vacation with Mummy." Lady Lydia reminded him, her hand firm on his bare knee.

"You had no other reason for wanting to go at this precise moment?" Fowey continued.

"No."

"You weren't going to meet someone?"

"Yes."

"Ah. Who?"

"Tony Cheevers' chauffeur."

"Is that all?"

"Yes."

George, a late comer to this interrogation of the boy, shifted uncomfortably in his place behind the snoring figure of Harry, slumped on a sofa.

"You hadn't arranged to meet someone else and take them to this Cheevers' house?"

"No."

"You planned this alone? There were no others involved?"

"No- I mean yes and no. I planned it alone and there was no-one else involved." Freddie crunched his face up and looked tearful.

George decided to step in. "Excuse me, inspector?"

"Mr Pender?"

"Are you accusing Freddie of something?"

"I am merely trying to ascertain if the young man knew anything of his sister's disappearance, sir."

"D'you mean Gaye?" Freddie's face relaxed.

"I do."

"I dunno where Gaye is. And I'd never try and meet her anywhere - she's weird."

"Weird?" Fowey did his rolling trick again.

"Spooky, you know."

"Now Freddie," Lady Lydia squeezed his knee tighter and he winced. "You know you love your sister and are just as worried about her as we all are."

"Excuse me madam, it may help me to discover in what way your son regards his sister as weird, it may lead us to her. Well, Freddie, how would you describe this weirdness?"

The boy shrunk and shrugged.

"I'm waiting...."

The room was so silent, the atmosphere so charged, that George could not imagine anyone, let alone a child, being brave enough to break it. Then Harry gave a particularly interesting snore - rising to a crescendo, stuttering, pausing for an unbelievably long time, before expelling the air through half closed lips. The noise broke the spell and Freddie murmured something.

"Pardon," Fowey leaned closer.

Lady Lydia gave a snort of derision and Freddie mumbled,

"Always looking at you... at me, in a funny way."

"The imagination of the young, Inspector." His mother excused him.

"Indeed," he agreed, "hardly a sign of weirdness." He pursed his lips and George was in a position to see the direction of his gaze, from Lady Lydia's face to her ample bosom and back.

"How would you like your sister always bursting in on you in the bath?" Demanded Freddie, determined to be believed. "Always trying to get a look...."

"Ah."

"What nonsense, Freddie."

Then George remembered a similar experience, "Actually," he interrupted and the inspector frowned at him. "That happened to me, too. After we'd found Aunt Hilda and I'd been out in the rain, I had a long, hot bath. Of course, it might have been Joye, I don't know."

"Well, was she taller, or not?" asked Lady Lydia.

"Um, difficult to say, really."

"We could ask Joye, it might have been her."

"Lady Lydia, if I may just interpose, here," Fowey smiled at George. "Once again, Mr Pender, your evidence seems to have some bearing on the case."

"I was just supporting Freddie's evidence, Inspector."

"We would be lost without Mr Pender," Lady Lydia turned round fully in her seat to face him and bestowed the most ravishing smile. "Without him I would have been unable to support my grief."

George blushed and had to get out a handkerchief to blow his nose and hide behind.

Harry groaned, jerked a leg and suddenly sat up, "I say, hello. What's happening? Someone dead?"

"No sir, just trying to clear up the matter of the gunshot and Miss Gaye's disappearance."

"Oh that; so we're no further forward. Would anyone mind awfully if I went up to bed? I've got a terrible head."

"No, I don't think we can achieve anything

more here tonight, eh Bacon?"

"Pardon, sir?" Bacon had been leaning distractedly against the door and straightened.

"Poor Bacon, you look awfully tired," Mags cooed at him, then slid a sly glance in George's direction.
He knew what she was doing and couldn't summon up enough interest to be jealous. George looked down at Jane, who was seated at his elbow - her dark hair shiny in the lamplight, her shoulders subtly suggestive under black silk - and the knowledge that she would be leaving soon with him, left him immune to her cousin's manipulations.

*****

In spite of Derek's careful instructions back in London, I am lost. I knew this would happen; I sort of willed it to. Getting into a state about being lost, a situation I can remedy if I want, is easier than getting into a state about James and Bibby. I have my mobile phone. I have a map. I have a car half full of petrol and in perfect working order. But I play with the idea of sitting here, parked up in a muddy lay-by on a bend in a winding lane; lost forever in time and space. How long will I have to sit here - uncertain of which unmarked road to take at the crossroads in front of me - until another car comes along? I haven't seen another car since I turned off the main road twenty minutes ago and the lane ahead is perfectly still. The autumnal trees are hanging limply, rusty brown, copper and dark olive green; the colours remind me of the painting behind me, angled in to my nifty little hatchback by poor Derek, all huff and puff and bruised knuckles.

I have never been to Norfolk before. It is not as flat as I was led to expect, but then people always lie about the English landscape, I find. The Lake District is supposed to be magnificent and brooding, but not if you've been to Norway or the Alps. And Cornwall with its laughable Riviera is damp, misty and closed in by hedgerows. Norfolk has hedgerows too - miles of them, neatly hemming squares of ploughed field and set-aside. There are red berries in the bushes beside me, bead bright in a watery sun. Like drops of blood.

Now why did I think that? It's made me shiver. What if a madman found me here, broke into the car and hacked me to death? Time to consult the map again and head my thoughts off in a more sensible direction. Right. This is where I turned off the A11, onto the B1135. Now both Aunty and my father have always said it was south of East Dereham and west of Norwich but I can't find it. Leatherboys? A weird name, faintly redolent of fetishism. But there are some other wonderful names round here; Clint Green, a failed movie actor, maybe? Or Brandon Pava, yet another actor- a martial arts specialist, pow! Zap! Carleton Forehoe, a hooray Henry without a doubt, face like a horse and acres of hedgerow to jump over. How about Mattishall Burgh? Or L'Atherbois-? L'Atherbois, Leatherbois, Leatherboys. Why did no-one tell me it wasn't spelt as you say it? It's like that English teacher we had in the third year, Mrs Cholmondenly - it was weeks before I was told to pronounce it Chummly. I thought they were two different women.

So, there it is, L'Atherbois village, at a T-junction and with the Hall where the antique writing says, 'Hall', I expect, but where am I? Which of the many crossroads on the map am I at? I shall have to plough on, I suppose. I dunno, two hours from London and already I am using country-based phraseology.

Oh bugger, bugger, bugger. I'm stuck. I've been out and had a look and the rear wheels are deep in mud. So am I now, or at least my boots are; beautiful, soft tan suede ankle boots caked in sticky yellow clay, all the way up the three inch heels.

What shall I do? I shall have to find a stick or something to scrape them clean. And I suppose I shall have to phone for help.

The AA man has said it's going to take ages to find me, since I can't give him directions. How unreasonable can you get?

I can't sit here for ages.

I'm a pregnant woman; I need the loo.

I'm bored. Who can I ring? Not Mum - she'd worry, not Aunty - ditto. Bibby is out of the question, now, but she would have been the one, she'd have made me laugh...

It's started to rain. I feel shut in by rain drops. Silvery trails all over my windows.

I might have been sitting here all this time and there's a house just round the corner. A house with a kettle and a loo and a nice woman inside who'd tell me where I was so that I could tell the AA man. Should I get out, and go round the bend to have a look? What if I go on too far and twist an ankle or get even more lost or the AA man arrives and I'm not here? What if I stand up and pee uncontrollably?

Ahhhhh! Another car!!!

CHAPTER 10

How very clever these country people are. Do you know, she had a tow rope in her boot and she knew how to use it? Her house was round the corner, she let me use her loo and showed me how to get to L'Atherbois Hall. How kind people are! Even the AA man sounded relieved and happy for me when I told him I was OK. So now I'm trolling down the windy lane humming along to the radio. It's stopped raining, the sun has come out and... yes, there's the rainbow... beautiful! Transparent bands of colour gilding the towers of a-

Yes, well, I must stop doing that. If I hadn't been going so fast, I would not have had to brake so hard and would not have ended up in this hedge. Above me a weathered wooden sign says, 'L'Atherbois Hall', and I've got an awful feeling that if I back out, which I must do, the sign will fall on my bonnet.

Ahh well, nothing ventured-

"Wait!"

I do hate that! People thumping hard on your roof! It makes me bellow, "What?!"

"Wait," he bends down to look in at me. "Are you OK?"

"Yes," I wind down my window a little, "I'm fine. I'm just going to back out."

"Well don't for a moment, let me just make sure the sign is not going to fall on your bonnet."

"Thank you." I know it's very wrong of me, it's very lookist, but I expect you're the same. You know how you can be really furious with somebody if they annoy you and they look like the back end of a bus, but you also know how, if that same annoying person is absolutely gorgeous, your anger melts? Well, that has just happened to me.

It's a pleasure for me to sit here and watch him slide his neat, pert bum across my bonnet to hoist up the sign, revealing a curve of tanned, smooth back under his ancient leather jacket, and manfully keep it aloft while he cranes round at me over his broad shoulder and calls,

"OK now, BACK out."

I don't even care about him emphasising the direction I am about to take. I put poor little nifty hatchback, all muddy and scratched, into reverse and manoeuvre backwards into the lane.

I park and get out, I am not going to miss this opportunity.

"I'm sorry about that, I know I was going too fast."

"You certainly were." He slowly lets go of the sign; it slips and settles further down into the hedge, drooping slightly in one corner. "Mm," He nudges it upwards and it falls back again.

"Perhaps if it was on a proper frame instead of just being wedged in there...?"

"It was on a proper frame, until a moron careered into it and broke it last week."

"Oh, sorry. It's an awkward bend and I just saw the towers there, at the end of the rainbow, and I thought, 'How poetic'. Then I thought - aha, this is where I'm looking for."

"Are you coming for some veg?"

"Veg?"

He points at the sign again, 'Organic Vegetables and Fruit', it says in swirly writing under the name.

"Oh, no. I didn't know you did veg. I've come to bring back a picture." Bright thought, "Do you live here?"

"Yes."

"Are you a Berenger?"

"Yes."

Oh, joy!

*****

"Joye!!?" The shout was loud and certainly

231

not modulated to take into account the lateness of the hour. "Joye!!!?" And it was difficult to locate. Was the caller inside or outside the house?

George went to his bedroom door and peered out. He didn't recognise the voice but it seemed to have a Celtic ring to it and not to go with the shadowy shape slowly shuffling towards him, bouncing off the walls as it advanced. "Harry?"

"Old chap... Old chap, I was coming to see you..." He stopped and sighed at the door and George stood back to let him in. Harry nodded his acceptance of the silent invitation and tapped George's chest, "The Bish's dressing gown suits you."

"Thanks. You look terrible, sit down- not there! The bed springs are through the mattress," he watched Harry shuffle round to the sofa and drop onto its unyielding chintz. "I can only offer you some water to drink."

"Nothing for me, nothing." He seemed to have shrunk inside his evening clothes, his glasses were smeared and lopsided, his shirt front stained with wine. "George, can you tell me how this has all happened to us? These last few days..."

"I know what you mean."

"Seems to me the old place has turned against us, you know? D'you believe in the spirit of place?"

"Never thought about it." He sat down

next to his visitor.

"I have. And it's always seemed to me that this house, built by one of us - one of the Berengers - has always looked after us rather well, until now. Awful time for you to come and stay here, I feel rather sorry for you."

"Not as sorry as I feel for all of you, believe me."

"You're very kind to say so. You're such a nice chap and I've done a really good job on you on the wall, you know. I'm very proud of it, you must come up in the morning."

"Yes, I will."

"But you know, even doing my painting these last few days, has not been as enjoyable as it used to be. I keep looking at the mural and seeing The Bish and The Beautiful Child up there, in all their glory, and now they're gone. I know Syb could be a bit of a pain, cutting up things and that, but she was the baby of the family and you know what happens to them..."

"No?"

"They get spoilt, dreadfully spoilt. It happened to me for a while, then all the ones who came after, because they'll be the last ones, you see?"

George nodded.

"Even old Aunty Hilda, she was part of it

all here. They've been here longer than all the rest of us, her and Mattie and Grace. And now Gaye has gone. Never knew how to deal with those two; typical twins I suppose, too close, incestuous, you might say. Though I doubt anything like that went on, Nanny kept too close an eye on them." He sank into a moment's reverie then frowned, "But Gaye had an unhealthy interest in men, you know."

"Did she?"

"Always trying to get a look at your tackle. I always kept the bathroom door locked.... she never got to see mine." Another short reverie was followed by a big sigh. "No-one's ever seen mine, actually." He patted George's knee.

"Ah, right," George got up and had a little walk about, making sure his dressing gown covered him completely.

Harry sighed deeply a couple of times, pulled his bow tie off and played with it then asked, "What is depression, do you know?"

"Well, it's feeling very sad all the time, isn't it?"

"Is it? Then that's what I've got, I think."

"Surely not."

"Yes, I think so. It's like carrying around a great black cloud. I'm starting to think that nothing good is ever going to happen to me. That I'll die here too, like the others. I know several of them want to get away, like poor Freddie but at least he's got to go to school. We never managed that. And then, when you tell me that you've been to galleries and all over London in your bus, I think, 'What the hell am I doing with my life?' My painting, yes, I know I have that but no-one else has ever seen it. And how can I paint, be really great and meaningful, if I've never seen life?"

"Well, that's true, I suppose."

"And now I'm getting paranoid."

"What about?"

"About going to sleep. I think I won't wake up in the morning-"

A knock on the door made them both glance round, George with some relief. He called for the person outside to, "Come in," and Nanny entered, but Harry carried on.

"I lay down, as usual and try to think happy thoughts, as usual but-"

"Joye has gone out of the window." Nanny reported.

"Yes," Harry looked up at her, eyes shining, "Yes, that's just how I feel."

"No, I'm sorry to confuse you Master Harry, but Joye has gone out of the window. Jumped."

"Is she dead too?!" Harry cried, leaping up.

"No, we are on the ground floor, as you may remember from your days in the nursery, my dear." She patted his head as he slumped back down again. "She'll be running round the grounds looking for her twin. She's taken Gaye's defection very badly."

"So, you are of the opinion that Gaye has run away?" George wanted to get this very straight, wanted to know that in this case he was completely in the clear.

"Oh yes, I'd sensed that we had reached a critical point in Gaye's development. Her behaviour last evening was most peculiar. It was a hard cross to carry, as I know only too well, and she fell at this latest hurdle. But I've come to ask you two gentlemen to help me search the grounds for Joye, she'll not have gone far and it's raining."

"Yes, of course," George assured her. "Harry?" Harry had sunk back into his crumpled dinner jacket and was shaking his head slowly. George shook him, "Did you hear?"

"Mmm?"

"We're to go and look for Joye."

"Ah, but will we find it here?"

A borrowed mac and tight wellingtons - a dark night and rain drops in his torch beam. George had been here before. He could hardly believe it was only last night. It had been a very long day. He shivered and his torch beam juddered. The spectre of pneumonia raised its head again and the more obvious possibility, of finding another dead body, made him shiver again, inside as well as out.

Harry had been sent to search the outbuildings. Nanny was of the opinion that Joye would not want to be out in the rain too much, nor would she head for the woods,

"Because of the bogie men," Nanny nodded and Harry had raised a hand to ask a question, but she had forestalled him, "No, they're not there any more, Master Harry."

"Ah, right, because I was going to say, George and I didn't see any sign of them yesterday."

"Well, you wouldn't. I personally know that they left in 1914."

"Yes, I remember you telling us. Right, I'll do the stables and yards and meet up with you both in," he consulted his wrist-watch, "half an hour."

"Twelve-twenty," Nanny confirmed and watched him shuffle away. She was wearing a huge and enveloping yellow cape with arm slits, and matching sou'wester and the sound of the raindrops on so large a surface area was quite deafening.

"I beg your pardon?" George had seen her whiskery lips move in his torch beam but not heard the words.

"I said, 'Poor wee man,'" she shouted.

"Yes. He's very upset by all this. He was saying when you came in-"

"We must get on, Master George, no time for chit-chat. My little song-bird will be soaked and frozen, she went out in her jim-jams and dressing gown only."

"Ah, I didn't realise that."

"We were having our night-time story and she just... Ah, me..."

"Never mind, Nanny, we'll soon find her."

So here he was, traipsing the sodden lawn, playing his torch beam in all directions, calling, "Joye? Joye?" and hoping every moment that Harry had already found her. One day soon he would look back on all this and it would be like a dream, or a nightmare, depending on how it turned out. No-one would believe him, so he would never be able to share his experiences with anyone. He would have to keep it all contained, inside him, for ever and ever. And when he was old and ga-ga, he might ramble on about Berengers and bizarre deaths, wide long galleries and butlers with a lisp and 'they', his family, would whisper about him losing his marbles and necessity of putting him away....

The dog came as something of a surprise; panting out of nowhere into his torch beam, eyes glittering, coat starry with raindrops. George had only seen one live dog during his stay and, as he raised his beam, he came face to face with the same old man, following on, his pipe in one hand

and a bright umbrella with pink and green water-lilies printed on it, in the other. He nodded, "A nasty night."

"Yes," said George.

"You'll find her by the front gates, in the porter's porch. Come on, boy."

"Thank you."

The dog padded away, the man followed him, and though George called after him, "Who are you?" and chased them both with his torch beam they had disappeared from sight. The rain had eased to a mizzle and there was a dull point of light over to his left, back towards the looming and unremitting blackness of the house. George ran towards the light, hoping it was Nanny and that she would know how to get to this porter's porch by the front gates.

His jolting beam soon picked out the shiny, yellow massiveness of Nanny; she was standing under a tree, facing the trunk and doing something under her cape. As he got nearer George could see a shining silver arc of liquid spouting from under the cape to splash into the knotted roots. He stopped suddenly. His heel slid on the mud- slicked grass and he fell hard onto his backside, losing hold of his torch.

"Oops-a-daisy," Nanny smoothed down her cape and hurried over to his side. "Up you get now and no more running on all this slippery turf," she extended a hand down to him.

George lunged for his torch and shone it up

into her large, concerned face, "You're a man!"

"Now, Master George, we're not going to let a little thing like that ruin our friendship, are we?"

"It's obvious now I know. The walk, the voice, the hands and..."

"But you'll keep it to yourself. Or Nanny will know and she'll be very cross indeed. Now, up you get or you'll get piles sitting on all that cold wet mud."

George allowed himself to be helped up, "This place," he began to laugh, "it's unbelievable, I mean, it's crazy." The laughter began to get the better of him, welling up from inside. "I never know what to expect next! Posthumous children! Wide galleries! Male nannies!"

"Master George! Control yourself. We are trying to find Joye, remember?"

"She's in the porter's porch."

"Of course!"

"The old man told me." He was only giggling now.

"The old man?" Nanny grabbed his arm and hauled him after her.

"Yes, the one with the dog and pipe and umbrella. Didn't you see him over there, just now?" He flailed with his torch in the general direction.

"There's no-one like that here."

"You all say that," George skidded and stumbled after her. "I don't believe any of you anymore."

They hit the drive almost running, shingle under his feet instead of slippery mud. Nanny set off at some speed and George had to go up into another gear to keep up with her, "So," he puffed, "why are you dressed as a woman?"

"I'm in hiding, if you must know."

"Who from?"

"Police."

"Why?"

"Murder."

"Murder?" He stopped but Nanny didn't so he had to run to catch up with her. "Who?"

"I can't say."

"Does Lady Lydia know?"

"She suggested it. Hush!!" She put her thick forefinger to her lips and they both stood still, straining into the wind to listen.

Some way ahead of them a thin, reedy voice quivered, "Whoooo issss Sssylviaaaa....?"

"It's my babe!" And Nanny was off again at top speed.

*****

He has opened the squealing gates for me, the gorgeous Berenger, and is closing them behind me now. A little hut, barely more than a porch with ivy growing over it, sits lopsidedly beside the gravel drive, with boxes and crates arrayed in front of it and all of them full of the most beautiful pumpkins and gourds, red slashed with orange, yellows and green and the most wonderful slatey blues. And the shapes, the usual round plump cushions, and more exotic bottle shapes and ovals and spiked octagons, flat and tall, honey coloured and mottled. I'd like to buy them all and varnish them to go in my fake fireplace at home.

"Right," he leans in and I give him all my attention, "carry on down here for about half a mile then, when you get to the circular drive in front of the house, turn right then left between the house and the stables, turn left through the stable yard and you come to a pump yard with washing hanging up in it. Park there by the bins and knock at the green door, someone will let you in."

"I've been told to ask for Ethel."

"Yeah well, she's in her room."

"I'll need help getting this painting out, will you be following? Or can I give you a lift down there?"

"I'm going into the village, someone else will give you a hand. Bye."

Oh, he's gone. Well I did try. I watch him in my rear-view mirror as I creep along the drive, almost going off the edge, actually. But then he disappears through a side gate and out of sight.

The drive is long and straight with incredibly old trees lining it, you know the type, all gnarled and snaked over at odd angles. Some are missing, only mossy stumps remain. But I'm finally here and

I get the shivers thinking of my Great Uncle George coming down this very drive fifty years ago.

*****

Joye was pathetically pleased to see them. She was huddled in the meagre shelter of a fake Palladian porch with a door in the rear wall and a hut behind. She was icy in her damp dressing gown, her teeth chattering. George was instructed to take off his mac, remove The Bish's thick jumper and put it over her. While he put back on the clammy mac, Nanny arranged his cape to cover Joye and picked her up in his strong arms, but gently, as if she was the most precious thing on earth.

"There my wee lambkin, now let's get you home."

George took charge of both torches and lit their way. The rain had started up again and he remarked, "We need the old chap who doesn't exist and his jazzy umbrella."

"Mmm," Joye agreed from the shelter of Nanny's arms, "he's my friend."

"You've seen him? And his dog?"

"Oh, yes," she snuggled against Nanny's massive shoulder, "lots of times."

"See," George told Nanny, "he does exist."

Nanny ignored him and hurried on, "We'll get you home, give you a nice hot bath and get you into your cosy wee bed."

"Is Gaye there?"

"No, Hinny."

"Will she come back?"

"I don't know, sweetheart."

Joye was silent for a while and George thought she had fallen asleep, then there was a small voice, "I feel like half of me has been torn away, Nanny."

"I know dear…"

George wondered what it must be like to be a twin. Pretty intense, he supposed, especially in this odd house with a male nanny to look after you. He only had a brother, Reg, who was three years younger and a partial stranger, with his soccer teams and passion for toy trains.

"Master George?"

"Yes?"

"Can I ask you to do me the great favour of keeping mum about all this?"

"About you," George lowered his voice, "being a man?"

"No," he tutted fussily, "about Joye running off. I only told you and Master Harry so let's keep it that way. I don't want to alert persons to my existence any more than is necessary."

"D'you mean the inspector?"

"I do."

"Didn't he ask you about Gaye?"

"I was indisposed and he has forgotten about me

by now."

"I doubt that, Bacon has everyone down in a little black notebook. But if you have to see them at all, make sure the room is dark and that you speak softly and they'll never guess. They're not the most brilliant of plods."

"Thank you for your advice, Master George."

After a moment's thought he asked, "You don't think they'll still be after you for your murder, do you?"

"They never close a case, so I hear."

"When was it, exactly?"

"1901."

"Helluva long time ago, Nanny."

"Master George!"

"What?"

"Do you watch any of those so-called gangster films?"

"I do, actually."

"I thought so. 'Helluva', indeed. Now what have I told you about proper pronunciation?"

"Sorry, Nanny."

"Where were you last night?" Mags hissed over his shoulder as he sat alone at breakfast the next morning.

"Out."

"I know you were out," she took her plate of

kedgeree to the other side of the table and sat facing him. "I went to your room. Who were you with?"

He buttered his second slice of toast and replied, "Harry and Nanny."

"Harry and Nanny? What were you doing with them?"

"We were following up a few ideas about Gaye."

"Did you find her?"

"No." He spread the marmalade thickly.

"I shall check up on you."

"Do."

She picked up her knife and fork, "You are getting out of hand, young man."

"Everything here is out of hand."

"I've noticed it. You've been throwing yourself about as if you own the place. Well you don't and you'd just better remember who you are - a bus conductor from Palmers Green."

"Mmm, that reminds me, I need to make a phone call. Where is the phone?"

"Who'd you need to call?"

"My parents, they're expecting me home this morning."

"The phone is in Daddy's office but I doubt you'd be allowed in there. I believe Smears has one too."

"Right, I'll pop down and ask if I can use it."

"Oh yes, I forgot, you're very chummy with Smears, aren't you?"

"Margaret-"

"Oooh, we're being very formal."

"-neither you nor I believe we are engaged so let's forget we ever imagined it could-"

"Georgie!" She was up and round to his side of the table in an instant. "Darling, don't be cross with your Mags, just because I was cross with you." She pushed his plate out of the way and sat on the table in front of him, leaning forward to try and kiss his mouth, tousle his hair but only succeeding in reaching his cheek as he turned away. "I came to your room wearing my best birthday suit and hoping for jolly good fuck and I found the cupboard, and your bed, bare. You can't blame me for being an itsy bit jealous. I want you all to myself for ever and ever," she kicked one leg over his head, locked her ankles and trapped his neck in a vice grip between her shins. "I won't let you go."

"Mags," George rasped, "you're strangling me."

"Promise to marry me. Promise Georgie. I won't let go until you do," her grip tightened.

"Mags!" he pulled at her ankles and his fingers slid on her slippery silk covered legs.

"Promise."

"Margaret! What are you doing?!" Lady Lydia had come in and was at George's side. She slapped Mag's calf and the pressure weakened. "Poor George... and at the breakfast table, too."

"He says he won't marry me Mummy."

"Well I should think not, if you treat him like that." She sat down in her place at the head of the table and flapped out her napkin, "Pass the marmalade, George."

Mags slumped, her legs fell to either side of him and George was able to reach for the marmalade pot at her hip and get up to take it to her mother. He was rather wobbly from the pressure of blood in his head and tottered against Lady Lydia, who dropped her hand to stroke the back of his thigh and buttock.

"Thank you, George. I think you must come up and see me later for a chat, I feel I've been neglecting you."

"Not at all, I've never felt so wanted, anywhere." He gathered himself and rubbed at his throat. "I must go and telephone my parents. And I must thank you for writing that letter for me."

"I had it sent off this morning."

"What letter, what are you muttering about?" Mags had straightened her back and was frowning up the table at them.

"I wrote to George's employers, explaining his absence from work. We can't have him losing his job because of all our troubles, can we?"

"I don't know," Mags bounced herself off the table. "It's a silly job anyway, I'm sure he could find something better."

"I like my job." He informed her.

"Better than you like me, it seems."

"I'll go and make my call," he excused himself and ignored Mags' grimace at him as he passed her on his way out.

Downstairs in the servant's corridor he cleared his bruised throat and asked at the kitchen door for a glass of water. One of the scullery maids went to fetch it for him and he had the opportunity of studying the tall, spare frame of the cook. He was obviously Alponse, the Bish's, father. The likeness was there; dark hair, olive skin and almond shaped eyes. Even the seductiveness of movement as he rolled out the pastry was similar to his son. George sighed and took his glass along to Smears' room, he knocked quietly. A chair scraped, footsteps approached and the butler inched opened the door to reveal himself in shirtsleeves and open waistcoat, his hair was mussed up and the waft of air from the room smelt very stale, for so early in the day.

"Ah, Mr Pender," he cleared his throat and pushed back his hair, "what can we do for you? I trust breakfast was satisfactory?"

"Yes, thank you. I was wondering if I could use your telephone to contact my parents?"

"Of course," he opened the door fully onto a table piled high with papers and an ashtray over-flowing with cigarette stubs, several half full bottles of wine stood side by side on the shelves to the right of his chair. "Excuse the mess," he began to stack the papers into piles, "I've been up all night; household accounts. I understand from Ethel that you went up to see her last evening?"

"Yes, it was all above board."

"Oh, I know that. She tells me everything, a little dancing, a sherry and a chat. I see no harm in that, except that you seem to be learning all our little secrets." He staggered slightly as he leant across to clear a space and move the telephone into it.

"There are plenty to discover. And there's no need to do that."

"What?" Smears paused in the act of transferring a peppermint from his waistcoat pocket into his mouth.

"I know you have a problem."

"Who told you?" He had to support himself on the chair back, "Ethel?"

"No, it's obvious, and quite common, I believe. I've read about it and it's only to be expected, I suppose. Dealing with drink all the time, ordering wine, serving up brandies-"

"Brandies?"

"All those half-finished bottles," George waved a hand at the shelf. "Lots of butlers have a drink problem."

"A drink problem?" Smears shook his head and straightened, "I'll have you know, sir, that I am tea-total."

"Denial is quite common, Smears, but don't be ashamed."

"I'm not in the slightest bit ashamed of being tea-total, young man, and I'll thank you not to go spreading unfounded rumours upstairs." There was something in Smears's manner which caused George to waver.

"You're not an alcoholic?"

"Have I ever shown any signs of being one?"

"Well... I thought... all the peppermints?"

"The peppermints?"

"Yes."

"I like peppermints."

"Oh."

"That's why I eat them."

"Right, I'm sorry."

"So I should think. There's the phone." He un-hooked his jacket from its peg by the door as he marched out.

George puffed out his cheeks and put down his glass of water. Perhaps Mags was right, perhaps he was rather throwing his weight about, jumping to conclusions. He would find Smears after his call, apologise and hope to get back into the butler's good books.

There was no telephone at 26 Linden Avenue, Palmers Green. To contact his parents, George would have to call the house of a neighbour, Mr Morris, ask him to go and knock at his parents' door, bring one or the other back to his house and then

George would ring again. An annoyingly, round-about procedure, made worse by Mr Morris' deaf-ness.

He picked up the phone.

"L'Atherbois exchange, what number please?"

"Palmers Green 251, thank you."

"What a lovely sound that has, Palmers Green. Is it a London exchange?"

"It is, yes." George frowned at the operator's impertinence.

"It's ringing for you now, sir."

"Thank you," they both waited while the tele-phone rang in the Morris' long, dark hallway. They waited for so long that George felt he had to explain, "The person I'm ringing is deaf."

"Rather a waste of time, then."

"Well, not completely deaf, I'm hoping he or his wife will hear something- Ah." The receiver was lifted and George bellowed into the echoing silence "Hello!!" Knowing that Mr Morris and his wife never answered unless spoken to.

"Oh, my," the operator complained.

"Hello?" Came Mr Morris' wavery reply.

"Hello, Mr Morris?!"

"Hello?"

"Mr Morris?!"

"Who's this?"

"George Pender!!! From number 26!"

"Oh, George, have you got your own phone now?"

"No, I'm calling from Norfolk!!"

"What poor folk?"

"Norfolk, the county!! I'm in Norfolk!!"

"Oh, I didn't know you'd moved. Your mother never said and I saw her yesterday."

"I want to speak to Mum or Dad!!! Can you go and get them for me?!! I'll ring-"

"I'll go and get them."

"Thank you. I'll call back in ten minutes! Mr Morris?! Mr Morris?! Oh, bugger!" Down the other end of the line, in Palmers Green, George heard the Morris' front door shut.

"I'll have you know, young man, that in fifteen years on this exchange I have never heard such language!" The line went dead.

He put down the phone and checked his watch, nine-forty, he'd ring back in ten minutes, if the operator would accept his call.

"What's all the shouting, Dad?" Ethel opened the door, "Oh, it's you."

"Yes, I'm sorry, I'm trying to call home."

"Can't you get through?"

"Yes, it's just- well it's complicated. I have to wait for ten minutes now. Ethel?"

She had been threatening to go, "Yes?"

"I've upset your dad."

"Have you? How?" She came fully into the room and closed the door.

"I accused him of having a drink problem."

"Why?"

"Because I thought he had."

"Dad's tea-total."

"I know that now. I need to apologise to him."

"Yes, you do." She looked at him and slowly began to frown, "Why's your neck all red?"

"Is it?" he felt his throat gingerly.

She came nearer, "All bruised looking," and touched his skin gently, her close-up face all concern.

"Mags tried to strangle me."

"Why?"

"Because I tried to tell her it was all over between us and she wouldn't have it."

"All over? You don't love her anymore?"

"No. She's warped and needs help. I mean, trying to strangle me with her legs..."

"I'm so glad you've seen through her," she beamed. "I thought you would eventually."

"Well, I have, and I can't wait to get away. D'you think the police'll have the autopsy report by today? Once I'm in the clear over that, they can't keep me here any longer, can they?"

Ethel's beam slowly faded, "Don't you like it here even one little bit? Isn't there anything that might tempt you to stay?"

He took hold of her hand and held it tenderly, "Ethel, look at it from my point of view. Ever since I came here on Friday there's been trouble, deaths and disappearances and I'm involved in them all, well, not Gaye's disappearance. I'm in the clear over that."

"No, you're not."

"Not?"

"Oh, George, I'm sorry to tell you this but Dad saw her - saw Gaye - go into the bathroom and after that, well, it was the final missing piece in the puzzle."

"What puzzle?"

"Her puzzle."

"Ethel-?"

"You'll have to speak to Nanny. I can't say any more."

He dropped her hand and turned away to rest an elbow on one of the shelves, "I think quite soon that I might wake up," he rubbed his forehead, "either that or I've gone completely mad and this is the asylum."

"Don't say that. It's not very flattering."

"I don't mean you, you're the only sane one here. Although, working your fingers to the bone when you're actually one of the 'knobs' isn't totally sane, is it?"

"I hardly work my fingers to the bone," she looked down at her chapped hands, "Though I could do with some hand cream, I suppose..."

"You're very sweet," he told her.

"Am I?" She hid her hands behind her back and blushed.

"Sweet sixteen."

"And I have been kissed," she smiled.

He smiled, and they stood like that for some moments, a few feet apart, smiling. Then he remembered Jane and sobered, "Now I have to make this phone call..."

"Yes, I'm sorry, go ahead," she opened the door then paused. "You do know I love you?" and was gone.

George had to wait for some time before the operator deigned to answer,

"Hello?"

"Hello operator, it's me again."

"So it seems."

"I'm sorry about the language, can you get me that number again, please?"

"I'll try."

"Thank you." He stood, listening to the clicks and the operator's affronted breathing only to get the engaged tone. He swallowed the expletive of his choice and only tutted, "Oh dear."

"Yes."

"I was hoping they'd be intelligent enough to put the receiver back on the cradle at the other end." He checked his watch. "I'll give it another five minutes."

"I'll try for you then."

"Thank you." He put down the phone.

Ethel.

He collapsed into her father's chair and sighed. Ethel loved him, Jane loved him and Mags was mad to marry him. Their mother just wanted to fuck him, he hoped. Or rather, he wished she had no carnal desires at all in his direction, but most of all he hoped that she didn't love him too. And now that Ethel had opened her heart to him he had no-one to share his thoughts with. And how was he responsible for Gaye's disappearance? Had the sight of his naked body sent her mad with desire and off in search of sex, like her younger sister? If so, why hadn't she pounced on him in the bath, got it over with there and then? Mags would have done and so would her mother.

He picked up a wooden ruler and idly flicked at one of the piles of household accounts surrounding the telephone. Two pages fluttered free and he bent down to rescue them from the floor and return them to their place. As he did, his eye lighted on the embossed heading of one sheet, 'Sampson and Tuck, Debt Collectors'.

He checked the door and lowered the sheet to his lap so that anyone coming in would not see it, 'Dear Mrs Berenger, We are acting on behalf of Messrs. Digby, Digby and Gaskin, Jewellers, whose accounts show that they have not received payment of the invoice they sent you in April; item - £100 4s 10d for the repair of two tiaras and one pearl necklace.' He put the letter back on top of the pile, then covered it with another and put the ruler on top. The ruler tipped the balance and the whole pile came down, white and blue sheets floating and slapping to the floor all around him.

He sat perfectly still for a moment.

He could attempt to pick them all up and re-make the pile but what if they had all been in order? What if they were all unpaid bills and dunning letters? He didn't want to know that Mrs Berenger – Mrs? Was she not a real Lady then? – that the Berengers were in debt, probably bankrupt, with all the staff relying on them and half the children dead and missing over one awful weekend and him involved in everything. Just like the inspector said.

The phone rang and he made a grab for it, "Hello?"

This time a wonderfully familiar voice answered,

"George is that you? Where in God's name are you?"

CHAPTER 11

"Hello, Mum, it's Clover. Just ringing to tell you I'm here."

"Where, dear?"

"You know, I told you I was taking Aunty's picture back to Leatherboys Hall this weekend?"

"Oh, yes. That's this weekend is it?"

"Yes." I'm at a bit of a loss, I expected her to be slightly more interested, or at least to remember what I'd told her three days before. "I'm sitting outside it now."

"Outside what?"

"The Hall. Mum are you OK, you seem a bit vague?" I hear male voices in the background. They've got the TV on very loud.

"I'm not vague - whatever gave you that idea? Now I hope you're going to be careful and not carry that picture about. Is there someone who can help you?"

"I'll find someone. It's a fantastic house-"

"I have to go now. We've someone here."

"Oh. Don't you want to-?"

"Bye-bye dear."

Well, I don't know. It seems to me that

when you grow up your parents lose all interest in you. All those years of hanging on my every word, nagging me and worrying about me and then phut! Nothing. I no longer seem to exist for them at all. I won't be like that with my baby. I shall always be interested and love him dearly. He will be the centre of my life, but I must remember not to stifle him and to let him go when the time comes. I've read about that, the importance of letting go...

I suppose I'd better go and knock at the door as instructed. It's a fabulous place, huge and rambling with turrets and balconies. I've been sent round the back to the tradesman's entrance, and to reach the green door I've got to duck under wet sheets and knickers, here goes.

There's no knocker so I've rapped quite hard on the door but no-one is coming. It's very draughty in this yard and I'll catch my death if they don't answer soon. Have you noticed how it's always colder in the country? I'll knock again. I can actually hear the wind moaning round the rooftops; it's very Wuthering Heights, except not in Yorkshire, obviously. Oh, bugger this, I wonder if the door is...?

"Hello?!"

I'm in a kitchen. It's nice and warm with a big, black Aga thingy taking up almost all of one wall. There's food laid out on the table, four plates, knives and spoons and a saucepan of something steaming on the hot plate; lovely crusty looking rolls in a basket and a pretty cream and green butter dish with a rusty coloured cow on top as the handle.

"Hello? Anyone there?!"

"Hello," a voice behind me, could be male or female.

I turn, "Hello."

"Is that your car?" she asks brusquely.

"Yes."

"Well, you'll have to move it because Davy'll be back with the van and won't have nowhere to park and unload." She's young; big and imposing, with wellingtons and an ancient Barbour, but I won't be intimidated.

"I have something to unload too."

"What?"

"A picture."

The face changes, all hostility melts away to be replaced by quite a nice smile. "THE picture? Are you Clover Berrow?"

"Yes, did Aunty phone you?"

"She did. Gran was quite overcome. Well, let's get it out," she turns towards my car, "I can't wait to see it."

"I can't help I'm afraid, I'm-"

"Just unlock her and I'll manage."

Yes, she looks as if she can and as I unlock and open the boot, she hauls the picture out as if it was all just polystyrene with no weight at all. She's stronger than Derek and more agile.

"Hold the door open," she instructs as I close the boot and lock it.

So I hurry to the back door and hold it open against the buffeting wind and she angles the frame through, no problem. Then I have to scamper after her across the kitchen to open the next door - as instructed by a curt nod - and out into a wide passageway. As she scoots off with my great aunty's portrait I feel alarm and panic,

"Hang on, where are you going with it?"

"Upstairs, where we've got room and light enough to see her by. Come on."

After a long, dim corridor we come to a narrow wooden stairway and she motions me ahead of her, "Can you manage?" I ask and she snorts her assertion that she can. At the top of the stairs a baize door - a real, padded baize door with diamond studding - swings open into a long wide room with windows all down one side and dark panelling to all the other walls. A great marble fireplace dominates the centre of the window facing wall and a glossily polished table reaches almost from one end of the room to the other.

"Here we are," she props the portrait up against the back of one of the chairs ranged along the table and strips off the Christmas wrapping. "Well, I never!" She steps back and beams, just beams.

And I can see that Aunty belongs here. She was cheapened by the modern surroundings of my flat, looked awkward and unhappy above Great Uncle George's little tiled fireplace. But here, in her home, she is just perfect.

"I did wonder why Aunty wanted to send this back here, but now I see why. And anyway, she's got plenty of pictures of herself as a young woman to look at and remind her how she was."

The woman frowns at me, "This isn't your aunty."

"It is."

"No, it's not; it's Mags."

*****

"Who's Mags?" His mother's voice was impatient, breathy.

"My ex-fiancée."

"Ex-fiancée? George, what are you playing at? First of all, you tell your Dad and me that you're going fishing with the boys, then I see Stan in the High Street and he tells me that you've gone to see your gran. And I sincerely wish you had because we've just heard that she's died."

"Died?"

"Yes, on Friday night, all alone. Now if you'd been with her maybe she could have been revived, if you'd got an ambulance or doctor round, but no. You're not even in Eastbourne, you're in Norfolk, of all places, and now you tell me that you've got an ex-fiancée. We don't even hear about her until she's 'ex', you notice. What do you think you're playing at and how on earth are you going to get back to London in time to do your shift this afternoon?"

"I won't be back. I've written to explain, or rather, Lady Lydia has."

"Lady who? George, are you having me on? Because I won't stand for it. If there's one thing your father and I have drummed into you over the years it's to tell the truth; to be straight with us, because we will always be straight with you. What does your father always say? Play a..."

"-straight bat. I know Mum and I'm sorry. I'm so sorry about Gran. How's Dad taking it?"

"Nice of you to show an interest."

"Don't be cross, Mum."

"Not cross? What else can I be? We don't know where you are, no-one does for days and now you tell me you can't get home in time for work. What'll you do if you lose your job? Mmn?"

"I can't come home yet because the police won't let m-"

"The police?! What have you got mixed up in? Are you in danger of going to prison?"

"No Mum, not at all. It's just that there have been several strange accidents since I arrived at the house and the police have been called in to investigate. They don't suspect me. I don't think they suspect anyone. It all seems to have been accidental."

"What sort of accidents?"

"Someone fell off a balcony. Someone else had a heart attack in the woods and then a bison fell on a little girl."

"Not bison, basin. Didn't I send you to elocution classes to get rid of those dreadful flat vowel sounds?"

"Not a basin. A buffalo type creature, a bison."

"Oh, poor little girl, is she alright?"

"No, she's dead."

"Dead?"

"It was a big bison."

"George, how terrible for you! Are you alright?"

"Yes, Mum."

"And the mother?"

"Lady Lydia? Well, she's upset of course."

"Of course, poor woman. I hope you'll do all you can to help; I know you can be very kind, George..."

"I do my best."

"You always do, dear. Are there many bisons in the house?"

"No, just that one."

"I was going to say, steer clear of them, Georgie."

Having let his parents know his whereabouts, having received the expected comfort and homely advice, George wrote a quick note of apology and explanation for the mess on the desk and left Smears' office. He had yet more things to ponder over, the mounting debts, Smears' lost good opinion and the shocking fact that Lady Lydia might just be a normal 'Mrs'. He was such a snob; as reprehensible as it had been to make love to his fiancée's mother, it had seemed almost allowable while she was a 'Lady'. Now he suspected that she was just a plain 'Mrs' it all seemed very tawdry indeed. Was Mags even an Honourable?

And then it sunk in. Gran was dead. Dear old

Gran, always ready with a humbug and a giggle, a very girlish giggle, and if he had gone to visit her - had been with her in her hour of need - he could have maybe saved her. He was a veritable Angel of Death, even his absence seemed to cause disaster. He began to worry about his mum and dad.

He wandered upstairs into the main hall, to find the family all issuing out of the drawing room and the two police officers being guided into the morning room by Smears with the offer of,

"Shum light refreshment, officersh."

He opened his mouth to call out to Smears but the butler shut the door behind him and George closed his mouth again quickly. Mags snubbed him as she ran upstairs but Lady Lydia smiled at him and trailed her hand along the banisters as she followed more slowly. And then, out of the gloom, resulting from the closing of the drawing room door, Jane appeared before him.

"We've had some news," she told him softly.

"So have I."

"Bad news?" She peered at his face, "You look sad."

"My gran has died."

"I'm sorry. Was she very old?"

"Yes, but even so..."

"I know," she touched his sleeve. They stood in silence for a moment, then he sighed and asked,

"What was your news?"

"Would you like to go out for a walk? I need to get out of this place."

"I know what you mean. Yes, let's walk and you can tell me."

"We can find coats in the lobby."

George went with her to the lobby and helped her into an old fawn rain coat that came to her ankles. He put on his usual mac and a trilby, which he thought might suit him. They strolled out together into the cool, damp morning and both took a very deep breath of fresh, clean air, then laughed, embarrassed.

"I needed some air so much," Jane explained.

"What's your news?" He could not relax until he knew.

"The inspector has had a report from the local railway station. The porter there saw a young person answering Gaye's description - tall, thin, white blond hair - boarding the Sunday morning train for Norwich. The porter said he thought it was Gaye, but in men's clothes and when he addressed her as such, the young person answered in a deep voice that he was a Mr George Pender of London."

"Me?"

"Yes, but the porter is sure it was Gaye, because of the height."

"That extra inch?"

"Yes, he's known the family for years; he used to be boot boy here."

"So, Gaye has escaped, dressed as a man."

"Dressed as you, it seems."

"But all my clothes were cut up."

"Maybe she just wanted to pretend to be you."

"I don't know why. I don't think anyone would want to be me at the moment. Apart, of course, from the fact that I am walking across a soggy lawn with the most beautiful girl in the world."

"Do you say that to Ethel too?"

"No," he took her hand and squeezed it, "I told Ethel she was sweet, which she is."

"Yes, I suppose she is," she sighed. "And what about Mags?"

"Mags tried to strangle me this morning at breakfast."

"What?" she turned to him, a frown only making her forehead more desirable.

"Look," he raised his chin and pulled down his shirt collar.

"Poor George," she cupped his face. "You must get away, before she does anything really - I mean, if she's that cross with you..."

"I told her I considered our engagement over and she tried to make me say it was still on, but I didn't."

"How brave," she smiled and moved even closer, "but I worry for your safety."

"Why?" He put his arm round her waist.

"Mags has been known to... well, she can get violent if she doesn't get her way."

"Like The Beautiful Child."

"Just like that, because they've all been so..."

"Spoilt. I know, Harry told me. But what about you, weren't you spoilt too?"

"Hardly," she spun away.

He followed and renewed his hold on her, "Tell me."

"I never talk about my childhood."

"Perhaps you should."

"It only makes me unhappy."

"I can't bear to think of you being unhappy."

"Then I shan't tell you."

"But I need to know, Jane."

"Why?"

"Because I need to know all about you."

She sighed again and rested her forehead on his shoulder, "Not here."

"Where?"

"At the boat house. I'll take you."

Across the springy green turf towards the woods, then right, across a little track leading to the stables and through a broken wooden gate into a vegetable garden. He held her hand and marvelled that he should be doing so; should be side-by-side with a young woman so lovely that all the movie stars he had yearned after for years palled in comparison. With her hair tossed about by the breeze, her old fawn raincoat soaking up the wet from the ground, her cheeks pink from the chill in the air, no-one else could match her in his eyes. She led him though a fringe of straggling trees and to the edge of a sizable lake. The water was still and grey, decorated with the few orange and yellow leaves that had fallen so far and the flat, green pads of a fading water-lilly.

It was silent and sheltered and, in the lowest corner of the lake, where a stream trickled over a wooden dam, a dank shingled boat house crouched behind looming bull rushes.

"This is my place," she told him. "This is where I came to hide and be myself when I was little; where I still come, sometimes."

George had to lift the door to open it because the wood was so wet and warped. Inside it was dark and she warned him about the little dock, empty of any boat, and taking up the central portion of the space,

"Up here."

He followed her up a rickety ladder to a boarded loft, where a square of cobwebbed window allowed in just enough light to see her by, to see the tears standing in her beautiful eyes. She sat down on a dusty old rug and hid her face in her hands. He sat beside her and put his arms round her until she had control of herself and then she began,

"There's only two days between Mags and me; Mother had me on the Monday, Lady Lydia had Mags on the Wednesday. We should have been great friends, being so close in age and even closer in blood...you see, my father was Mags' father too."

"You're sisters?!"

"Half sisters. Lady Lydia was furious; she wanted to give birth first, she did everything to bring it on and Nanny is of the opinion that some of the methods used have damaged Mags... You see, Mags and I are the only real Berengers."

"Yes, of course."

"And the eldest would inherit."

"That's you."

"Mm, but Lady Lydia is still alive and is desperate for Mags to marry and have children, and she is equally desperate that I should not. She's spent years trying to convince me that no-one would ever want me because I was so plain, but the irony is that she needn't have bothered. I'd never bring children into this evil world to suffer as I have suffered.... The other thing she doesn't know is that Mags has been pregnant several times..."

"All the dead babies in the mural."

"Has he put them in? I'm surprised... but then, I shouldn't be. It's very possible that Mags is barren, Mummy and I have discussed it, she hasn't had a pregnancy for some time now. It's all so wicked, she thinks nothing of killing... and of course The Bish helped her out."

"An abortionist?"

"He said that as a so called 'man of the cloth', all Mags' sins would be washed away because he would intercede for her. But now he's gone she's got to mend her ways. You're the chosen father; I don't know why - she could have had her pick of the local gentry, but we don't really mix. Perhaps she thought that by choosing someone she felt so superior to, she could get away with marrying, conceiving and then leaving you in the lurch."

"She feels superior to me?" He tried to sound put out, but he knew it to be true.

"No, I don't think she does now, you've turned out to be more of a challenge than she thought. Though you are woefully easy to seduce."

"I'm sorry about that."

She smiled at him, "Overwhelmed."

"Yes. I was. And now I'm overwhelmed by you."

"I'm not going to seduce you."

He felt a swoop of disappointment, then continued cheerfully, "But you're going to come away with me?"

"If I may."

"You may. Although, this house belongs to you more than any of the others."

"I don't want it! I hate it. I want to go away and never ever see the wretched place again as long as I live." She rifled underneath the rug and pulled up a loose board, "Here, read this," she handed him an exercise book, faded and damp. "Put it back when you've finished and I'll see you later," she got up and stepped over him to go back down the ladder.

"Wait," he caught at the trailing skirt of her macintosh.

"No, I can't be here while you read it. I'll see you outside." She climbed backwards down the ladder.

"Jane?" He called to her disappearing head, "Jane?" But she carried on down without looking at him. He heard her walking across the floor boards downstairs, then nothing. So, he opened up the exercise book.

'This book belongs to Jane Berenger, aged eight.

Once upon a time a beautiful princess lived in a fairytale castel with her mummy and daddy who were king and queen. She had a pony to ride and a cat to cudle and as many books as she wanted to reed. No one upset her becose the king would have there heads chopped off if they did. They did not hurt her cat or burn her books up and all the peple in the castel beleeved her when she said they had tryd to do those things. Her big brother was a santly boy who red the bibel all day and sang hims. But she did not have a sister becose she had died of a terribal acident a long time ago.'

The story did not continue overleaf. Instead there was a small fold of tissue paper glued to the page with, 'Dimples fur all I have left of her' written underneath. He did not doubt that the tissue contained Dimple's fur and had no wish to unfold it to find out. He turned the page,

'I am so fed up with mummy crying all the time. I cry to but I don't sniff and blow my nose all over her. Daddy will come back. He said he wood and he always dos. Grownups allways make things dificult. He can stay if he wants to. We culd go with him. I wuold like to go away from here. Mags has said she will cut all my hair off wile I am asleep if I don't give her my new red shoes. They won't fit her.

She has new shoes as well but mine are red so they are better she says. I think I can stay awak for one night at leest.'

On the next page a big red heart drawn in red wax crayon with an exaggerated and terrible crack through the centre of it, and underneath the plea 'DADDY PLEESE COME BACK'.

There was much, much more, the whole exercise book reeked and wailed of misery and fear,

'She says she'll come and get me one night and cut out my miserable heart with one of cook's knives. She's got the knife, she's shown me.'

'Harry made Gaye eat the paint crying, fight back, fight back you coward all the time and I had to run away. I should have stayed to help poor Gaye but she said later that she forgave me. She was very sick and Nanny was so worried she kept falling over.'

'I am to go to a dentist to make my teeth better, I didn't know my teeth were bad but Lady Lydia says something must be done to improve me. I don't think I'm so very bad looking. I look a bit like Mags and everyone says she's so lovely. Joye and Gaye say I look lovely too. I wish I could say the same about them. They have terrible spots, all crusty and bleeding then Gaye laughs and skweezes one all over the mirror. Horrible, but I have to laugh too.'

'Mags has been very ill. I hope I don't catch it, she keeps breathing all over me and laughing that it's not contageous. She kept being sick then put on wieght then lost it suddenly and now she doesn't look very good at all. The Bish keeps on going into her room and I hear them whispering and her breathing all funny. I told Nanny but she said to leave well alone.'

He could read no more. He shut the book, returned it to its hiding place and hurried down the rotting ladder. Jane was waiting for him outside, swishing her long mac across the wet grass, she looked up.

He opened his arms.

*****

I am engulfed in a big, whiskery hug. My ribs hurt and I can hardly breathe. This introduction to my newly discovered but distant relatives is proving a painful business.

"At last," my overwhelming host exclaims, and lets me go, "we've had to wait so long to meet anyone from the other side."

They keep saying that, 'the other side' indeed, you'd think I was a ghost. Brian and Gloria beam at me, they have decided that we are cousins, of a sort and I assume they know what they're talking about.

"You'll stay for lunch," Gloria informs me, setting another place at the table, "Mum will want to see you. And you should stay the night, it's a long drive back down there and in your condition..."

"Eh?" Brian immediately looks concerned,

"are you ill?"

"Expecting, Bri," she nods at my stomach.

"Sit down," he pulls out a chair, "sit down."

I sit. This unprepossessing pair are the parents of the muscular Bronwen - who unloaded the car - and, unbelievably, of the gorgeous Davy who unlocked the gate for me. There are even more 'Berengers' waiting to be met. The matriarchal Gran, for a start, and a couple called Guy and Joye, also incredibly old; Stephen, a brother of Brian's, and his family in the east wing, and another lot called collectively 'The Grahams' in the stables. This, and the fact that the stunner in the painting is not my great aunt but someone called 'Mags' is all quite a lot for a girl in my condition to take in. Quite unexpectedly I find tears running down my face.

"Ah, she's overcome," Gloria enfolds me in her baggy red cardigan and pats my head. She smells of onions and root vegetables and some floral talc I can't put a name to. But it's very comforting, so comforting that I feel dangerously close to losing control completely. I could do it, I could let go and wallow in my emotional bog for a good half hour and I reckon that Gloria would listen and condole and soothe. She's that kind of woman. Welsh, she told me when we were introduced, 'And I met Bri at Stoneleigh.'

I connect the roar and gravely grate of a vehicle driving into the yard with the expected arrival of Davy and decide to reign myself in,

"I'm alright," I insist and draw back to find a

hankie, "it's all been a bit much."

"Ah, well you're here now," Bri sits down on the opposite side of the table, reassured now he knows I'm not going to give in. "So nice to finally meet someone from the other side...." He nods and looks to his wife.

Gloria has returned to the bubbling saucepan on the Aga thingy, her back firmly turned to us, shoulders hunched in her cardigan. Bronwen clomps in from the passage and grins at me, shy suddenly, and Bri does his beaming. There is an awkward silence. Four people, all related with so much to say and enquire about and not one of us can find the words. They must think me odd, they must assume I know things. Oh, how I wish my family had been more communicative over the years. I give my nose a final pat and pocket the squelchy lump of tissue, "Well...."

"Yes." Bri agrees, glances towards his wife's back and rubs his bristly fat knuckles, hand over hand.

The backdoor flies open, "Is that daft bitch still-? Ahh."

"Oh, this is our Davy," Gloria explains, "Davy, this is your cousin, Clover. She's brought the painting back."

I am pleased to see him so disconcerted. I smile serenely as he slithers out of his leather jacket and goes to the sink to wash his hands. He mutters something, his mother hears and asks,

"What?"

"I said, what do we want with the bloody thing anyway?"

"It belongs here," his sister reminds him.

"We managed very well without it for sixty years."

"Don't be ungracious, Davy," Gloria gives him a threadbare hand towel and a meaningful look.

He dries his hands intently then suddenly asks, "Did she tell you about the mishap?"

"What mishap?" His mother frowns at me.

I'd better jump in here, "I skidded on the corner and knocked into your sign, I'm afraid."

"Are you alright?" She's all concern again. "No wonder you needed a cry. Do you want to see a doctor? Should he check that the baby's OK?"

Davy cranes round, and narrows his eyes at me for an instant, an electric instant.

"No, I'm fine." I wonder how to play this, I could go one of two ways…. I plump for the brave little woman act. "It's just it's been a long journey, and then I got lost and when I parked to look at the map, I got stuck in the mud and had to be towed out of the lay-by, and I was sidetracked by the wonderful rainbow and skidded on the corner. I'm sorry I knocked your sign again but there was quite a lot of mud on the road."

"You should have been looking at that, not the rainbow," he seems determined to upset me. "And anyway, we've got a sign for that too."

"What?"

"'Mud on the Road' it says."

"I didn't see it."

"Well, never mind - no harm done if you're sure you're OK, Clover?"

"I am, thank you, Gloria."

"Let's have some lunch now," she begins to ladle soup into big green bowls. "Davy sit down and stop prowling. What are you looking for?"

"You said something about a baby."

I lean back and pat my tummy, hoping he notices the tan and the still relatively sylph like waistline.

"Ah. Even more reason to keep your eye on the road."

The soup is excellent, the rolls delicious, I am full but the offer of fruit cake, the family recipe, is too good to resist. In spite of all this the meal has not been a success. Davy is the fly in the ointment, or more properly, the chicken bone in the potage.

"He's not usually like this," his poor mother tries to laugh off his rudeness.

"This is exactly how I am. How many times have we sat here and bad-mouthed bad drivers? City folk who don't know a country curve when they see one. It's all you lot who're being on best behaviour. They're not usually like this, cousin Clover, and your name'll be mud when you go."

"Davy," his father wades in. "I'll not have you speak to a member of the family like that."

"It's because she is a member of the family that I can speak to her like that, surely."

"He's never been the same since he went away to college," his mother tells me.

"Where did you go?" I ask politely.

"Aberystwyth Agricultural."

"Wales! Your mother's homeland, how lovely for you."

"Not really."

"He didn't get on-" Gloria began.

"They didn't get on with me, not the other way around." Davy cut across his mother.

Gloria pulls a face and takes a bite of the moistly fruity cake.

"Would you like to see the picture, Davy?" Almost Bronwen's first words, though hardly a topic he seems much interested in.

I smile at her and explain to them all, "We've always thought the painting was of my Great Aunt Jane, but it's not. You'll have to tell me who Mags is, Aunty has never mentioned her."

They all look at each other, ruminating slowly, so I flail onwards hoping to rescue the subject,

"I've always loved the painting but it never looked right at the Palmers Green house, far too big for the room. She looks in scale here, if you know what I mean."

"How is your aunty?" Gloria asks on a dying fall.

"Well, getting on you know, and a bit dotty, and missing Great Uncle George terribly."

Bronwen sniffs, Davy bows his head and

Gloria pulls out a hankie,

"We all miss him dreadfully."

This is odd, according to Great Aunt Jane, he has never been back here - but didn't she say something about an anniversary? I had dismissed all her ramblings as.... ramblings, but maybe...

"You knew my Great Uncle George?"

"Of course. He's Bri's father."

"No. No, that can't be... He never had any children."

"He had five."

I laugh, "No, we're talking about different people, I think. My great uncle, George Pender, former bus conductor and later bus inspector, and his wife, Jane, never had any children."

They all exchange complicit glances,

"I think you need to go and speak to Mum," Gloria tells me and turns to her daughter, "Will you take Clover up, love?"

"Of course. She can't wait to meet you again," Bronwen assures me. "I'll take you when you've finished your tea."

I swig it down, still scalding, and stand up. There are certain things that can't wait for a cup of tea to cool down.

You have to walk fast to keep up with Bronwen, she's as fit and robust as her brother but much nicer.

"I like your boots," she tells me as we cross a huge expanse of murky hall and begin to climb a wide and rambling staircase leading up and up. "I went to Norwich last year but I didn't see any boots like that."

"You don't leave the Hall much then?"

"Hardly ever. I don't mind, I like my work here and I don't like big cities."

"What do you do here?"

"Work on the veg."

"The organic vegetable farm?"

"Yes, we all do. We got proper certification two years ago and it's really taken off, but then we don't pay ourselves much, we plough it all back in. Davy says that in five years we might be able to take a holiday."

"He seems a bit of a hard taskmaster. And he doesn't seem to like me."

"He's very moody at the moment." We've reached a landing; she pauses and I'm grateful because my thighs are quivering. The house is vast and ugly, the walls are hung with dreadful muddy tapestries, rippling in the many draughts that come up the stairwell, along the corridors and now from a lighted doorway with a gaunt figure emerging. "It's alright Guy, it's only me."

A puce hankie drifts from an expressively limp hand and the door shuts again.

"Who was that?"

"Guy." She moves on and round to the next lot of stairs.

"So," I haul myself up after her, "why is Davy so moody at the moment?"

"He's broken up with his girlfriend."

"Oh." I suppress a smile, "Why's that then?"

"She said he was moody."

"Oh."

We are coming up to the second floor and a giant suit of armour glowers down at us from a plaster archway. Various portraits line the panelled walls now and I search the pallid faces for a Berenger likeness.

"Are these all family?"

"We've no idea who they are. When the Hall was built in the 1830's, it was fashionable to buy in old portraits, to pretend they were ancestors."

"How odd."

"The only real Berenger portrait is the one you brought back with you, that's why we're so pleased to have it back."

"Who is Mags, then?"

"It's all very complicated, Gran will explain. Along here," she leads me down the second-floor corridor to the right where dim wall lamps provide some light to see the way. It's all rather dusty and down at heel, but then they obviously don't have time to keep it clean, who would, you'd need an army of servants. "In here," she knocks at a door as she opens it and calls, "I've brought Clover to see you Gran."

CHAPTER 12

"Can I come in?" George peered nervously round the door.

"No."

He ignored Joye's instruction because Nanny got up from the nursery table and came to let him in,

"Now then, darlin' we mustn't be uncharitable."

"He's a rude man."

"All men are rude. Come in Master George and join us in some lemonade," he went to fetch a clean glass from one of his cupboards and Joye stuck her tongue out at George as he sat down opposite her.

"I'm sorry you had to see your mother and me, Joye. Perhaps if you didn't spend so much time hidden away and spying..." He stopped himself as a glass of lemonade landed heavily in front of him. "Thank you, Nanny. Anyway, I've come with some good news."

"Gaye's back?!" Joye's face lit up and she half rose from the table, then she saw George's expression and sank down again.

"Not back, I'm afraid, but she has been seen."

"Where?" Nanny sat in a flurry of talc.

"At the railway station yesterday morning."

"Gaye likes trains, doesn't she Nanny?"

"Yes, darlin'. Safe?"

"Boarding a train, dressed as me."

"Ahh," Nanny rubbed his chin and nodded.

"Ethel said you would explain."

"I don't understand. Why has Gaye gone away without me?" Joye's lips wobbled, tears blobbed into her eyes. Nanny reached over a comforting hand but looked at George,

"Can you not guess?"

"I suppose she just wanted to get away and decided that a disguise would be the best way, so she stole some clothes from the laundry room and cut her hair. But she's so distinctive looking, even with it cut short, the colour," he gestured at Joye's bowed and glossy white blond head, "and the extra inch."

"That was what gave her away, I expect..." Nanny sighed. "Och, well, it's time I suppose, and Joye you must be brave and listen to what I have to tell you. Sit up straight now, no slouchers in this nursery." He cleared his throat theatrically, "Many years ago, when everyone was very much younger..."

"Is it a fairy story, Nanny?"

"No darlin', it's true. Just listen. Lady Lydia was mother to two fine boys, Alphonse and Harry and she was expecting another child. Now, much as she loved her boys, she'd always desperately wanted a girl and she had decided it would be a girl this time; a girl she could dress up and make a fuss of, someone she could pass on all her own winsome ways to. She ordered new pink baby clothes and dolls for the nursery and chose a name. She was so desperate it was pathetic to see. So desperate that she threatened to- well, do some violence to herself and her child if it was yet another boy. You know how your Mummy gets an idea into her head and it won't shift? We were all very worried about her. Well, the time came and she had another boy. 'Is it a girl?' She screamed and poor Mrs Pearce, who was midwife here then, was so alarmed by Mummy's manner and by the dagger she had concealed under her pillow and was now waving about, that she lied and said it was. I remember the look on the poor woman's face, Master George - total terror. Because, although you may not know it, Lady Lydia can be a very domineering person, even with her legs in the air and smeared with birth blood. And then we thought that poor Lady Lydia would die, because she still screamed about the pain and rolled around, and she still had the dagger, we couldn't get it off her. So, I was sent off for the doctor and while I was gone, and while Mrs Pearce was concealing the baby boy's sex with a napkin, another child was born. Lady Lydia delivered it herself and cut the cord with her dagger. That child was you, Joye."

"Me? I was delivered with a dagger?"

"When Mrs Pearce returned to the room there was Lady Lydia holding up this second child - this twin - and proclaiming, 'Two girls, I have two girls

now to go with my two boys! Two lovely girls!'
She went on and on like that for days. The doctors
said the balance of her mind was disturbed. For that
reason we didn't dare tell her that one of her twins
was a boy and so, we made the dreadful decision…"

"Dreadful indeed! How could you do that to
poor Gaye?" George stood up; he was appalled -
of all the ghastly things that had happened in this
place this was surely the worst.

Tears ran down Nanny's puffed and bristly
cheeks, "I had done it, Master George, and I con-
demned that poor wee child, my poor wee child, to
the same fate…. It was wrong, I own it. More girls
came later, we could have righted the wrong but…"
he gestured at Joye. "She's not of the brightest and I
feared for her."

"But Gaye found out? He must have done."

"Eventually."

Joye turned her face from one to the other,
confusion twisting her mouth and clouding her sore
eyes. George felt such pity for her that he sat down
again,

"She just doesn't understand, does she?"

"No, and I think that Gaye knew what a dreadful weight that simple-mindedness put upon him.
That's why he waited until he was twenty-five and
could stand the agony no longer. My poor boy; I am
responsible, I am at fault. I took to the skirt to save
my own skin, I was old enough to know what I was
doing. I had no right to impose it on my only son."

It took George a moment to fully understand

the importance of Nanny's last sentence. Then he closed his eyes and let his head fall forwards onto his crossed arms upon the table.

Later, on the stairs up to his room, he sat down to think. Mags' expensive wristwatch told him it was only eleven o'clock and all the clocks within hearing confirmed the fact for the next five minutes, but George felt he had lived a whole day already. The events and discoveries of the morning had numbed his mind and he found himself humming a nursery rhyme. It was suddenly important that he re-tie his shoelaces, so he leaned forward over his knees and pulled the laces loose. Wandering around in almost constant gloom, it was vital that he didn't fall over a straggling lace and tumble to his death. Because death lurked everywhere in the house and grounds, death and awful secrets. He wished himself back to the cheerful, if nervous, youth who had entered these ghastly walls on Friday afternoon; but that George had gone, he had changed, he had done dreadful deeds and seen terrible sights. 'Georgie Porgie pudding and pie, kissed the girls and made them cry, when the boys came out to play, Georgie Porgie ran away...' That's what he must do now.

He stood up and was immediately blinded by the beam of a flashlight.

"Argh," he shielded his eyes, "who's that?"

"Who's that?" The voice was instantly recognisable.

"Inspector? It's me, George Pender."

"Mr Pender," the light left his face and hovered around his middle as the Inspector mounted the stairs towards him, "was that you singing?"

"Singing?"

"I thought I heard singing just now."

"It might have been me..." he blinked, his vision a mass of dancing lights, "I'm not really sure. I'm not really sure of anything anymore."

The inspector joined him and sniffed, "I know what you mean." He was breathing hard and kept playing the torch around the stairs and walls, making George feel dizzy. "Odd place this, and so big."

"Yes, and I'd rather like to leave, if I may?"

"Not yet sir, I'm expecting to hear from the mortuary by luncheon and depending on what they have to say... The thing is...." He swung the torch back to George's face, "I've lost Bacon."

"Ah. I see." He squinted and covered the beam with his hand.

"We had breakfast together, spoke to the family about the report we had received concerning the sighting of Miss Gaye at the railway station - you did hear about that?"

"Yes, from Miss Jane."

"Right. Then we had coffee and biscuits in the morning room and discussed the case. We decided to interview the Nanny, to see if she had aided and abetted the runaway and whether said runaway had anything to hide, vis-à-vis the spate of accidents. So

I sent him off to do that while I contacted the mortuary to hurry them along with the toxicology report and I haven't seen him since."

"I've been with Nanny for the last half hour or so and he didn't come in while I was there."

"Perhaps he's there now, you might have passed him in the dark and not seen him."

"I suppose I might have done."

"Well, perhaps as you know the way, you might accompany me up to the nursery to ascertain his whereabouts."

"The nursery's not up there, it's on the ground floor."

"Unusual."

"Everything here is unusual, Inspector. I'll take you." He tried to move his feet, found them unresponsive, and lurched forwards. Only the inspector's quick reactions saved him from the hurtle into oblivion he had dreaded. "Ahhh!"

"Watch it! Watch yourself there!"

George freed himself from the inspector's embrace and sat down, his legs quivering and strangely hindered. "I feel quite odd. I think I've become paralysed."

"Paralysed? Has this ever happened to you before? Ah, no," he squatted down next to George, "I see what's happened. Look," he drew George's attention to his feet, "your laces are tied together."

George stared down at his well-polished brown shoes, glowing in the torch light like freshly fallen conkers. Each lace was neatly and tightly tied, in double knots, to its fellow on the other foot. He grabbed at the inspector's arm,

"If you hadn't come, I'd have fallen to my death."

"Well, taken a nasty tumble, certainly."

"If I don't get out of here soon, I'm going to die here."

"Now, now, you're getting a little paranoid, I think."

"Well wouldn't you be? Since I've arrived here, three people have died in bizarre circumstances and two have gone missing."

"Two?"

"Gaye, and now Bacon."

Inspector Fowey drummed his fingers on his chin and then straightened his shoulders,

"We must be sensible about this, Mr Pender. Who would want to kill you? Find the motive and we have our assailant. So, who do you think tied your shoelaces together? "

"I did."

"You did?"

"Yes, I sat here on the stairs to think, and thought I might as well make sure my laces didn't come undone, in case I took a fall and... It sounds mad, doesn't it? But it's dark and it's an easy mistake to make. One shoelace feels much like another..." He glanced up and saw the Inspector's expression. "Just shine the light on them and I'll do them properly then we'll go and look for your constable."

"Yes, sir."

They arrived at the nursery door and, in the improved lighting, George could now see that the list of rules pinned up on the outside of the door included: 'No spitting, no partaking of alcohol, no gambling, no fighting and no women, By Order of His Majesty's Armed Forces.'

He knocked and opened the door, keeping the inspector behind him, "Nanny, are you there? I have the inspector here looking for his constable."

"Oooh," a high-pitched, girlish coo came from Nanny's thick lips, "there's no-one here but me and wee Miss Joye, Master George."

"Right-oh." George made to shut the door but the inspector pushed him aside and marched into the room.

Nanny rose from the nursery table, all female confusion, and Joye rushed to seek comfort in his solid bosom.

"Excuse the intrusion, Madam. I sent my constable to interview you nearly an hour ago, did he arrive?"

"Master George came to tell us that Gaye had been seen at the railway station, which set my mind mightily to rest, I can tell you. I have been fair mad with grief and worry, after The Beautiful Child's dreadful accident and the poor Bishop..." The effort of speaking in so high a pitch was making Nanny's face puce, "But no policeman has been here at all. Have they, my darlin'?" He applied to Joye for confirmation, she shook her head fiercely.

"Would you know why Miss Gaye would want to run away, at all?"

"Why? Well, no," sweat was breaking out on his upper lip and forehead but he smiled in a game - if untimely - way.

"Are you feeling unwell, Madam?"

"Oh, women's trouble, you know..." He flapped a hefty hand, helplessly.

"Ah, yes, Mrs Inspector Fowey is similarly... Well, I can see you're busy with young, um... How old exactly are the twins?"

"Twenty-five," Nanny grinned, his face glowing.

"Ah. But not quite, um..."

"No, no, ha-ha-ha-ha."

"Must be difficult for you."

"Very."

"Tragic for Lady Lydia, too."

"Absolutely."

"Well, shall we carry on looking, Inspector?" George indicated the open door. "He's obviously not here and I think that Nanny needs to sit down before she falls down. Such a very trying few days for her."

"Yes, indeed. Thank you, Madam." He bowed out and waited for George to join him.

George heard the thump and scrape of Nanny's chair as he shut the door on him.

"Brave woman," the inspector confided as they retreated up the corridor, "confused and shocked by the weekend's events but still smiling for the sake of her charge."

"Yes. Nanny is very attached to Gaye and Joye. She treats them as if they were her very own, as she does all her charges."

"So, where is Bacon?" The inspector stopped and turned off the torch, a shaft of sunlight cut across the corridor at that point, revealing line upon line of busy etchings upon the walls. All were framed in black and most seemed to be concerned with executions. "Lost probably, like us."

"No, I know where I am." George had spotted the paved courtyard where Joye had danced and sung for him. "We can get up to the main hall through here. Perhaps we can find Smears and ask him about Bacon."

But Smears hadn't seen Bacon. He was patrolling the main hall like a sentry; occasionally glancing up the stairs, then down at his watch and seemed tetchy when the inspector asked when he had last seen the constable.

"Not shinsh I showed you into the morning room for coffee, shir."

"What about the rest of the staff, Smears?"

"I will enquire downstairs, shir." He bowed to the inspector and then stopped by George and tapped him on the shoulder, "I did, however, resheeve your note shir, and will shpeak to you later."

"Right." George could not for the moment recall a note, but then remembered the phone call and the bills on the desk and nodded.

"Luncheon at one o'clock, shirsh. Perhapsh you would wait in the drawing room."

They agreed and were making their way there, but as Smears disappeared below stairs an eerie glow began to bleed down from above. George went to the newel post and peered up. The whole stairwell was suffused with the warmth of candle-light.

"What's going on?" The inspector joined him. Now they could see several many-branched candelabra approaching, held aloft by black-gloved hands. Lady Lydia appeared above the first-floor banisters, veiled in deepest mourning, followed by Aunt Suzy, and two indistinguishable slender, younger figures, either of whom could have been Mags or Jane. Behind came Harry and Freddie, the latter looking troubled and uncomfortable, because they carried between them a red, velvet covered board, with the dead and immaculately dressed Beautiful Child laid upon it. The two sobbing black huddles bringing up the rear had to be the two remaining old aunts. Only Nanny, Joye and Ethel were missing.

"My God." The inspector hurried across the echoing tiles towards the drawing room.

Ethel emerged from below stairs in her smartest uniform, wearing three black bands on her sleeve. She kept her head down, ignoring George as he stepped back to allow the weird procession to come down into the hall. He watched Ethel join them and then, as Mags passed him, noticed the satisfied smirk on her face under the spotted net veil. He ran into the drawing room and called to the inspector,

"Quick! I think I know where Bacon might be."

Even so it took a while to find him. They opened several first-floor bedroom doors before they found the right one.

"Good heavens, boy!"

"I'm 'orry, Uncle, 'on't 'ell gum," Bacon's speech was muffled and slurred by the gag across his mouth. He tried manfully to cover his private parts with his hands but his handcuffs, looped round one of the posts of the four-poster, hindered him.

"How on earth did you get into this state?!"

"Where are the keys?" George enquired untying the gag, since the uncle/inspector was too stunned to move from the bedroom door.

"In my pocket," Bacon nodded towards the tumbled pile of clothes on the floor beside the bed.

George began to sort through the discarded uniform and woollen underwear.

"Who did this to you? Are you hurt?" The inspector finally shut the door behind him and walked towards the trussed-up figure on the bed. "You were supposed to be interviewing Nanny. How on earth did you end up here?"

"Don't tell Mum."

"Of course I'm not going to tell your mother. What would I say? Well, Audrey, I finally found your son naked on a bed, handcuffed to the bed post, his feet tied up with..." he leant closer to investigate, "black stockings... and- saints preserve us! Lipstick imprints on his bare buttocks. Lionel!!"

"I've found the keys," George stood up and began to unlock the cuffs. "You do his feet."

"I don't know as I want to touch him. Here," instead he threw his nephew's long johns onto the bed. "For the last time will you for God's sake tell me who did this to you?"

Bacon bowed his head and rubbed his newly released wrists, "I can't say."

"Well I can," George told them. "It was Mags, wasn't it?"

"I'm so sorry, Mr Pender." Bacon hurried into his underpants.

"Don't be sorry on my account, my engagement to Mags is off, has been since breakfast. Feel free to do what ever you want to her."

"It wasn't what I did to her-"

"I don't want to hear this," his uncle interrupted. "And all I have to say now, Mr Pender, is that my constable and I will be eternally grateful if you could forget what you've just seen and the fact that Lionel here is my nephew. Nepotism is a nasty word and I can see how all this could be misconstrued, but you have to understand that in a small town with a tiny police force, these things tend to run in families." He sniffed and pocketed the handcuffs.

"Don't worry, I won't say a word, but I have to warn you, everyone will know about Bacon's exploits. Mags never keeps these things secret; staff, Lady Lydia... everyone will know by now."

"Oh my God. How could you let yourself be used like this, Lionel?"

"Well Uncle, I'd like to see you try to resist her." Bacon was beginning to resume his confidence with his uniform. "She gave me the come on like a- a whore."

"Language, Lionel, we're talking about a member of the nobility here."

"I know what she can be like," George told them, "he's not to bla-." He started as the dinner gong sounded, very loud. "Have you two noticed that, wherever you are in the house, that gong sounds as if it's just outside..." he flung open the door, "...the door?" The hallway was dark and empty.

"I have as a matter of fact and I put it down to acoustics. Are you ready constable?"

"Ready, sir." He picked up his helmet and cradled it under one arm. "Ready for anything," and certainly there was more of a sparkle in his eye and a suggestion of a cockiness to his walk as they went downstairs for lunch.

*****

"Let me take your tray, Gran. And I've brought Clover to see you," Bronwen picks up the neatly stacked tray of empty plate, bowl and dish and stands aside.

"Clover, this is our Gran, your Great Aunt Ethel and Jane's half-sister."

The little lady sitting in the armchair by the fire smiles at me and beckons me closer. I edge nearer avoiding all the delicate china arranged on the many draped tables and put out my hand to shake hers. But she takes my hand and pulls me to her for a kiss,

"Hello dear, it's nice to see you again. Do you remember me?"

I shake my head. Bronwen lifts the tray over me and squeezes out,

"I'll leave you two alone, Clover wants to know who Mags is, Gran." She pulls the door shut with her foot and I'm left alone with Great Aunt Ethel.

"I'm very sorry, I don't think I've ever…"

"At the funeral, dear. I wasn't supposed to be there, but if a girl can't go to her own husband's funeral then, what's the world come to? Sit down."

"Whose funeral are we talking about?" I sit in the armchair opposite hers and get myself comfy among the cushions.

"George's funeral, of course. And before you say, 'He's not your husband', take a look at that marriage certificate on the table at your elbow."

I do as I'm told and read that, 'George Edward Pender, bachelor of Palmers Green, London, married Ethel Marguerite Berenger, spinster of this Parish, on the fifteenth of May 1937'. "But what about Great Aunt Jane?"

"Shall I start at the beginning?"

"I wish you would."

She smiles and clasps her dry little hands together; rings sparkle and I notice that she is wearing pink nail varnish though she must be nearly eighty.

"George first came to this house in the autumn of 1936. He was a guest of one of my other half-sisters, Mags - or Margaret as she was called when she was being naughty - which was often. They were lovers, but her attention had been drawn to him by Jane, always a sly one, although she was shy then. She knew that if she mentioned this handsome young bus conductor who took her fare every time she went up to London to the dentist, then Mags would be alerted and do what she would never dare do; attract his attention and bring him down here for one of her lewd weekends of sex and..."

"Hang on a minute, excuse me, but my Great Uncle George was a dear, sweet old man. He would never!"

"Ah, but he did. He was young once, like you, and I suspect that you do.... Don't you?"

I feel myself blush. "Yes- but, this is way back in the nineteen-thirties when people were very.... prim and proper."

"Oh, some were, no doubt about that but others weren't. The Berengers have never been very prim and proper, especially mother and Mags and George certainly wasn't. Have you never seen a picture of him as a young man?"

"I don't think, well, no I haven't."

"Hang on," she shunts herself up out of the chair. I try to help but she shoos me away. "If you don't use it you lose it, I always say. There," she straightens, smoothes her pale blue knitted skirt and hobbles this way and that between all the furniture, to open a bureau set against the far wall. Then she has to find her glasses, put them on and heave open one of the long, heavy drawers. "Here we are," she hauls out a thick, brown album and returns with it cradled in her arms. "You open it and have a look. I still get too emotional seeing him again. He was so lovely." She hands me the book and I open it.

No need to ask who is who. Ethel and George smile out at me from every page; amazingly fresh, happy, attractive young people. My great uncle was certainly very good looking, even in those awful dull clothes they wore then and especially in his army uniform. On the beach you can see he has sex appeal, good legs - and there's Ethel, cute and girlish with fair curls and a sleek wet bathing suit. And now there's a baby in the pictures, babies and toddlers growing to childhood. Their doting father carrying them, pushing them on their tricycles, sitting amongst them on the riverbank fishing; his hairline receding slightly and a pipe clamped between his teeth.

"This is amazing, he's never really all in the pictures Jane took of him."

"She was always useless with technology."

"But if he was your husband and you had all these children..."

"Five."

"Five children together, then how come we only knew him as living with Jane and never guessed about you and the children?"

"It was part of the deal my father struck with him. I'll explain it all, but where was I?" She frowns and I can see a likeness, a flicker of something of Great Aunt Jane. "He came with Mags and I first saw him properly in the long gallery that evening, although we had met briefly on the stairs. But even in that short meeting - a few seconds together in the dark - I knew he was the one. And then when I saw him in the proper light, all dolled up in his dinner suit, a scabby cut on his hand and so nervous, my heart went out to him. Of course, he never noticed me, Mags made sure of that. She was all over him and only wearing a slither of satin, you could see everything through it, and he was looking. Well, you couldn't help it with Mags; she just oozed sex appeal...."

*****

George didn't think he had ever found anyone intolerable, until now. But Mags, her hair in disarray, her lipstick – and the memory of where those lips had been – thickly red, her mourning dress wrongly buttoned and her black stockings twisted, quite repelled him as she glided across the dining room to greet him.

"Darling, we've been to put Sybella in the chapel."

"I know," he swerved to avoid her hand, raised ready to caress his face. "I saw you, remember?"

"Yes, you were with the inspector, has he had any news? We really missed the darling Bish. No-one knew what to say over Sybella's poor, dead little body." She followed him across the dining room as she spoke and finally got her hand round his arm to halt his retreat. "I'll need to see you after luncheon." She tried to press the back of his hand against her pubic bone, but he snatched it away.

"I'll be too busy packing to leave."

"Leave?"

"Yes, the toxicology report has come, that's all I was waiting for. The inspector's looking at it now and you know as well as I do that it won't show any poison."

"You can't leave," her grip tightened. "Mummy's sent a letter to your silly bus people, you can stay as long as you like."

"I don't want to stay any longer, Margaret. There's no point." For the first time he noticed a flicker of doubt in her gaze; she had always been so sure of her power over him that he had been sure of it too. He straightened his shoulders and glanced over to where Jane and her mother sat at the damask covered table, waiting for their lunch to be served. "Shall we sit? I think we're keeping everybody waiting."

"Mummy's not here," Mags blocked his way and hissed. "You know there is a point. You know this will be your home when..."

"Will you please try to get it into your head," he spoke at normal volume, "that we are no longer engaged."

"George, you're making me cross." She narrowed her eyes and the subdued hum of conversation, which had formed a background to their intercourse so far, stopped. He noticed over her shoulder that all eyes were now upon them; Harry was in the process of passing a roll to Freddie, Jane and her mother hunched closer together, Hilda and Grace were almost under the table, only Joye, involved in her own little world of misery without her twin, was sipping from her water glass unperturbed. George knew he had to assert himself, although at that moment his stomach rumbled audibly, he had to show Jane he was not weak - that he was worthy of her and would look after her in the outside world.

"Did you hear me?" demanded Mags.

"Of course. I was just wondering-"

"Sorry to keep everybody waiting." Lady Lydia rushed in, brushing passed him, leaving a wake of fruity perfume. "Come along you two, let's sit down. The inspector has received his report on the poor darling Bish." She took her place at the head of the table, "Margaret, please sit and allow Mr Pender to get to his place. The inspector wants to talk to us all after dessert. You may serve, Smears."

"Yesh, my Lady."

George sat down and blew out his cheeks. Jane's gaze was lowered as she smoothed out the napkin in her lap. Mag's still hadn't settled; she came up behind Joye, jiggled her chair and snapped,

"Out toad, I want to sit next to my fiancée."

Joye rose to obey.

"Leave her be," George protested. "I don't want to sit next to you."

"Tut, tut," Lady Lydia called, "what's this, lover's tiff? Come and sit by Mummy, Joye, let the two love birds bill and coo."

Joye hurried to obey her mother and Mags slipped in next to George, "Now," she squeezed his thigh with a hard hand, "what were you wondering?"

"Mm?" Smears was just serving his soup and as he leaned away from Mags, he caught a warning gleam in the butler's eye, which he decided to ignore. "I was just wondering how you have the gall to be cross with me."

"Jeshush," Smears hissed under his breath and his ladle clanged against the side of the tureen.

"Because," George continued, "I know what you've been doing this morning and with whom."

Mags burst out laughing, a ridiculously shrill and over the top bout of laughter which drew all attention to her. George tried to sup his soup with it all going on next to him, but she jogged his arm twice and he was worried about spilling cock-a-leekie all over The Bish's superb tweed jacket.

"Good heavens child," soothed her mother, "is it a joke? Tell us, we need a joke, don't we Harry?"

Mags calmed herself with exaggerated difficulty, her hand at her bare throat, and managed to get out that, "George is jealous, Mummy dear, green with jealousy."

"I'm not jealous. I'm disgusted."

"He's such a lovely little prude!" She made to cup his face but he shied away.

"And you're such a whore!" The accusation was out before he had time to think of the consequences but it certainly stopped her laughing.

"A whore?!"

"Yes."

Her voice dropped to a throaty rasp, "Have I ever charged you money?!"

"No, you demand a higher price!"

"What? Your putrid little soul?"

"My self-respect!"

"Ha!! You are so suburban and common! Listen to him! His self-respect? You're only a bloody bus conductor!"

"Margaret!" her mother boomed, "Go to your room! Now!"

George was somewhat surprised to see that Mags did subside a little, put her napkin carefully on the table in front of her and move back her chair preparatory to getting up out of it. She was pink under her make-up, biting her lower lip and breathing fast. She turned to him, about to speak but unable to get the words out. He watched her struggle for a moment, then she was gone, running to the door and wrenching it open with a gasp.

"Dear Mr Pender, please let me apologise for

my daughter. You have been through quite enough with this family over the last few days and I hope you will put down poor Mags' peculiar behaviour to the strains and bereavements of this weekend. We are all a little on edge over this report of the inspector's and Mags was so devoted to The Bish. She misses him terribly, as do we all. Personally, I can't believe that he won't walk through that door," she gestured towards the still open door and everyone turned to regard it warily, "at any moment, raise a hand in blessing and tell us it has all been just one of his practical jokes."

"Poor Mother," Harry got up to go to her.

"I know what she means," Aunt Susie shook out her handkerchief.

"And poor Hilda..."

"She should be here..."

"I want Gaye!'"

George sat and watched them all guiltily, but took some comfort from the fact that no-one had mentioned The Beautiful Child. Jane got up to go and comfort Joye and, as she passed behind his chair, she touched his shoulder so lightly it might have been nothing.

The soup was cold by the time the family had calmed themselves enough to eat it. Mags did not return, her mother asked Smears to send a tray up to her. The cold cuts were consumed in silence and George found himself unable to swallow without effort, a hollow of foreboding in his belly. The plum duff was just being doled out as the inspector barged in with Bacon in tow looking round expectantly.

"My lady, if I may just interpose?"

"Interpose all you like, Inspector, it sounds such an interesting occupation."

Everyone stopped what they were doing and watched as the inspector shook out a crackly sheet of paper and held it taught, "I have here the toxicology report on Alphonse Berenger. It shows there to have been a large quantity of alcohol in his system at the time of his demise along with three lead toy soldiers and a small key. No poison shows up at all."

"The key," Lady Lydia enquired, "does it have a heart-shaped loop?"

"It does, my lady."

"My jewel box key! And the little devil denied any knowledge of its whereabouts! Do you remember, Susie?"

"Yes, I do, dear."

"Do you have the key, Inspector?"

"Not on my person, no, but it is at the lab if you should require it."

"Oh, I do. I haven't been able to get into that box for years. I've quite forgotten what's in it."

"I'm prepared to bet one of those lead figures is of Napoleon," grumbled Harry.

"Surely Alphonse would have passed that, dear?"

"Not necessarily mother, he was mounted."

"Ahh."

"Would you like me to find out for you, sir?"

"Yes, if you would, thank you, Inspector."

"So, as far as I can see there was no foul play in any of the cases. Tragic accident is what I shall put in my report, Madam, as I think we can reasonably assume that the amount of alcohol imbibed is responsible for the poor gentleman's instability on the balcony. I see no need for my constable and I to trespass on your kind hospitality any longer, my lady."

"As you wish," Lady Lydia waved a regal hand.

"Does this mean I can leave?" George asked hopefully.

"Whenever you want sir, thank you for your forbearance." He nodded all round and turned to Bacon. "Come along, constable, our work here is done."

With one more disappointed glance round the room Bacon followed his uncle out into the hall.

"It's best I think," Lady Lydia addressed them all, "not to muddy the inspector's waters with the information that darling Alphonse was permanently smashed and quite able to carry on normally. It will just make it all the more difficult for poor Mags. Don't you agree?"

The family did agree and the plum duff was plunged into. George managed a couple of mouthfuls before he heard his name called and raised his head to the lady of the house.

"Dear Mr Pender, are you really going to leave us?"

"Yes, I am."

"I do hope that before you go you will come and see me to say goodbye."

"Of course."

"Smears will show you the way to my room..." there was something about the way she trailed off and the way that the rest of the diners watched his reaction that made George wonder if he wouldn't rather just say goodbye here and now.

"Um, I was wondering if I could leave after lunch, actually."

"Impossible."

"Ah. Right."

"You can leave in the morning, when you've sorted things out with Mags."

"Oh, well, actually-"

"Someone must go and tell her about the inspector's report. Would you like to do that, George?"

"Oh, no. No, I can't. I've er... I've got to um- Yes, I've got to go and see Harry's portrait of me."

"Yes, indeed you have. I thought you'd forgotten all about me."

"No, of course not."

"Excellent, we'll go up after lunch."

That was it as far as the plum duff was concerned and it was only the plucky smile which Jane flashed to him across the table that stopped George from losing the will to live.

CHAPTER 13

I really don't know what to do. Great Aunt Ethel has just dozed off. Well, at first I thought she had died, but I checked her pulse and it's up and running. She was almost in mid-sentence, just getting to an exciting bit about George and Mags when she began to nod and slow down and then stopped, her head lolling back alarmingly. She's snoring now, so that's alright. But what should I do, sit here or leave? The awful thing is I don't know my way back downstairs. And what if I do leave and she wakes up and finds me gone and thinks I'm terribly rude? Old people get affronted at things like that and I don't want to upset Great Aunt Ethel because I rather like her. Although her story is certainly strange... I know old people can get confused sometimes and I think that must be the case here. I'm taking it all with a pinch of salt, but it's very amusing and she looks very sweet, with her beautifully manicured hands neatly clasped.

I suppose I can look through the album for a while and wait to see if she comes to again. I find old photos very sad, even my own, time passes and we change in so many ways. Goodness me, I've changed in the last few months. I'm half a stone heavier, for a start, and fuller round the face. Look at this picture of George and Ethel; he must be in his mid-twenties, I suppose, and she's only in her teens. They look so young and happy on a windswept seafront with a grey sea and a dark smudge of pier behind them. He's got one arm round her and is grinning into the camera; she's hunched up close to him - for warmth probably - her hair blowing about and her smiling face angled up to him, no-one but him. I don't think I've ever been that young or that happy, and I've been to Mexico and Spain and Italy and oh... everywhere. They're probably in Great Yarmouth or somewhere equally dire.

This isn't doing me any good.

I'll put the album down and have a wander round the room, a nose. There are some very pretty bits of furniture, all fragile and inlaid, and some quite monstrous dark veneered pieces. Little china statuettes and dishes are dotted all over the place, you have to be very careful how you move between them. There's a box of Belgian chocolates on the sideboard, half empty, a bottle of cough medicine, a few white packets of pills and a box of Kleenex, all alongside a lovely etched glass vase that must be worth a fortune. The pictures on the walls are frankly ghastly, all puppies and kittens in baskets looking cute, but they all appear to be original oils-Oh!

"Hello."

"Hello. Great Aunt Ethel's fallen asleep I was

just waiting for her to wake up and looking about a bit..." Why do I feel like I've been caught stealing the family silver? I have a perfect right to be here and the person who's come in - I can't say man, I can't say woman - seems to be as embarrassed as I am.

"Afternoon nap."

"Yes, I suppose that's it. I'm Clover Berrow, a sort of cousin. George's great niece."

"Ah, George, dear George, we miss him so dreadfully."

"I think everyone does."

"I've been sent to find out who you are- I'm Guy."

Male. OK- I'll overlook the shoulder length white hair and the floral blouse, or shirt but whichever sex, he shouldn't still be wearing jeans at his age. They hang off his angular hips and sag round his bottom and he appears to be wearing high heeled boots underneath. "Pleased to meet you, Guy."

"So nice to see a new face." He shakes my hand, he has a surprisingly strong grip and his hand is warm. "We don't see many new faces. George was a new face, all those years ago."

"Yes, I've been hearing all about that. I've brought the painting back the one of Mags. Great Aunt Jane wanted me to return it."

"Jane? Oh, how lovely. Is she coming home?"

"Oh, I don't think so. She said she never liked it here."

"No, she had a rough time, we all did, but Jane

was nice to us. We were fond of her. We haven't seen her for, oh, about sixty years. How time flies. Is she still beautiful?"

And I can see, as he asks with a wistful smile, that he must have been quite beautiful himself, once. "Yes, she is."

"Good! We Berengers always keep our looks."

"Where do you fit in? Are you a cousin or something?"

He laughs an attractive laugh, almost feminine but with a masculine edge that I find very appealing, "Yes, we're cousins. Oh look, Ethel's stirring. I'll go and report back. Pop in and see us before you go. Ta-ta."

Great Aunt Ethel is puffing up her perm and checking to see that she hasn't drooled. I don't watch, it's not decent, so I pretend to be studying the paintings, hoping she remembers I'm still here.

"Sorry, dear."

"That's alright."

"It's the pills, they make me so dopey. The family tease me terribly about it and it's very embarrassing."

"Not at all. I've been looking at your paintings."

"Rubbish, George called them, sentimental rubbish. But I like them and this is my room." She smiles a cheeky sort of grin, very girlish.

"Of course. Men, they're always throwing their weight about."

She tilts her head, "Man trouble?"

"Oh, well, not really," I go to sit down again.

"It's life, isn't it? Men and women. And how bored we'd all be if we weren't so different. That's what we used to say when all this unisex came in. Where's the fun, we used to say, where's the fun?"

*****

"Well, that's what I think, don't you agree?" Harry led the way up to his studio, positively bounding with excitement.

George trailed after him, trying to convince himself that this visit would be the lesser of three evils, but knowing that he would have to see Mags and Lady Lydia soon. "Yes," he agreed, dully, "oh, yes, life has to be fun."

"And that's what I think I've got to concentrate on now. Having you here, us making friends, has been a great eye-opener. I've never had a friend before."

And the smile on his face and the tone of his voice made George wonder just what Harry understood about male friendships. He waited, resigned, while Harry unlocked his studio door and ushered him in. The air was a little fresher than before and George noted an open window; flies buzzed over a couple of drooping grouse, laid artfully across the gun which had dispatched them, and an easel displayed the beginnings of a sketch of the dead birds. But Harry was intent on showing him the latest addition to the encircling mural.

"See if you can find yourself. I'll give you

315

three minutes," he actually checked his wristwatch.

George walked slowly round the room, scanning the family vignettes; the adoration of the Berenger Christ, Mags on her manger, the twins twining out of the same tree root with twigs for fingers and Nanny, vast in her yellow sou'wester, thumping up the terrace with a switch. He really didn't want to find himself and dreaded the moment. When it came, two minutes and twenty-one seconds into his allotted time, it was worse than he could have imagined.

"I say."

"It's arresting, isn't it?"

"Yes. I do feel you've rather taken liberties, Harry."

"But that's what friends are for, old boy. Friends forgive you anything and make allowances."

"Well if that's the case, then I hope you'll forgive me saying that I think that's obscene and make allowances for my prudishness."

"But it's so true, can't you see?" He pushed his glasses up his nose and bent closer to his work. "You came here and ravished us."

"But not all at once."

"Mags keeps on about you being common, not seeing that it's your very essence, as the common man, that is your charm, your power over us. You rushed in here like a breath of fresh air and nothing will ever be the same, thank God. I'm not talking about our losses over the last four days, they will, of course, make a difference to us all. But I especially feel that you have unlocked doors for me, hence the key," He indicated the large golden key being wielded by one of the painted Georges. "And Joye! Joye spoke to you!"

"But that's all she's ever done, Harry! This... this is pure fiction."

"It's a metaphor, don't you see?"

"It just makes me feel very uncomfortable."

"Nobody likes to see the truth about themselves. That's why we have artists. Artists reveal all our truths, they have a special licence to do so. I am an artist, I know that now, not just a dabbler but a real artist. I have a purpose in life and you have given it to me. I could almost say that I love you."

George glanced at his enraptured face and then back at what Harry was allowing a George to do to him on the wall, "Mmm. Well, I suppose I'd better go and see your mother."

"I shall search for friends and like-minded people the world over," Harry continued. "I shall leave here and travel to seek out other artists. Before you came it had never occurred to me that I could do this but hearing about you and your bus and your visits to art galleries... if you can do all that, just a common sort of chap, then so can I. I shall never forget you and you shall never be forgotten here," he indicated the wall. "You belong here."

"Mm, well, I'm glad to have made some difference. But I must go now, so I'll say cheerio..."

"Yes," Harry was peering closely at his work. "Just a little more purple here, I think, and a highlight on the glistening drop-"

"See you later, then." He slipped out and closed the door. A shiver coursed through him and he ran full pelt down the turret stair.

The last person he wanted to see was Mags; the second to last person he wanted to see was her mother, but he had to decide. Politeness and a rather imperious invitation demanded that he go and say his thank yous and goodbyes to his hostess soon. But the last few times he had been alone with Lady Lydia he had given in to her in a most craven way, because politeness and her imperiousness had demanded it. He was unsure as to how he would react if she tried to seduce him again - he should resist, but could he? He dithered in his bedroom as he opened his suitcase and found what he could of his own things; two odd socks and one handkerchief, all that The Beautiful Child had left him in one piece. The knock at his door made his legs go weak,

"Who is it?"

"It's me."

"Ethel?" He ran to the door and opened it. "Ethel." He almost hugged her and she almost looked as if she wanted him to, then she saw his open case.

"Are you packing already?"

"The inspector says I can leave, I'm in the clear and quite honestly, I can't wait to go. I'm sorry Ethel, I can't pretend that I've enjoyed my stay here, apart from you and..."

"And?" She gently closed the lid of the case

and sat down on the sofa.

"Harry has done the most awful painting of me," he gabbled, "I think he has feelings for me."

"Jane, is who you were going to say." She looked up at him and her lower lip trembled. She was so sweet, with her curls and her frilled cap and plump, tight little body that he sat down beside her.

"Can you keep a secret?"

"She's going with you."

"How did you know?"

"She told me. I'm to pack all her things."

"But you're her half-sister. Why can't she pack all her own things?"

"It's what she's used to. Someone to pick up after her. Are you prepared to do that?"

"She's not said that she's going to stay with me - just that she's coming away with me."

"To her it means the same thing. Where else would she go? Who else does she know? Apart from the dentist, of course."

This news thrilled George to the core; Jane was his, that was what it meant, his forever and alone. He was being rewarded beyond his wildest imaginings. He only wondered what he would have to do to earn such a reward. Then he noticed that Ethel was crying. It was a quiet kind of crying, tears slipping out under her lashes, and a rush of tenderness towards her made him put an arm round her shoulders and give her a squeeze.

"Oh," she moved slightly away, "don't."

He took his arm away and felt for her hand

instead, but she moved both hands out of his way, sitting on them and said,

"Don't," again.

"Well, what can I do then?"

"Nothing."

"I don't like to see you upset."

"Why should me being upset bother you?"

"Because I like you. You've been a good friend to me here - so kind."

"It's my job."

"Is that all it's been, just a job?"

"Why are you interested?" She sniffed. "Why should you care about me? You've got what you want, Jane. Because she's beautiful, she's no nicer than me, just more beautiful."

"You're beautiful too, in a different, special way."

"Am I? Lotta good it's done me."

"Please," he pulled one hand out from underneath her and kissed it, "don't cry."

"Give me a good reason not to, then."

"It makes your face blotchy."

She gave a little laugh, "Then I won't even be beautiful in my 'special' way, will I?"

He smiled and kissed her hand again. Of course, Ethel was the sort of girl he should end up with; not a rare creature like Jane, but a comfy, caring sort of girl who wouldn't frighten his parents. Chance had put both girls in his way and given him the choice. Was he to be penalised because he had decided to go for rarity? More to the point, was

Ethel to be penalised because of his ambitions?

He got up and opened his case.

"Not much in it," Ethel remarked.

"It's all Sybella left me. Mum'll be furious."

"Take some of The Bish's stuff."

"I can't. I wouldn't feel right about it."

"Even though you're in the clear?"

"You haven't told anyone about that ticket?"

"Of course not."

"He was drunk too, you know."

"He was always drunk. Couldn't live with his conscience."

"All those babies..."

"Six at least! Wicked! Anyway," she stood up and wiped her face with the back of her hands, "I was sent up to remind you that Dad wants to see you."

"Oh, right. I've also got to go and see your mother at some time and I'm not looking forward to it. You know what she's like."

"No, I don't." She turned away and flicked the bedcover straight as she went towards the door. "Just behave like a gentleman."

He nodded and watched her close the door carefully behind her.

Always the coward, always taking the easy route, George left his packing and hurried down to the servant's corridor to knock on Smears' office door. He could see him through the glass window; hair standing on end, an unsmoked cigarette burning to ash in a big, brass ashtray, while he turned over page after page of a thick accounts book, a deep frown on his forehead.

"Come," he barked.

George opened the door and announced himself as the butler had not looked up, "It's me, George Pender, Ethel said you wanted to see me."

"Yes," he looked up now.

"I'm sorry about the mess on the desk. I was-"

"I should never have left you alone in here. You noticed it all, I suppose. Read in detail of the decline in fortunes, the mounting debts?"

"Well, no, I didn't like to pry."

"Then you are either something near a saint, Mr Pender, or a liar. Shut the door and sit."

George did both.

"The family are unaware of any problems. If they were, do you think they'd be trying to snap you up for their daughter?"

"There's no snapping up going on. Mags and I are not engaged."

"So you say, but no man has ever escaped this place without giving something of himself - leaving something of himself here. If indeed they escape at all."

"I'm leaving tomorrow and wondered if you could arrange for me to be taken to the station."

Smears raised one bushy eyebrow, "Have you been to see her yet?"

"Who?"

"Her ladyship?"

"Not yet, no."

"Then I will await your return from that meeting before ordering the car to be got ready for you."

George pressed his hands between his knees, "Do you think that she might...?" he changed his mind. "Jane's father escaped."

"And left her and his wife behind."

"Do you ever hear from him?"

"Why?"

"I just..." he squeezed his knees tighter. "I can't be made to marry Mags if I don't' want to."

"No, indeed." He licked a finger and turned over another page in the ledger, pursing his lips and whistling tunelessly.

"Why hasn't the family got any money?" It was time to fight back.

"Because the bottle factory and the tannery are both out of date and failing. Lack of investment has finally caught up with them as I said it would."

"Is there nothing you can do?"

"What you have to realise, Mr Pender, is this; although nominally in charge of both enterprises, my suggestions and warnings over the years have been systematically ignored. I go off with sheets of accounts and profiles to prove my point and I return flattered and soothed, satisfied and happy, but with none of my proposals either listened to or acted upon. I know this, yet I still battle on and the factory still makes a loss and the tannery workers still fall ill at an alarming rate and I cannot recruit more, for obvious reasons. The only thing that can save the family finances is a war and I hardly think that we can arrange for one to come along just to suit us."

"I don't know anything about business, I can't give you any advice."

"Nice of you to offer, though."

"All I can say is that Lady Lydia must be made to see-"

"Do you think I've not tried?"

"But if there was no soup, no beef, no food to put on the table, wouldn't she realise?"

"Four years ago, I put the whole household on starvation rations for a month. Her ladyship praised my economy because she said they were all getting too fat and that everyone needed to lose the weight. I tried to sack members of staff; she went to their houses and brought them back again. No-one must leave her, Mr Pender. Death is the only way out."

"Nonsense." But a shiver ran down George's back.

Smears sighed, "Another bit of nonsense for you. Ethel is smitten."

"I know."

"What are you going to do about it?"

"What do you mean?"

"If you are not going to marry Miss Mags, can you be persuaded to marry my poor, infatuated daughter?"

"Um, well, Ethel is very nice..."

"Enough. Just swear to me that you've kept your trousers done up around her and I'll say no more."

"I swear."

"Been too busy in other quarters...." He muttered then sighed again, "Lady Lydia..."

"Yes?"

"We've been through sho much together," he made to get up and sank back again, "Sho much..." He gazed down at his hands, as they lay spread out over the pages of columns and red figures. "Life never turns out how you expect it to."

George cleared his throat a couple of times in the ensuing silence, then got up slowly, "I'd better go and see her then, I suppose..."

"Mmm?" Smears glanced up.

"I need to know the way to her room."

"Yesh." He stood immediately and unhooked his jacket from the back of his chair. "I'll take you now, shir."

Neither man spoke on the long and complicated journey to Lady Lydia's room. George, because he was bracing himself for the meeting and trying to remember the way back, in case he should need it; Smears... George looked across to the man beside him, a darker solid in the gloom - who knew what Smears was thinking? Their route took them by way of the main hall and stairs, a thickly carpeted corridor with views out over the woods, a spiral staircase with padded treads and a carved wood banister, a double door concealed behind a heavy tapestry and another, lighter corridor with red velvet drapes at the high windows and giant, green and pink Chinese vases posted like sentinels every few yards. The corridor led to a carved, gilded door with a huge ornate lock plate. Smears straightened his jacket, smoothed his hair and cleared his throat. He gave the impression of an uneasy schoolboy calling at the headmaster's study, and his nervousness made George suddenly aware that he hadn't been to the lavatory for some time.

Smears knocked, three reserved and respectful taps with one knuckle. They both waited and George could see a pulse in the butler's neck, above his stiff collar, it was going at quite a lick.

"Enter." The voice was low, coaxing but quite audible.

Smears opened the door, "Mr Pender to shee you, my lady."

"Show him in."

George stepped forward. Of course, he had expected something extraordinary. A woman like Lady Lydia would not have a neat cosy, pink bedroom like his mother's, for instance, or a cold, spartan room like his gran's down in Eastbourne. But nothing he had ever seen could have prepared him for such opulence. It was, quite frankly, a room furnished for fucking. To enter it; to breath in that scent, and touch, albeit involuntarily, the soft lilac curtain at the door, to sink into the carpet and see the sheen of warm candle light on the satin upholstered bed and sofas, was to immediately want to roll naked, to press heated flesh with your own and give oneself over entirely to self gratification.

George dropped limply onto a slippery pouffe and almost slid off. He was only half aware of a whispered conversation at the door behind the curtain, of a stifled giggle, a sigh, a rhythmic swishing of the diaphanous fabric and a groan. A painting above the fireplace caught his eye, a beautiful young woman in an oyster satin dress which clung to every curve, with one languid hand upon the head of a hairy dog. It was Jane.

He was so surprised to find her here that he looked quickly away. There were other paintings - mostly of nude women in what his mother would call 'unseemly' poses - and one of Lady Lydia, younger, naked and lying along the grey silk covered sofa on his left, a challenging gleam in her eye.

"So," the door clicked shut, "you've come at last." She came to stand in front of him and such was his low position on the pouffle that his gaze was in line with her barely concealed, heart-shaped fluff of pubic hair. She swept away, her silvery negligee gaping over bare flesh as she turned and bent over to toss a cushion from the sofa on to the floor at his feet. She sank down on to the cushion and threw back her head. Her dark hair was loose - everything was loose - and she wore diamond encrusted tassels on her nipples, which shimmered and sparked in the candle-light. "What do you think?"

He watched the swing of the tassels slow to a halt. "Abo..." he cleared his throat, "about what?"

"About my room? What else?"

"It's very nice."

"Isn't it? I spend hours up here. I've been wanting you to come and visit me here ever since I first saw you. Mags has no idea about us, you know, she thinks you're her private property. She thinks I'm too old to attract and hold a man your age. Smears, Cookie, Nanny, all the others have been older - but we've had some fun, haven't we? Of course, downstairs I have to maintain a certain decorum, but up here," she gestured around and the tassels started up again, "up here I can be who I want to be, who I still am." She fixed him with a heated gaze, "A very passionate and still very supple, sexual being." She ran her warm hand up inside his trouser leg and squeezed his calf muscle, "Go and pour me some champagne, darling, it's over there on the tray."

George started to obey. If something is offered so openly, so wantonly and there's no-one to know, then why shouldn't he oblige? The tray of champagne was borne by a naked Nubian boy in glowing bronze; life-sized, his eyes blank, his slim loins tied with a golden belt and a chain around his finely modelled neck. On the wall above, Jane stared down into George's questioning face. He put the bottle of champagne down, un-opened, on the brass tray. "This is not going to work."

"It's a knack, darling. Strip off the foil."

"No, I mean this seduction business."

She smiled, "I've already seduced you, darling, this is a continuation. We are further down the path than you realise, George. We are lovers now and we shall go further still. I will introduce you to such delights-"

"I've come to say goodbye and to thank you for your hospitality."

"Well, come and thank me properly and to do that you must shed those silly inhibitions of yours, along with that awful sports jacket and tie."

"These are your son's clothes. Your dead son's clothes."

Her smile faltered, "Let's not think about that now. I never think unhappy thoughts here, Georgie darling." She reached out a hand to him and one large breast flopped out of its fragile restraint, the tassel dragging on the Chinese carpet.

He put his hands in his pockets and turned to look at her properly. He saw a plump, middle-aged woman, attractive still, but past her best, sprawling on the carpet in a skimpy nightdress, one tit hanging out. "Get up and sit on the sofa so I can talk to you properly.

"What?"

"It's been a very upsetting weekend for us all and frankly I can't wait to leave. My engagement to Margaret is over, if it ever existed."

"Wait," she was getting up, hampered by her trailing chiffon, and stuffing her breast back to where it had come from. "I understand. You love Mags-"

"No."

"-and you think that we shouldn't be intimate. I can understand that you might think that, and with her looking down on us," she glanced up at the painting above his head. "But let me tell you, there's nothing unusual in it; I slept with my husband's father for several years after his death."

George gaped, "Your father-in-law's death?"

"No, my husband's, silly. Mags, I know, can be trying, and that's why you need me."

"I don't need either of you. I'm going home where I belong."

"But you belong here, you know you do." She came to hang on his arm and caress his cheek. "You can't leave, Leatherboys Hall is in your blood. Look what's happened since you came-"

"That's what I mean, three deaths and a runaway."

"But you can't blame yourself for any of that, accidents happen, I was thinking more of you saving my life...." She stared into his face, so close he could feel her breath on his skin. Her face changed, her smiled firmed up. "But you do blame yourself, don't you?" She tightened her hold on his arm and forced his face round so that she could study it. "Hilda died of a heart attack, she had been warned - no excitement," her eyes narrowed, "but you and Mags were in the woods too, having a very exciting time. Do you think she saw you?"

"No."

"And The Bish called to you, and you wouldn't go to him, you just sat at that table, with

Jane."

"I told him to come down and talk to me."

"He took you too literally darling, drunk as he was."

"He over balanced and fell. The inspector said so."

"And Sybella, my dear little Sybella....?" Her gaze bore into his eyes. He stared back; of all the deaths this was the one he felt most easy about.

She let him go suddenly, turned away and picked up a silk shawl to drape about herself. She tied it tight under one arm and turned back to face him, "Alright, let's be practical about this; Mags needs to marry, to settle down, and she's chosen you. I would have preferred someone with a little more class - no, let's be honest - much more class. But I have been open and hospitable to you and you owe it to me to do as my daughter wants. Otherwise I'll tell her about us."

"Tell her. I don't care. You don't seem to understand. I don't want to marry her. I don't want to carry on with you."

"Carry on? Carry on?! Mags is right, you are a dreadful little prude and snob! I offer you what most men would die for; my body and expertise and the run of a fabulous house, and you refuse to 'carry on'! How common and very dirty your mind is. You men are all the same, cowards, afraid to live life to the extreme. The only real man amongst you all is Nanny. He did what I asked, what I needed him to do, without question, and we had such a time together, you wouldn't believe it. But then the police came and there were questions and he had to go into hiding and since he put on a skirt, he's never had quite the appeal he always had for me in his regimentals..." Her eyes glazed slightly and she forgot herself enough to let her hands run up her body before she snapped to attention again and focussed on George. "Are you still here? Get out!"

"With pleasure. I'll ask Smears about the car."

"Who the hell do you think you are? You'll go on the donkey cart, with the post."

"Fine. I'll just be pleased to leave this fucking place, Mrs Berenger." George pushed past her and fought his way through the lilac curtain to the door. He ran down the Chinese-urn-corridor, came up against four identical doors and then got lost.

*****

I knew this would happen. Great Aunt Ethel was very precise with her directions to the toilets, but I can't remember what to do to reverse the route and find my way back to her room. It's so gloomy, and rather creepy. And I'm beginning to wonder about Aunt Ethel; surely all this rubbish about strange accidents and Great Uncle George having an affair with Ethel's mother, Lady Lydia, can't be true? Although I have to admit that most men I know will try their luck with anyone still breathing. I suppose I don't want to believe it. I really loved old Uncle George and I've always admired Great Aunt Jane, so elegant and aloof and lovely. But then again, if what Aunt Ethel says is true, then all this really belongs to Jane, not to her. So why isn't Jane living here? Oh yes, because George didn't like it. Well, I don't blame him. I don't like it either.

It's so cold! I'm stuck in a long corridor lit by two twenty-watt bulbs, at least fifty yards apart and there are doors everywhere. I'll just have to try each one until I find Great Aunt Ethel. Locked... locked... ah- empty... locked... open!

Ahh!.

A stuffed bear! Fancy putting that there! I can't take shocks, not in my condition.

Oh, this is better, a lovely big room with french windows onto an ivy festooned balcony. How romantic, it only needs a four-poster bed to make it the complete Sleeping Beauty room, cobwebs and all. The only nasty thing is a moth-eaten tiger skin on the floor covering a stain, but he's a boss-eyed tiger and actually rather funny. Everything else is under dust sheets and the curtains are mouldering into heaps on the floor. But the view of the garden and the tree-tops beyond, is the same as from Great Aunt Ethel's room, so I need only check the doors on this side of the corridor. What a clever piece of detective work.

Someone's coming, I can hear footsteps. Why am I hiding behind this wardrobe? I want to be found, don't I? But the whole place has made me feel so unsure and vulnerable. What if it's a weird nutter, usually kept locked up in a turret, like in

Jane Eyre? I could be murdered here, stuffed in this wardrobe and never found. This is silly, I'm just a bit spooked by all of Aunt Ethel's ghoulish tales but those footsteps sound very purposeful...

"Who's there?" Davy appears in the open doorway, scowling.

"It's me," I wave, stupidly.

"What're you doing in here?" He is so rude, but gorgeous.

"I'm lost. I'm trying to find Great Aunt Ethel's room."

"Why didn't you wait for someone to come and get you?"

"I had to go to the loo."

"Oh." I've embarrassed him - good. "Have you been?" Well, really.

"Yes, thank you. Now if you'll just show me where-"

"It's supper time." He holds the door open for me and I slip through, "I've come to bring Gran down."

A gong reverberates around the house and in my ears, then a door opens further along the corridor and light spills out,

"Clover?"

"It's alright Gran," he closes the door quickly, "I've found her."

"Oh, Davy dear, was she lost? I did worry."

"No need to worry, I'd have found you eventually," I joke as I follow him up the hallway.

"It's supper time now, dear. Are you staying?"

She looks so small up against her grandson.

"Mum's invited her to stay the night," Davy takes his Gran's arm, she gives me her other and we set off down the corridor at a very slow totter.

"How nice," she squeezes my arm against her side. "You know, I can see something of Georgie in you, my dear. Something around the eyes."

"She's only a niece," Davy reminds her.

"Don't worry darling, you still remind me of him most." She squeezes my arm again.

At the top of the stairs Davy straps his Gran into a stair lift and presses the button; we walk down at the same pace as the chair descends, a sort of procession, side by side, step for step, down into the warm well of light, accompanied by the whine of the chair and our mutual silence.

Supper is served in the grand dining room, in my honour, it appears. I wish I'd done my face in the bathroom, I'm sure I look a mess. Bronwen has put on a skirt, a shabby cotton thing with faded flowers and thick tights in a matching orange. She hopes she's done her best and I have to say, "Nice skirt," as I sit down at the beautifully laid table. I have the best view of Mags from here; she's been put up on the wall and Brian tells me,

"We had a helluva job, it's very heavy."

"I know."

"Well I hope you used good strong nails. We've a history of things falling down on people, Bri."

"I know Mum, don't worry." He pats his mother's shoulder and leans over to give her a kiss. "Gloria's made a nice stew and your favourite pudding."

"Plum duff," Bronwen informs me, still blushing from my compliment.

Davy sits down next to her and there are still two places empty, not counting Gloria, who must be in the kitchen. "Are 'they' coming?" Davy asks in hopeful disbelief.

"We thought it would be nice," his father replies. "'They', are Gran's half-brother and sister, Guy and Joye."

"I've met Guy."

"Have you, dear?"

"He came in while you were dozing," I tell her.

"Yes, I'm afraid I fell asleep again. Poor Clover, what must she think of us all! Does Jane doze off?"

"Oh, yes." This seems to please her.

Gloria struggles in through the baize door with a delinquent trolley and Brian rushes to stop her colliding with the mahogany sideboard, "Worse than them super market trolleys," she laughs.

"Dreadful places, supermarkets." Aunt Ethel shakes out her napkin then glances towards the hall door, "Oh, hello Joye, dear."

I turn to look and there is Guy, in a dinner jacket no less and puce silk cravat, but still with his jeans on underneath, and the strangest creature on his arm. Thin and bent, with her white hair in a bun adorned with black feathers, a low-cut black evening dress displaying a bony old chest criss-crossed with ropes of pearls, and white socks and trainers on her feet. Her face is skeletal and her eyes bulge with excitement, yet I can see her resemblance to the still-handsome Guy.

"Where is the new girl?" She asks, all high and trembly.

"Here I am," I half-rise and she is led over by her brother. To my amazement, he guides her quivering old fingers to my face and I realise that she's blind. I take one of her icy hands and press it to my warm cheek, she smiles in my general direction and I am filled with such a protective surge of affection for her it quite overwhelms me. Guy smiles at me encouragingly, so I say, "It's lovely to meet you Joye." And I realise that this is the twin who lost her brother and who sang for George in the twilight courtyard and all Great Aunt Ethel's strange tales suddenly come to life.

"A young face, warm and smooth and so pretty. I like you already. Shall we be friends?"

"Yes, I'd like that."

"Guy, let me sit near her. We must have whispered conversations."

Guy laughs and pulls out the chair next to mine. I sit back and notice Davy's eyes on me; he rolls them and turns away, but I know I've embarrassed him again.

Joye certainly likes her 'whispered conversations'. We sit forehead to forehead all through the first course and she asks, "Where do you live? Is it nice and green and open? What sort of furniture do you have? What do you do? What are you wearing and what colour is your hair, your eyes?" And finally - they all get round to it eventually - as the plum duff is served she asks, "Is Jane still beautiful?"

"She's old now of course, but still very lovely."

"You brought the picture back."

"Yes."

"Where is it?"

"On the wall in front of you."

"Between the dead grouse and the bowl of fruit?" She means the other two paintings on that wall.

"Yes."

"They all think it's Mags, you know," this in a tiny hiss, "but it's not."

"No?"

"No." She giggles and misses her mouth with her fork full of nothing.

Davy opposite tuts audibly and every woman at the table, except Joye, but including me, glares at him.

"Who is it then?"

"When he came to paint it, the young man with the floppy bow tie, he was supposed to paint Mags. She sat for him and they did other naughty things too, I saw them. First of all, he painted her with no clothes on, then he painted over to make the dress, but he got cross with her. They were shouting one day and he threw paint at her. I saw it - I could see then - I was younger and had good eyes. I saw too much though, that's what I think, so I was punished, but it's no good because it's all still in my head."

"So, what happened?"

"He put Jane's face on, he-he-he. No-one could admit it you see. It was supposed to be of Mags, therefore it must be. But George knew and that's why he wanted the painting, although Jane never believed it. She never really knew how lovely she was, they ruined all that for her. They ruined a lot of things...." She puts down her spoon and fork and announces out loud, "Now I shall sing."

"Oh, my God."

"Shut up, David." She looks straight at him and you would swear she can see him. "Whoooo issss Sylviaaaa? Whhhhat isss shhhhe?"

It is bad. I can understand him not wanting her to do it in front of a stranger. But she's enjoying herself and all the grown-ups at the table, I do not include Davy, listen with fixed grins, although she cannot see them. We all clap at the end and she bows and nods, her smile stretching her taut skin even further over her prominent bones.

"I used to sing that for George. He liked it better than the other song that Mags taught me."

"Oh, not that one, Joye dear," Guy intervenes.

"No, no I won't sing it," she assures him, then turns to me, "I think it's rude, but they won't tell me. They want to preserve my innocence, you see - I am the innocent one, there has to be one and I'm it."

"Yes, innocence is precious," I tell her and suddenly I know that it's true. I've said an absolute truth and it makes me feel very special. Baby kicks, it's his time for kicking, about eight o'clock every evening. I lean towards Joye and whisper, "I'm pregnant, expecting a baby, and he's kicking inside me. Would you like to feel him?"

"You will keep it?" She's alarmed.

"He's got a cot and little bootees already, I'm definitely going to keep him."

"Then, I would like to feel..." she puts out her hand and I guide it to my bump and we wait a moment. "Yes, there! There it was, I felt it. Guy there's a baby kicking in here. Come and feel."

CHAPTER 14

George found himself in a warm, dark room. He had stood for sometime at the end of the corridor, confronted by the four identical doors and deciding what to do, but had eventually been forced into action by the sound of Lady Lydia's distant door closing and her hurried footfalls on the soft carpet. Now he stood, breathing heavily, just inside the door and listened as she passed. Then, because it was warm and because there was a pleasant, faint scent in the air, he allowed himself to slide down the door and on to his haunches. He had upset his hostess, but he had remained true to himself. Would anyone ever know or praise his gallantry? And how was he to get through the rest of his time here, dinner especially, without Lady Lydia on his side?

The sound of a match being struck very close by made his heart leap, "Who's there?"

"Oh, it's you," a pale face appeared above the whipering flame, barely an arm's reach away.

"Jane?"

"Yes. Shush." She applied the match to a candle and a feeble glow illuminated her and her immediate surroundings; a bed hung with gauzy material and an empty bedside table with a marble top. "This is my room."

"Why are you sitting here in the dark?"

"Why are you here?"

"I'm escaping from your aunt."

"Quiet. Yes, I heard the summons at luncheon. How did you get on?"

"Not well. But why are you sitting here in dark?"

"I wasn't sitting, I was lying, thinking. I think better in the dark, don't you?"

"No. Draw the curtains, I can't see you properly."

"There aren't any."

"No curtains?"

"No windows."

"What?"

"Shush! It wasn't thought necessary for me to be able to see anything in my room, so I was given this dressing room off my mother's room. She's just there, through the double doors."

"This is appalling," he stumbled towards her, fell over something hard and heavy on the floor, and tripped on to the bed. The springs squealed.

"Are you awake, Jane?" Aunt Suzy called tremulously and alarmingly close.

Jane put her finger to her lips and they sat, still and silent for what seemed a long time until Jane felt it was safe to whisper, "Was she cross?"

"Who?"

"Lady Lydia."

"Fairly. I didn't succumb."

"You didn't? She will be cross. Oh dear."

"Well, aren't you proud of me?"

"Of course I am."

It was lovely, sitting shoulder to shoulder, thigh to thigh on a squishy bed with Jane. It was natural for him to put his hand on her leg and for her to let it rest there. He could now see that what had tripped him were her cases, packed by Ethel presumably, and ready to go. As his eyes adjusted, he could see the double doors to her mother's room, a seeping of light along the floor, the empty rail where her clothes had hung and a small chest of drawers bearing only a lace runner, all within four feet of where they sat.

"Are you really coming away with me?" he whispered into her hair.

"Do you really think I could do anything else?"

This was not quite the answer he had expected, but he pressed on, "And will you stay with me? Marry me?"

"Yes, and no."

He swallowed, "What d'you mean?"

"I will stay with you if you want, but I won't marry you."

"Why not?"

"It doesn't mean anything."

"It does."

"Not to me." She turned to look at him, "I

think you're lovely, and I'll do anything you want except marry you and have children."

"Oh." He knew that this offer should be the answer to his dreams, to any man's dreams, but somehow it wasn't. "I see," but he didn't. Now was the time to ask her about her strange offer; to tell her that he'd always really wanted to have children of his own, that he intended to get to the top at the bus depot, but still wouldn't ever earn much, and that he could never give up his fishing trips with the lads. Instead he kissed her cheek softly, and she sort of collapsed against him and they slowly and quietly fell sideways on the bed together. He wrapped his arms round her, she lay her head on his shoulder, her hand over his heart and they stayed like that as the candle wore down and the darkness grew deeper all around them.

"Where have you been?" Mags' imperious demand greeted him as he entered his room. She was sitting on the sofa at the end of the bed, arms folded.

He was full of warm, fuzzy romantic longings and heroic impulses brought about by his afternoon on the bed with Jane, and in no mood for any of Mags' games, "Oh, shut up and get out," he told her.

"You're very good at giving orders all of a sudden. Mother told me about your wanting the car to leave in. But I find it quite attractive in you, that cocky, cockney arrogance."

"I'm not a cockney." He picked his suitcase up off the floor where she'd shoved it and placed it on the bed. "Did she also tell you about her attempt to seduce me?"

Mags laughed. She was wearing a tweed skirt and a jumper. She looked completely ordinary, but he should have taken note of the abnormally shaped lump on her right hip as she stood up to face him. "That would never happen. If mother decided to seduce you then she would have done so but she knows to keep away from my men."

"But I'm not your man. I'm my own man."

"What nonsense, you have a very annoying independent streak and I can't decide whether I want you or not. Sometimes you really excite me and sometimes I'm appalled by your common little ways. Mother says I'm to forget you, that she never liked you. But I thought she did, at first... And I wonder now if that's why," she sidled up to him and stroked his cheek. "Did she try it on and did you rebuff her? That won't have happened to her before; she always gets who she wants, but maybe she's losing her touch. She's getting older and fatter, she really should act her age." She kissed his neck, licking up round his ear, something he used to find very arousing but now he pushed her away.

"So should you."

"Georgie, you know I like it when you tell me off. That's not how you're going to get rid of me."

"Then tell me how to get rid of you, please, because all I want is to get shot of you and out of this place." There must have been something about his face, manner and tone of voice because, for the second time that day, he felt he had actually got under her skin and touched a nerve.

"I don't think you know what you're saying." Her voice was quiet, she turned away and put her hand in her pocket. "I don't think you're brave enough to know what you're saying."

"Mags' I'm tired of your games. The gong has gone. Go down and have your tea and give my apologies to your mother, I'm sure she'll understand my absence. I will see you at dinner, until then I want to be left in peace."

"Peace?"

"Yes, peace, do you know what that is?"

"No." She turned and pointed her hand at him and then at her own head, and he realised that she was holding something.

At first, he couldn't believe it was a gun because this was a very small and pretty looking gun - that was why he laughed.

"You think I won't do it?!"

"What?"

"Kill myself."

"Don't be silly."

"I've been sitting here thinking and I thought, first of all, that I would kill you. But then I decided that it would be letting you off too easily. You'd be dead; no guilt or misery for you and perhaps prison for me, if they ever found out. After all Nanny's got away with it, why shouldn't I? Then I thought, what have I got to live for?"

"Plenty-"

"No, nothing now he's gone. I miss him so much."

"Who?"

"The Bishop. He was my reason for living. He knew me through and through! I was his creature and without him I don't know what to do. I thought I could get by with you, because he approved of you, as you know. He hated all the others and so did I, eventually but I always left them and this time it looks as if you're leaving me. Why did he do it, why did he fall?!"

"Mags, put the gun down and I'll tell you."

She smiled, "That won't work."

"It will because I know. I know why he fell and I'll tell you if you put the gun down."

"That would work with someone who didn't really want to kill themselves, who didn't want to leave you feeling guilt ridden and unhappy for the rest of your boring little life. But I want to do all those things, very much."

"I know that you do, I believe you, but I know what he was reaching for - what he'd seen tangled in the ivy below the balcony..." he spoke more and more slowly because she was lowering the gun, equally slowly. "He spotted it and I spotted it when I came into his room and drew you away from the balcony rail and I couldn't believe it."

"What? What was it?"

"I went back," he moved gradually towards her, the gun now down at her side, "and I reached through the rail and I picked it up."

Her eyes were wide and her lips open with suspense.

"A number 24 bus ticket," he put his hand over hers and took the gun from her.

"A bus ticket?"

"He asked me for one."

"I remember!"

"I didn't think I had one on me. But I cleared out my pockets that first afternoon in my room, and obviously I did have one. I threw it away over the balcony and it must have got caught in the ivy below his room."

"You did have one?"

"Apparently."

"And you didn't give it to him? You didn't do it to please him? You just threw it away? How could you be so cruel? You bastard! You killed him!"

"Of course I didn't!" He was too surprised by the turn of events to resist as she snatched the gun back from him.

"You deserve to die!"

"This is stupid! Mags! A bloody bus ticket!" He raised his hand and fortunately deflected the first shot. The sound of it switched on some instinct for survival and he began to fight her. He had fought her many times - rough sex fights which she loved - but there had never been a gun involved before and she was strong, he knew that. And suddenly he was fighting for his life. A life with Jane. A life that he wanted very much. He hardly noticed the scratches to his face, or when they both crashed onto the metal coils of the bed - tearing the thin bed covers as they twisted and squirmed for possession of the gun - tearing their own flesh on the rusting tines. He did notice the look of ecstasy on Mags' face beneath him, and that he was becoming aroused despite of, or maybe because of, the terror of his situation. And he did notice the sudden silence and stillness after the second, muffled, shot.

*****

I've never heard a gun shot that close before. It made me jump.

"Poachers," growls Davy.

"Oh, now, Davy, leave it be."

"That's why they come here, Mum. They're laughing at us, because you won't let me go out and get 'em."

"They're more likely to get you, that's why, and then where'd I be without my baby," she tousles his hair.

"Get off."

But I think he likes it. He's spoilt. I've seen it before, James was spoilt. I spoilt him and I spoiled it, what we had, which was good, for the most part.

"Clover?"

"Mm?"

"Any more tea, dear?"

"No thank you, I'll never sleep."

"Are you tired?"

"I am a bit, yes." I'm exhausted, supper was over an hour ago and I've been helping Gloria and

Bronwen clear up. Davy's been hanging around getting in the way, but I like to think it's because of me that he wants to stay in the kitchen.

"Bronwen'll take you up to your room. Have you got a nightie?"

"Oh, well, no. I don't use one, actually…"

"You'll need one here, it's a big, draughty old house. Bronwen'll find you one, won't you?"

"Yeah. You can have one of mine."

The thought does not excite me and, though I hoped the thought of me without a nightie might excite Davy, he never raised his head from the sports page of the Daily Mail. Who am I kidding? Even if Brad Pitt and George Clooney came to my room tonight, I think I still might prefer sleep.

To be honest, this room, the brushed cotton nightie Bronwen has shyly presented me with and the brown mug of warm milk Gloria has just delivered, all leave me feeling very odd; a strange mixture of excitement and, almost, fear. I don't think I shall sleep. I don't think I shall even take my clothes off. The thought of being naked in this barren green room, with its plastic lampshade drifting eerily in the draught from under the heavy varnished door, is quite horrifying.

I wish I was at home.

I wish I'd been brave enough to say to Gloria or Bronwen, 'Don't go and leave me'.

I crawl into bed fully clothed, just my boots kicked off, and I wish I could leave. Get in my car and drive away back to civilisation and busy streets, amber lights and cars, people leaving the pub down the road and sirens. Friendly sirens.

At least the bed is soft.

"You are a gentleman, a Christian gentle-man...Blood, blood!...Quick. What? Mags, no. Yes, now!...Joye has gone out of the window...Dad's tea-total. Yes, I know that now...Georgie, darling...Just be a gentleman...I'm my own man... Where have you been?....Just shut up and get out...You bastard!"

Wow. A dream. Just a dream! That moaning is the wind and with the light on I can see that there is no-one here. I'm drenched. Cold sweat. It's all that rubbish great aunt Ethel's been telling me but the voices were so real. Not inside my head, real people's voices and near-by. Young voices, clipped, posh, but I can't remember what they were saying. It's only three o'clock. I'll have to get out of my wet clothes or I'll catch a chill. I can't be ill here. I can't stay another night. Oh, Great Uncle George, I wish you were here with me. You hated this place too, we could console each other. Were you as frightened as this? Did you want to get away just as badly? The bed is wet so I'll have to lay on the other side, the cold side, to try and get warm again. But I don't want to sleep. I'll leave the bedside light on, just in case. In case of what? Oh, baby, baby, you're still with me. I can feel you move. My precious little son, I'll protect you.

I wish James was here. I've got my mobile but

I can't ring him at this hour, he'll be asleep. Warm and comfortably comforting. I don't want to wake him. He won't want to hear from me, he hates me. Oh, I know I shouldn't have. I know Mum is right, everyone's right but me. I'll go back to sleep, I'm just being silly.

Wow. Blood on the floorboards. That was what the stain under the tiger skin rug was. Brown, a puddle of it, a big puddle judging from the glimpses of it all round the skin. Who died there, in that room? And where are all the people from Aunt Ethel's stories; Harry, Freddie, Gaye and Mags? I know what it is, this feeling I have, it's that I'll never get away from here, it's like glue. This place can suck you in....

"James?"

"Who's this?"

"It's me, Clover."

"What's wrong? Is the baby alright?"

"It's fine. I'm in this awful old house in the middle of Norfolk and I keep having nightmares about all the things that are supposed to have happened here in the past, when Great Uncle George - you know, the one who died recently - and Aunt Jane, were young here. People died, accidentally, all over the place..."

"Clover, have you been drinking?"

"I can't, not with the baby. He's kicking. He knows I'm scared and it's bad for him to absorb negative emotions from me. I don't want him to be paranoid."

Sigh, "What do you want me to do?"

"Just talk to me and tell me I'm being stupid. That there's no such thing as ghosts and it will soon be morning and everything looks better in daylight."

"You've just said it all yourself. You've not left me anything to say, as usual. You'll be fine, read a book or something."

"There aren't any. Are you alone?"

"Yes. Clover, I went to see your mum and dad today, did they tell you?"

"No."

"I wanted to talk about you and the baby and I don't seem to be able to get any sense out of you."

"Excuse me, I've been quite sensible."

"Whatever. I need to know that I will be able to see my son."

"Of course you can see him. I've said so."

"I don't know what to believe about what you've said and- oh, I don't know. It's half-past-three, can't we talk about this at some sensible time, some sensible place...?"

"We did have some good times, didn't we, James?"

Pause, "Yes, we did."

"I've been thinking about them. Do you ever...?"

"Yes, of course I do."

"Did you ever love me?"

"You know... yes, I loved you."

"It makes me so happy to hear that. Even if you hate me now, you did love me and this baby, our son, was born of love."

"I don't hate you, Clover. I was angry with you. Very, very angry."

"I know. You had every right."

"And then I started to think; why did she do this? Was I missing signals? Did I give out the wrong signals? I had what I wanted from our relationship, but obviously you wanted more. I'm thirty-six. I've got to stop playing games and grow up...."

"You're fading, and I want to hear what you're saying."

"Why are you in the middle of Norfolk?"

"I'm returning the painting for Aunt Jane."

"When will you be back here?"

"Tomorrow, if I don't get lost again."

"Have you got the map book with you?"

"Yes. But you know I'm not very good..."

"Do you want me to come and get you?"

"Yessss...."

"Don't cry. Where are you?"

"Leatherboys Hall, but it's spelt, L-apostrophe –A-T-H-E-R-B-O-I-S."

"I'll set off now."

"Thank you, Jamie..."

It's alright if James is coming. I know I can cope with all this now, I was just being silly, that's all. Why is it, I wonder, that in scary films at this point the terrified heroine gets up and wanders about all over the house in the dark? Just to make a spine-tingler, I suppose. Well, I'm not going anywhere. I'm warm again and cosy and James is coming. If he's coming then there's hope. He says it's time for him to grow up but I need to grow up too. I'm going to be a mummy. I'm going to be a mummy....

I need to go to the loo. I shall ignore it and it will go away.

I cannot ignore it I shall wet the bed!

Ohhhh, the bathroom is several doors away down a long, dark, windy corridor....

I've gotta go!!

Someone has kindly left the hall lights on and it's perfectly alright. I know where I am. Bronwen is next door but one, she showed me her room, but not inside, and Brian and Gloria are one door further on. Here is the bathroom and- Oh, shit, the door is locked. Shall I knock? No answer. I'll call, "Hello?"

"What?"

"Who's that?"

"Is that you, Clover?" Davy's voice. Oh, Lord. "You're always bloody going to the toilet."

"I'm a pregnant woman."

The door opens, he's got his shirt off and is holding a towel over his arm. There's red on the towel.

"What have you done?"

"The toilet is free," he stands aside to let me in.

No time to make a fuss, I'm desperate. I go in and shut the door, lock it, and in the basin are thin trails of blood and wodges of red toilet tissue in the loo. I do what I have to do, pull the chain and wash my hands, then I open the door and drag him back inside. "Show me."

"It's just a graze." It's more than that, a chunk out of his forearm and a loose flap of skin, barely attached, and blood still oozing out from under it. "Don't tell Mum."

"Did you go out after the poachers?"

"Don't get all hoity-toity."

"It's a simple question."

"Yes. Alright?"

"Is this a gun shot wound?"

"No. Bow and arrow."

"Bow and arrow?"

"It's quieter, it's what all the pros use."

"You need stitches."

"I know. Will you do 'em?"

"Me? No way! You need to go to hospital."

He thinks for a moment. His mouth twists and he looks pale, "Will you take me?"

This is what it must be like to have a brother, a naughty younger brother. He's all brave now, in front of the young nurses in A&E, but in the car he was quite anxious. "Will I get blood poisoning? Will I have to stay in? I don't like the smell, makes me sick. I think I'm going to be sick…" He wasn't, thank goodness. Bad enough to have possible blood stains in the car, I don't need sick smells as well. It's nearly six and getting light, there's a trace of pale green on the horizon, as we leave the warm brightness of the hospital and he takes my arm.

"I feel a bit dizzy. Loss of blood I expect."

"I suppose it could be, or shock."

"I'm not shocked."

"No, OK."

"I'm not."

"OK."

"This is our secret, OK?"

"So, where shall we tell them we've been?"

He see's the problem and scowls, he's such a one for scowling. It ruins his good looks. "You'll stay like that one day, when the wind changes."

"Gran says that."

I let him into the car, "Davy, she's been telling me some tales…"

"They're not tales, they're all true."

"Honest?"

"Yeah. We Berengers are quite a crew."

"But you're not Berengers, are you? You're Penders. There were only two Berengers, Jane and Mags. What happened to Mags?"

"He shot her."

"Who shot her?"

"Grandpa."

"Great Uncle George?!" I can't start the car till I know, I turn to look at him, my cousin, Davy.

"Tell me."

"She was gonna kill herself because he was leaving and she missed her half brother, Alphonse. There was something going on there, I think - incest or something - Gran won't say, perhaps she doesn't know. Anyway, they fought for the gun and it went off in her, up through her chest to her heart. Horrible lot of blood, all over the bed and floor, you can still see the stain in that room you were in this afternoon. Grandpa was going to leave with Jane, but she wouldn't marry him or have children, for some reason, so Smears, my great-grandpa, made a deal with George. He'd cover up the death and make it appear a suicide - which it sort of was - if George would marry Grandma. Any children they produced had to be registered as Berengers, to carry on the line. So he married her. He did love her and they were very happy when they were together, which wasn't much, but it was enough for Gran, and he got to have children. Jane got away from here and lived as his wife, so it all worked out."

"So it's all true."

"Oh, yeah."

"And what happened to everyone else, Freddie and Harry and Gaye-"

"Well, that's Guy, of course. You've met him. Freddie died during the D-Day landings and Harry drank himself to death in Tahiti, trying to be Gauguin, or something. I dunno about the others Not interested, really. It's all in the past, nothing to do with me."

"But it is to do with you, and with me. It's our history."

"You make your own history. Can we go home now? I'm tired."

Amazingly L'Atherbois Hall is only fifteen minutes from the nearest A&E. Coming at it from the direction I did yesterday afternoon it had seemed in the middle of nowhere, but there are housing estates almost up to the front gates. Shame really, it sort of spoils its Hammer House of Horror appeal. And what a lot of horrors! I suppose I have to believe it all if Davy says it's true. I don't think he's a romanticist. Great Uncle George, killing someone? Poor man! It must have left him with an awful guilt about them all, he always seemed to have an air of otherworldly melancholy about him. It didn't stop him laughing or enjoying a joke though - or his pipe or his fishing - and perhaps it added to his appeal as a dear old man. What a bitch that Mags must have been! And poor Ethel, having to make do with half a husband all those years and not even welcome at the funeral. Aunt Jane has got some explaining to do.

Nearly there, the main gates are still open. I had to open them on our way out earlier and I can't be bothered now to get out and close them, I might wake up sleeping beauty here. How very grand, swishing in through elaborate wrought iron gates and a porter's lodge and on up a gently curving drive in the early morning-

Shit. Where did he come from?

"What? What's up?" Davy lurches, winces and nurses his wounded arm. I pull on the hand brake,

"That dog. Did you see it? It's gone now. It just shot out of nowhere and straight across in front of me. I didn't hit it, thank God. Did you see it?"

He looks at me woozily, "What sort of dog?"

"A 'dog' dog. Black and a bit shaggy"

"White face and chest, white tip to the feathered tail?" He makes me think of Crufts, but the description is good.

"Yes." We've skidded off the drive on to the grassy edge and I'll have to coax the wheels to grip and return to the straight and narrow.

"Anyone with it?"

"I didn't see anyone."

"He must be around. Wait," he gets out and totters.

"What are you doing? Davy?"

He stands for a while, holding on to the open door, then turns, scanning the flat open expanse of lawns and shedding trees. The air is cold, I shiver, its daylight, but grey and misty. "Davy, I'm cold."

He gets back in and signals for me to continue, there's a smile on his face now, a bit of colour in his cheeks, "Well, well..."

"What?"

"Nothing, Cousin Clover. Let's get home and have some breakfast, I'm starving."

James' BMW is parked under the washing in the yard. I've forgotten all about him coming. He's out of the kitchen door, Gloria behind him all concern and crumpled jumper, before I've switched off the engine.

"Clover, where've you been?"

"What's happened? Davy, you alright?" She gapes at the sling.

"It's alright," Davy tells her. "She took me to hospital."

"Hospital? What've you done?"

"Nothing."

"Come in this minute and let me take a look," she hurries him off.

I turn to face James, he looks awful. Well, anyone would, having been woken at three in the morning and asked to drive two hundred miles by someone who's betrayed your trust once already. "Have you had a coffee?" I ask, shy all of a sudden.

"Yes," he doesn't come any closer, just stands soberly regarding me from under some large, pink knickers. "Gloria has been looking after me, along with worrying herself sick over her son. What's he done?"

"Silly boy went out after poachers and was shot in the arm by a bow and arrow."

"That's what all the pros use these days, apparently."

"Yes." I finally lock the car and take a step towards him, "Thank you for coming. I was just being feeble last night I know, but…"

"I can see how someone could be a little nervous, here."

"And if you knew the stories…"

"Well, some old queer has been filling me in a bit."

"Guy. D'you know, he was brought up until the age of twenty-five to think he was a girl, just to please his mother."

"Ah, well that would confuse a chap. You look tired."

"I am."

"Let's go in," he takes my arm.

Gloria has insisted that we stay for lunch and to my amazement, James has agreed. I really didn't think this place would be his thing at all, but he and Brian and Davy have been sitting in the cosy morning room talking all about markets and products and growing seasons. And Guy has been dithering across the corridor between them and the kitchen, where I've been making a lemon roulade to help Gloria out. Guy told James what I was doing and I overheard him say,

"You're in for a treat then; I've never tasted anything as good as one of Clover's puds."

And I sort of glowed with pleasure. Gloria must have noticed because she asked if I was too hot and opened a window for me. Now the men, Guy in tow, wearing a full length, riding Barbour and Doctor Who scarf, have gone out to 'look the ground over', and I have decided to go up and see Aunt Ethel.

I can remember the way and I've brought a cup of tea to ply her with. I need to find out every last secret this place holds, so that I can settle it all in my mind and feel at home here. I knock on the door and open it slightly,

"Aunt Ethel? It's me, Clover, can I come in? I've brought you a cup of tea."

"Oh, how kind, dear," she's been dozing, she's all pink cheeked with an empty sherry glass in her hand, but she doesn't seem to mind the intrusion. "Come and sit down. Bronwen tells me you and your young man are staying for lunch. I'm so pleased. I've always liked Sunday lunch at the Hall. We used to have five courses, I don't know how we managed it! They only had three upstairs," she giggles.

I sit down beside her and as I put the tea tray on the little table between us, she takes hold of my hand and looks at it. I know what she's looking for.

"Is he the father?"

"Yes."

"Is he pleased?"

I sigh, "I think so."

"I hope so, dear."

"Yes, I know."

"Babies have always been very important at the Hall. Mother always wanted lots of them, well, she had seven, but poor Aunt Suzy, she only had the one."

"Jane."

"Yes, who was the most beautiful of the lot,

unfortunately."

"You were very pretty, you still are."

"Flatterer." She frowns, "And poor Mags, who so nearly had it all...."

"Davy has told me."

"Has he?"

"About the shooting..."

"Mmm." She pats my hand and gives it back to me, "Pour the tea, there's a dear."

"Did he really shoot her?" The tea pot dribbles onto the white lace tray cloth and Ethel tuts.

"Oh, yes. It was an accident, of course."

"Of course, but he must have felt so bad about it."

"Yes, he did. How nice of you to think of his feelings first. It was very messy; all over the bedspread and covers and through to the floor. That's why he never could abide beds ever afterwards. He always slept on the floor or in an arm chair. It made life very difficult for me - for Jane too, I should imagine - but I don't like to think of that. At least I was able to help him ease his guilt, which was something she would never do. That's why we had the five children you see, one for each of the deaths he had caused." She sips her tea and I do a quick mental calculation.

"But Gaye only ran away. She- he- didn't die."

"No, and it was George who found him. He was going home late one night from work, just before the war started, and Guy propositioned him. Well, of course, George couldn't believe it, and nor could poor Guy. He'd been so unhappy since he ran away and fallen into all sorts of peculiar company. I never wanted to know all the details but I do know that he worked for some club, dancing and singing on stage, which is what he'd always wanted to do, of course. But it wasn't a very nice club and he got arrested. Prison was very uncomfortable for Guy, he's so careful in his personal hygiene and in those days, conditions were very bad, especially on 'F' Block."

"Poor Guy."

"Mm, anyway, George brought him home, he'd been too ashamed to come by himself. He was frightened of Mother, but by then she'd gone off to France with that contortionist and later got caught up in the war. She had a very good war, by all accounts and died here, at home, in 1950 of exhaustion. Aunt Suzy was with her to the end, running round after her as she had done all her life. They were sisters, did I tell you that?"

"I don't think you did."

"Sisters marrying brothers; it was all the rage in those days."

"What happened to Suzy?"

"Well, after Mother died, her husband Lawrence returned to her. She nursed him to the end with the help of Nanny and..."

"Did Nanny live the rest of his life as a woman?"

"Yes, he was still wanted for the murder, you see."

"But who did he murder?"

"Father."

"Smears?"

"No, Dad died in his bed, aged ninety. Nanny killed Howard Berenger. You see, he was Howard's tutor first then his batman in the army. He was specially trained to look after him because he was always a bit queer; prone to tempers and tears, smashing china and wanting to shoot things. When mother discovered how bad he was, she paid Nanny - whose name was Cyril, by the way, Cyril Curly - quite a nice name... She paid him to kill Howard. Which he did but they found the body and Mother was suspected of being involved, so she had to keep up this pretence of missing him in front of strangers. It was in all the papers at the time, so that's why the whole family had to lie low here in Norfolk. We're still doing that, I suppose."

"And Cyril had to stay a woman until he died?"

"Yes. They've put Cybil Curly on his tombstone in the churchyard."

I am intrigued, "How did he kill him?"

"He suffocated him, while he slept, then left him under a tree in lion country, to make it look like an accident. He cried, all the time he was doing it, so he said. It was a kind of mercy killing, you see. There wasn't much left of him when the natives eventually found him. Just his swagger stick."

"How horrible."

"Oh, I think it was the way he would have wanted to go. Mother always said so, it was apt, she said. He'd killed so many of them it was only fair that they should be in at his death. Of course, they had to sell the cocoa farm, the witch doctor put a juju on it."

"Yes, of course." Am I going mad? I can actually see reason in all of this. "So, there were three accidents and one actual death?"

"Mmm?"

"That Great Uncle George was responsible for, because he brought Gaye/Guy back home again."

"Yes, but you're forgetting the baby."

"What baby?"

"The one Mags was expecting when he shot her."

My lemon roulade has gone down a treat; Brian had two huge helpings and Gloria is cross that there's none left for supper. James and Davy are talking of new forms of advertising for L'Atherbois Organic Vegetables, and Bronwen, I'm sure, has got a sort of crush on me. I don't mind. I don't mind anything. James keeps on looking at me across the table, like he's seeing me for the first time and I'm full. Full of food, full of stories, full of wonder and full of baby.

Up above us, beautiful young Great Aunt Jane is smiling down, and the dog, the wolf hound, who was stuffed and smelly, Joye tells me, is grinning too. Guy, whose life was blighted so terribly, is fussing over his sister with such tenderness that I can't help but feel his poor tragic life has been worth while. And we must be going soon, back down the motorway to London to try and create our own history, as Davy said.

I make a move to go, James rises and shakes hands. I go round the table and kiss all my new found relatives farewell,

"God speed my dear," Aunt Ethel squeezes my hand, "and come back soon. People rarely leave here, you know. George never has."

"She nearly ran him over this morning," Davy laughs.

"What? I didn't, it was a dog anyway."

"See." He nods at his grandmother.

"Brandy?" She asks.

"Oh, no I mustn't, I've got a long way to drive."

For some reason they all find this very funny.

*****

"Ethel?!"

"What?"

"I'm just going out."

"Not now!" Ethel comes hurrying into the kitchen, tying her apron round her plump waist, "I'm just going to start on the potatoes."

"Lucky old potatoes," he makes to chase her round the kitchen table, but his knees are stiff and his chasing days are over.

"Stop it. Act your age," but there's a smile in the corner of her lips.

"I'll take Brandy," he flips his cap on and unhooks the lead from its hook by the door.

"Half an hour. Oh, and if you see Bri tell him that girl rang again, the Welsh one."

"She can't help being Welsh."

"I know."

"Well, it's the way you say it. It's obvious you don't approve."

"I'm sure she's very nice."

"I'm sure she is. Half an hour."

"Mmh."

He steps out into a wet glisten of sunlight in the yard, so bright he has to blink a few times. While his eyes adjust, he pauses to light his pipe, striking the match against the wall, puffing a few times and raising his gaze for an instant to a fourth-floor window where sometimes, just sometimes, he catches a glimpse of the young man he used to be. Brandy is dozing in the sun by the coal yard wall, George gives him a whistle, slaps his thigh and the old dog gets up slowly, hind quarters first, stretches and gives him a smile.

"Come on then boy, let's go and tour the estate...."

ACKNOWLEDGEMENT

Love and thanks to my husband for his patience and amazing tech skills - which I sadly lack: to Gemma for her proof reading; to Jacqueline for the cover design and her enthusiasm; to all the friends over the years who have encouraged me and read things and given such helpful comments, I must mention Christine and Kate here. To my sons who cam home from school starving but knew not to interrupt Mum if she was writing. To writing group tutors and members for all their support. Writing is great but it can be a lonely business, having friends and family like those above makes the whole process even more wonderful. Thank you all.

THE
BERENGERS

Death and sex on a country house weekend

LouiseVan Hamm

Printed in Great Britain
by Amazon